The Ultimate Zombie Hunter's Handbook

The Ultimate Zombie Hunter's Handbook

A Guide to Surviving Zombies ... Probably

By Matthew Collins
And Geoffrey Collins

Illustrations by
Brian Smith
Nick Main
Leslie Turner
Derek Chase
Brandon Barnes

iUniverse, Inc.
New York   Bloomington

Copyright © 2010 by Matthew Collins and Geoffrey Collins

All rights reserved. No part of this book may be used or reproduced by any means, graphic, electronic, or mechanical, including photocopying, recording, taping or by any information storage retrieval system without the written permission of the publisher except in the case of brief quotations embodied in critical articles and reviews.

iUniverse books may be ordered through booksellers or by contacting:

iUniverse
1663 Liberty Drive
Bloomington, IN 47403
www.iuniverse.com
1-800-Authors (1-800-288-4677)

Because of the dynamic nature of the Internet, any Web addresses or links contained in this book may have changed since publication and may no longer be valid. The views expressed in this work are solely those of the author and do not necessarily reflect the views of the publisher, and the publisher hereby disclaims any responsibility for them.

ISBN: 978-1-4401-9685-0 (sc)
ISBN: 978-1-4401-9684-3 (hc)
ISBN: 978-1-4401-9683-6 (ebook)

Library of Congress Control Number: 2010900463

Printed in the United States of America

iUniverse rev. date: 03/31/2010

To Stephen Colbert, for teaching us about the number one greatest living threat in America: bears.

But, Mr. Colbert, have you ever considered the threat of zombie bears?

Contents

1. List of Illustrations ix
2. "Chapter 1" 1
3. Zombies: What Are They? 9
4. Is This a Zombie? 35
5. Typical Human Responses 69
6. Weapons 86
7. When to Throw in the Towel 104
8. Preparing for the Zombie Invasion 116
9. Necessary Government Preparations 139
10. The First Forty-eight Hours—a Practical Guide 159
11. Applying Knowledge to Tactical Situations 208
12. Some Last Words Before You Start Rereading 219
13. Appendix A 221
14. Appendix B 225

List of Illustrations

1. Little Duck Cometh by Brandon Barnes
2. Branch Killer by Brian Smith
3. KFC Bucket o' Death by Brian Smith
4. Causes of Infection by Brian Smith
5. Running Zombies Never Quit, Neither Should You by Leslie Turner
6. Zombies Need Tums by Brian Smith
7. Tablets of Stone by Brian Smith
8. Rusty!? by Brian Smith
9. Grandma's Strawberries by Brian Smith
10. The Taco's Death Waltz by Brian Smith
11. Just One Gunslinger by Brian Smith
12. Bandits Love TVs by Brian Smith
13. Weapons Are Everywhere by Nick Main
14. The Right Weapon for the Right Job by Nick Main
15. Fast Food Will Kill You by Brian Smith
16. The Tragic Life of Hank by Brian Smith
17. Reasons for Building Better Fences by Brian Smith
18. Friends for Life—or the Rest of It by Brian Smith
19. A Political Revolution for You and Your Parents by Brian Smith
20. Blueprints with a Stamp of Approval by Brian Smith
21. A Weirdly Delicious Pretzel by Brian Smith
22. Escaping with What Matters by Brian Smith
23. Clowns Are Weird by Derek Chase
24. The Dodge Stratus Surprise by Derek Chase

"Chapter 1"

(Deciphered by Geoffrey from ancient texts)

> How many zombies does it take to screw in a lightbulb? 3,723. One to screw in the lightbulb and 3,722 to be terminated—with prejudice—by yours truly.
> —Paul

Once upon a time, there was a young watch repairman who loved to collect watches. He especially loved rare old watches that didn't work anymore because it gave him the pleasure of fixing them throughout the night. Over time, this healthy hobby became an obsession that he was unable to control. Whenever he found a watch that was not functioning properly, he stopped whatever he was doing and attempted to fix it.

Things went on like this for a while, until one fateful day when he walked into his local police department to dispute a parking violation. After the clerk noted his dispute and gave him a court date, he begrudgingly headed toward the door. As he passed a door of no particular importance, he heard the faint ticking of a watch and noticed that the watch was ticking slowly, losing two-tenths of a second each hour. It wouldn't take him three minutes to make the proper adjustments so the watch would run like new again. Kreil—that was the man's name—rushed through the door and immediately found the watch on a table in the middle of the room. Within two minutes, he had fixed the problem, and he smiled as he replaced the backing on the watch. It was at about that time that he noticed the brick of C4 attached to the watch. Exactly three seconds later, thanks to Kreil's improvements, the watch triggered a detonator, and the brick of C4 exploded. Despite the medical officer's best efforts, Kreil didn't make it. No one ever figured out what inspired a man to walk through a door clearly marked LIVE BOMB FOR TRAINING PURPOSES ONLY.

For the slow starters out there, you may not have realized how you have been tricked. Well, if I have to spell it out for you, I might as well give up now, but here it goes anyway. Chapter 1 is really the introduction. Chapter 2 is chapter 1. This simple pattern repeats itself until the ending of the book. The reasoning behind this is also very simple: we didn't want anyone to skip out on the introduction like so many of you probably would have if we had had one. You see, the introduction is usually boring and unproductive, so most people skip it. However, *this* introduction is vital to the understanding of the book and the enormity behind its purpose. If Kreil had just read the sign on the door before launching into a quest to fix the object of his attention, he would have been alive today, teaching his kids how to fix watches. Instead, he skipped the introduction. To ensure that this information was not passed over, we hijacked chapter 1, and the rest of the book followed suit.

Who, might you ask, are these diabolical geniuses running the show behind the print? Nothing more than a couple of brothers: Geoffrey and Matthew Collins. My brother, Matthew, almost became a ninja, but instead ended up studying codes and numbers after a tragedy when a samurai murdered his karate kid classmates while he was on the pot blowing zombies through the pipes. (This happened back in the early '90s at Tokyo Dongs Tae Kwon Do Shop. The only criminal evidence found was a single strand of red facial hair. Matthew remembers this because he had been very excited about the roundhouse kick lesson that he was supposed to have that day. He has since drunk away the rest.) Meanwhile, I went to college to study brains and business and left with a psychology major and business minor, making me the hugest double-threat ever. We have both made it our life, second to our real lives, but overshadowing all three, to prepare the world for the upcoming apocalypse. Thus, the creation of this groundbreaking, precedent-setting, lemon-squeezing survival guide.

Read this guide. Study it, live it, dream it. If you have any time left in your day, you screwed up and should immediately make a list of things you did incorrectly. (You'll learn about lists later.) Also, remember that there are certain people that cannot be trusted; this is crucial to your survival. While you'll find a lot of evidence from us describing who we would and would not trust, it is ultimately up to you to make this decision based on your knowledge and training. Just don't mess it up because it could mean the end of the human race. Also, I might kill you.

"But why?" cries the small girl who just got bitten by her zombie hamster, Flufficans. I'll tell you why, little girl from down the street. Because I don't enjoy taking pleasure in blasting the face off of former little girls who used to sell me lemonade but are now dirty zombies. I want people to live through the invasion long enough for me to save them. That will not happen if you don't read this book. That will not happen if your family doesn't read this book. That will *not* happen if your neighbors don't read this book.

Before we get too deeply into the book, each of us wants to explain how our different personal lives changed course and resulted in a monumental collision, the result of which is now known as *The Ultimate Zombie Hunter's Handbook*. When it comes to it, I suppose it all started when I was about five, and Matthew was about three. We were just two beer-drinking, tobacco-spitting, roughhousing young men walking along the yard when we discovered a heavy brown brick. Matthew decided to throw the brick, and it went pretty far. Being the manly man that I was (and still am), I told him I could throw it farther, so he went out to mark his spot, and I promptly hit him in the head with it. Blood was gushing out, and we were just sure he was going to turn into a zombie, but Mom soothed our worries when she said he wouldn't turn into a zombie for the simple reason that he was distraught about becoming a zombie, and zombies don't concern themselves over stuff like that. It made us feel better.

Well, now things have changed. First off, we now know that she completely lied to us. You can become a zombie even if you do worry about it. Second, and more disturbingly, she disarmed us for over a decade to the real danger of zombies. For this, she may never be forgiven. I think I'd rather be cut in half, nuts to helmet, from a spit wad from God, than be that dangerously ignorant again. But I digress. We each came back into our understanding of zombies, but at different times in our lives.

Matthew

"I think it all started back when I was young and still afraid of bullets. One warm fall day, as the leaves were bright in color and birds were preparing to fly south, I was walking on a path set between a small pond on the left and a lake on the right. There, in that pond, was a little duckling that had been left lost and all alone while the rest of its family had moved into the lake. I felt purposeful and benevolent as I scooped him up and set him in the lake on the other side, after which I paused to watch as he swam up next to his mother. She seemed pleased at his return, but immediately smelled the scent of man-danger all over him and suddenly attacked the duckling as if he were not her own. While I watched the momma duck drown the young fowl, I think I realized how fragile life was, and how sometimes, no matter how hard I tried, it just didn't make sense. I also thought about how sad it would be if that little duckling rose from the dead and tried to chase after me, ineffectually hungering for flesh and pecking at my shoes. I think that's about when I started to hate the zombies again ...

"There have been times since that day that I lapsed into complacency, into a frame of mind that isn't prepared to fight for my life against the unliving, a frame of mind that would have gotten me killed. Whenever I start to think that maybe there are no zombies, or that they won't invade during my lifetime, or that zombiism won't happen to me, I just remember those tiny little feathers floating across the surface of the water. It brings the hate back, keeps it fresh, and steadies my soul for the coming fight."

Geoffrey

"It was a dark, stormy night. About every twenty seconds, a brilliant flash of lightning would erupt from the heavens, illuminating the surrounding forests. I was alone, and there were strange sounds coming from the darkness all around. I could hear the pounding of my heart as I concentrated on the task at hand. It was the only heart beating there that night.

"Then, all of a sudden, I realized something profound. It wasn't nighttime. It was two in the afternoon. And it wasn't stormy; it was warm with a light breeze. And that wasn't lightning every twenty seconds; it was the sun for all seconds. I was out at the lake, with my camcorder, simultaneously practicing for my *American Idol* debut and taping my *The Real World* audition. My show name was going to be Raul Suarez, because Hispanic names were popular back then. I played a solo with my favorite flute while sporting a Band-Aid over a nonexistent cut on my cheekbone. I was also showcasing my songwriting skills with my own version of 'Somewhere Over the Rainbow," titled "One time, I Cut My Finger.'

One time, I cut my finger,
Watched it bleed.
Cut on a rusty razor,
Once by a Taco Bell.

I got food in my finger,
Beans and beef.
And I thought that I'd lose it,
Once by a Taco Bell.

No one really thought I'd be okay,
Or wake back up another day, despite me
Being tough as nails or rocks,
Wrapping it in dirty socks,
They need to respect me.

I got, meds for my finger,
To apply,
Germs die out of my finger,
Once by a Taco Bell.

I made those germs go bye, from my finger,
Die, baby—die, die, die.

"At the ending of my performance, a car came out of nowhere, careening dangerously out of control in the direction of a small boy. The driver's face had that kind of look on it. The kind that says, 'Seriously, a flute? A fucking flute?!?' Meanwhile, the boy was helping an old man get some fish off a grill while the man watched from the picnic table nearby, stroking a rusty spoon in anticipation. Luckily, I have the dexterity of a child (not this child) and the speed of a starving obese man with a bottomless spaghetti bowl. As the car came ever closer, with a fatal impact imminent, I had already leaped into action, helping the boy escape from certain death with a lightning-fast ninja roll. We tumbled clear of the mechanical monstrosity as it passed by me and crashed into a nearby tree. Close one.

"At first, I didn't know what to think and lay in the leaves of confusion, which also happened to be maple. I was in the midst of planning my next move when the door from the car began to open slowly. Behind the steering wheel was a slow, unstable individual with blood caked to its lips. A slight moan betrayed the enemy of nature for what it really was: a zombie. Before I knew what had happened, the zombie lay dead at my feet while I stood there, holding the bloody tree branch that I had bludgeoned it with.

"After the darkness faded from my eyes, I realized that it was nothing but a drunk woman who had previously been a living member of the society. Hey, mistakes happen, and I regret nothing, because if she had been a zombie, hesitation would have meant damnation. I know this now …

"Later that same night, I had a dream. In this dream, I was a pregnant woman. It was very odd, but everyone kept complimenting me on my glow and how pregnancy was a really good look for me. I had a baby shower with beautiful gifts from all my friends, and they all gave me hugs, and we laughed well into the evening. It was a wonderful party.

"The next day I went to the doctor for some checkups since the baby was approaching the due date. I sat there, thinking about all the wonderful memories I would be having with my new baby, gushing at the idea of its first steps and the first time it said, 'Mamma.' Then the doctor told me the baby was dead, which was a pretty huge surprise to me since I was expecting it to be alive. He told me that the umbilical cord had wrapped around its little neck, and it suffocated in my sleep the previous night. I was so upset by the worst news of my life that I went into labor.

"When the dead baby was born, the doctor got very quiet. After a couple of minutes, I decided that I had to look down and see what the problem was. That's when I saw it. My baby was a zombie, and it was eating the doctor's face. And I woke up.

"That day, I knew that zombies would be the end of the world as we know it."

But why do we care about you if we're already so prepared? If you are nothing but a liability, then why do we waste our time and effort to save your life? The answer is simpler than you might expect. It is the driving force behind every great accomplishment in the history of mankind. Success. We cannot live the rest of our awesome lives entirely alone in an undead world and go to sleep feeling a sense of victory. If every other human being on earth became fodder for the wolves, then what would the purpose of life be? Nothing. And there's always the need for companionship, the kind of companionship that no brother can provide. Think about it. We need it. I would rather throw a baby into a bear den than see it grow up in an empty world. You can take that promise to the bank.

While writing this book, a very important revelation struck us both at nearly identical times. There are only two types of people in the world today: There are the people who read this book, then study this book, then tattoo scripture from this book onto their skin and live their lives by the words written in this book. Then there are zombies. Dirty, stinky, horribly grotesque man-eating zombies. Only you can decide your fate. Who are you going to be?

Make your decision by setting this book down or by reading it from cover to cover. The knowledge in this book will help any man, woman, or child escape the hell that awaits all zombies. Read and reread it carefully. Take thorough notes, because not a detail can be lost in the translation. The information is all here, but it is up to you to put it to use. By the time you are finished, you will be ready to survive a full-blown zombie invasion. We will be waiting for you on the other side.

PS: *A quick note to anyone who has ever dressed up as a zombie for Halloween.* You risk your life wearing that shit. If we or anyone who has truly grasped our rhetoric is at that party, you will be destroyed before anyone even knows what is happening. The costs far outweigh the benefits in that equation, friend. I would kill one hundred innocent people dressed up as zombies just in case there is a slight chance one may be a zombie. To be honest, there is a pretty good chance they will all become zombies anyway. Matthew dreams about it.

PPS: If you chose something other than to read this book, I've already begun to hunt you.

> Oh, and I executed the zombie who screwed in the lightbulb too.

—Paul

Chapter 2   Zombies: What Are They?
(Written by Matthew on the back of a Dixie cup)

Seriously, what is a zombie? The definition can be hard to pin down due to all the media hype these days, hype that attempts to glamorize and mischaracterize. So forget everything you think you know, and let's start from the beginning, with the basics, and we'll build from there. What is a zombie? Well, a zombie *is not* your friend (this is important!). Furthermore, a zombie *is* a flesh-eater (kind of important!). Even more further, a zombie was originally a normal, hardworking, honest puppy-loving, cat-cuddling everyday neighborly human being. *Was*. Now, let's continue our investigation and look at what defines a zombie, how zombies are created, how zombiism can spread, and all the rest of that kind of crap.

Defining a Zombie

There is some debate over the life/death status of a zombie. Some have the idea that zombies are just mindless humans that appear internally motivated to destroy their former brethren, more or less like brainless cannibals without a sense of home. In this scenario, people suggest that a zombie need not die first but can shift seamlessly from human to zombie, kind of like a water slide that's really fun until you realize it goes to hell. (This whole idea is dumb, but an understandable mistake that will likely end in death.) Occasionally these zombies have internal motivation, like anger and the need to crap, but with the complete inability to relax the final sphincter. Really, I don't know what else to say about this bag of lies, so read on for the sake of truth. (Also justice.)

Other people, who are better, say a zombie is a human who had died and risen again as the "undead" to feast on living human flesh, much akin to Lazarus but with more chomping and less praising. This is what most people agree defines a zombie, and more importantly, it's how Geoffrey and I define a zombie. So let me clarify this, because everything hinges on this pivotal moment in all our lives of humanity crisis rainbow hearts. A person is not considered a zombie until he or she has first died, then come back to a state of motion many associate with "life," if you want to call it that, and when that person does, they have an insatiable hunger for man-meat along with significantly retarded mental capabilities. As in, there's nothing upstairs but moss and rocks. If the person does not appear to die, but instead goes straight to zombie, it's an illusion; there is a "death" at some point, but it just appeared so briefly that the corpse didn't have a chance to hit the ground. The implication of this idea is that the person, like any animal that has ever died, is gone forever; what remains is, at best, a moving target.

Lastly, just to be fair, there are some opinions (not credible at all) that I mention here for the sole purpose of mocking them. They propose the idea that zombies can be cured, whatever the cause, and turned back into humans. Do not listen to them! They want to steal your shit when you die! Sure, some people like to imagine there's a cure, but you'll never find one. Only in the movies will you ever see a cure, and it's bogus. It's deceit. It should be treason against humanity to mislead, to give false hope. Now, I think Jesus, with his Christian hocus-pocus and "miracles" or aliens, might be able to do something like "cure," but in my opinion it's all hogwash. Once a zombie, always a zombie. That's what I say.

So what do we have? We have a human—perhaps dead, perhaps not quite as dead anymore—that somehow or other became zombified. All right, class, it's time for a practical example. Let's say we have a man, and this man dies and lies down. If the zombiism is particularly vicious, he might stay standing while he turns, but let's say he lies down. He might look dead for a while, maybe even a few hours or days, but eventually he will get back up. At the point when he starts to get back up, it's safe to say he is a zombie.

It's also safe to assume he will want to eat you alive, ripping the skin from your flesh like some obese middle-aged bachelor with every fried drumstick in a bucket of Kentucky Fried Chicken, just because he knows no other way to drown out the loneliness of his meager, unprepared existence but to eat slowly and methodically until no meat remains. Zombies eat that shit up. Keep in mind that it's also possible zombies might not eat you, instead choosing to infect you with their own curse, whatever that might be, to make you a zombie too. This is especially the case when they are already "full." If this happens to you, skip the rest of this book and turn to the chapter on how to shoot yourself in the face.

Matthew Collins And Geoffrey Collins

On the History of Zombies

We should probably get the record straight at the beginning. If there ever was a modern zombie, in action, it was destroyed before anyone realized what it was. There have not been any reported cases of human zombiism that have withstood rational investigation, nor has there been any deadly outbreak to speak of. *Yet*. Historically, however, there have been rumors of zombies, from various parts of the world and in various periods of time, where people who were dead have purportedly been revived and subsequently risen from the grave. One of the world's major religions, for instance, maintains a belief in just such a "miracle." Other reports include the hopping zombie from China, which are completely ridiculous, and, more currently, slave zombies wandering around Haiti.

Concerning the matter of zombies in past history, I can only say that most of those weren't actually zombies, and some of them weren't actually real. For instance, it is a proven fact that zombies can't talk due to considerable deterioration in the faculties of the mind and so forth and who cares. This means that the Zombie Jesus we all know and love is actually not a zombie, but more likely some kind of ghost or spirit, as the case may be. In fact, almost all historical references to zombies can actually be converted into stories about ghosts and possession. Consider the classic Egyptian mummy reference. This is clearly not a zombie because the mummy has a purpose: to protect its tomb and booty from the injustices of thieving bastards. Zombies, on the other hand, have no purpose except to rend flesh and die miserably, and it would be illogical to suppose otherwise. The only reasonable conclusion, then, is that the mummy is actually a ghost in possession of a corpse.

Turning to more recent times, zombies have supposedly been found in Haiti, some existing for many years after being created by some kick-ass Haitian voodoo performed by a religious individual bearing the title of *bokor*. Supposedly the bokor could use his sorcery to create a zombie powder, which would then be applied to a person to turn the victim into a zombie, but a zombie under the bokor's control. Seriously speaking, it appears that these "zombies" are usually just normal people high on some amazingly psychedelic drugs contained in the powder, drugs that may cause paralysis, hallucinations, and the appearance of being dead. Mind control aside, it is my guess that since everyone in town insists they've come back from the dead, the victims just go along with it, maybe to get attention, as a response to social pressures and religious beliefs or to play a good joke on their mothers.

Lastly, though not really lastly at all, are those rumors from Chinese lore that bear some slight resemblance to what we typically might refer to as zombies. In these fairytales of recklessness, the Chinese talk of *jiang shi*, reanimated corpses that supposedly hop around to attack people for the sake of absorbing their life essence and perhaps in order to get back home where they can be buried in peace. In reality, these are no more zombies than mummies are but seem to be some hybrid of mummy-vampire baby. As such, the hopping jiang shi should not be considered a significant threat.

In the end, whether they are rumors of zombies from Haiti, China, or something even more mainstream, these rumors are, in all likelihood, only bedtime stories parents tell their children at night to scare the shit out of them, and I'm pretty sure they have no real basis in fact. For instance, I've heard these so-called Haitian zombies aren't very dangerous, which to me conclusively disproves their zombie status since we all know zombies to be a horrifying menace both to society and to the lives of sweet, innocent children.

Most likely, the only real zombies so far have been retarded zombie animals that were crushed beneath the tires of Bubba's eighteen-wheeled delivery truck of lard as they mistakenly stumbled toward the lights. All in all, we might not necessarily know a zombie when we see it, at least not right off. However, here's your first tip: it's pretty safe to say that if you see a human eating another human, it is one of two things—a psychopathic cannibal or a zombie. If it's the first case, get out your gun and shoot it in the head. If it's the second case, get out your gun and shoot it in the head.

How Could I Become Zombified?

Just how does one become zombified if not from another zombie? Is it possible to become a zombie without coming in direct contact with the "infection"? What actually causes zombiism? No one really knows (by which I mean that I don't really know). I just asked Geoffrey, and he said something long and complicated, which is something I was afraid of. I didn't actually listen, so I think it's safe to say that nobody knows. There have been some theories, I suppose, like that it could be caused by a viral infection, some kind of bacteria, radiation, meteorites, comet dust, aliens, rainbows, leprechauns, magic, or, even worse, science. Each possible cause might act differently, affect different organisms differently, or even spread differently. Even better, any of them could happen at any time, even the same time!

I'm not going to say I know which will be the real cause because that would be lying; instead, I just assume that they all will be the real cause, and I stay wary of each. I also wear around my neck a silver bullet that has a cross cut into the tip, and inside that tip is a lead bullet stuffed with some garlic and holy water paste. Just in case of emergency. Oh, and I also wear a pistol on another necklace made of gold. Gold barbed wire, that is, because I'm no girl (but I still like gold because it's liquid [which is to say that it is an investment that also has immediate value, not that it is in a state of matter which flows and can boil (that would be hot)]).

The real problem with not knowing the specific cause of zombiism is that each cause might manifest itself differently. For instance, some causes of zombiism might be sudden and widespread, affecting all people—dead or alive—equally, thereby creating an entirely hostile atmosphere without much chance of survival, much less quarantine. In other cases, the zombiism might be slow spreading, slow like dying old people running, and it might originate in one small laboratory, city, or countryside where the military could contain and prevent further outbreaks (assuming the government is prepared). As if that's not bad enough, each cause could create a different type or mixture of zombie, like leftover night after potluck Mondays, but on Thursday instead of Tuesday. Consequently, this uncertainty requires that preparations be thorough and well planned out, but I digress, as preparing for the onslaught will be discussed in later chapters. Further discussion on how zombiism spreads can be found below after the following statement.

Now, this doesn't make any sense to me, but if you're reading this section because you *wanted* to become a zombie, I would suggest you snort some more narcotics, throw a doughnut in the face of a cop, and drive at top speeds into a solid wall. And I mean *solid*. Why? Because doing that would be retarded, just like you must be if you *want* to turn into a zombie. Saying you want to be a zombie is like saying you want me to reduce your brain into a cloud of red vapor, and if that's how you feel, then you make me sick. Sick enough to go get a cupcake and wash it down with a bottle of warm tequila, which I'm going to do right now.

Ah, that's better. Now that we've all become more sensible, be cool and stay in school. Jackass.

How Do I Cure Zombiism?

If someone weren't quite a zombie yet, the closest thing to a cure, in my graciously humble opinion, would involve enough morphine to kill a whale followed by a bullet to the old thinker. If there is no morphine on hand, any similar type of powerful kill-you-on-overdose drug will do, or just skip that step and move straight to the bullet part. If the zombiism has already taken hold, it's again with the bullet thing. It may just be possible to amputate limbs fast enough to avoid a full-body infection, but that's always risky business. Sure, though I don't believe them and spit on their graves, some sources say zombies may possibly be cured by an alien-induced spray or some supervaccine, but I don't think the first encounter of the third kind is going to bring a cure for zombiism, and I haven't seen any supervaccine that has worked or was even made with curing zombies in mind, which I imagine would be like curing death and retardation with the same pill. No, I think it's only the bullet.

How Could I Kill a Zombie?

Now, since I'm mentioning it, I might as well go into how one might kill a zombie. Throughout the years there has been some speculation about exactly what it takes to kill a zombie, but most of that was between a few crazy hobos resembling some mixture of a Mary Kay lady hawking pink lipstick, a truck of fake beards, and a Goodwill bin overflowing with crusty used underwear, with everyone making out and dry-humping everyone else. Needless to say, we didn't take them seriously. We did give each of them about, oh, three fiddy and then went on our way.

No matter how weird things get, or what zombie you face, you can always kill a zombie by destroying its brain. Sometimes taking off the head is all that matters, but not always. Taking off the head is sure to render the body useless, and any movie where that isn't true isn't a movie that should be watched, sober or in a good humor. Let's use some simple science here, people. The body's muscles are controlled by electrical impulses. From where, you might ask? From that organ known as the juicy, blood-engorged brain. If any part of the body is cut off from the brain—be it a hand, an arm, or the whole thing—those electrical impulses just won't be there anymore. Sure, it's possible the body still might shake a bit, but that's not living or undead. No, I think that's something else. Something you don't have to worry about, just so long as you don't pick up a zombie's hand to scratch your ass with it.

So you see that the body is just a tool of the brain, which is pretty much true for all of us. However, it's worth taking note that the brain cannot be completely removed from the head without a lot of work or a big rock, so keep in mind that a severed head might still be a bit feisty. Again, there's no real danger unless you put a finger in its mouth, or it somehow falls into your lap. If you want a souvenir zombie head, you might consider knocking the teeth out of it. Think of how helpless that poor zombie would be, bodyless and toothless—it would be hilarious, and members of the opposite sex would find themselves oddly more attracted to you. The best it could do would be to gum you to death, and I don't see that happening. If it could, people wouldn't think babies were so cute.

Now, the best way to destroy the zombie's brain is so painfully obvious to Geoffrey and I that we often forget the average person doesn't spend the majority of his or her day considering it. Quite clearly, the easiest and most effective way is to combine one part zombie skull with two parts bullets, the bigger the better and mixed at high velocity. These bullets are usually fired from guns or cannons or something of that sort. This kind of combination, that of the zombie head and bullets, is a match made in heaven and generally results in what we in the business call "pink mist." If done right, it really is a beautiful sight to behold, and I often drink to the memories I have of it. For the most part, the exact type of bullet is not a large factor in the fate of that zombie's useless gray meat loaf, just so long as the head is blown clean from the shoulders in a smattering of hairy confetti. *Bam!* Another dead zombo. And yes, it is that easy.

If you can't explode the brain through traditional ammunitions, there might be other methods you could use in a dire situation, but not fire. Fire would be useful in purging the land of the bodies, but this is best done if the zombie is already dead. It could take up to several hours before the fire works its way inside the head to consume the brain, and while the fire's working, the zombie could still be wandering about. Now, I'm not an expert on forest fires, but this sounds like a good way to start a forest fire. I am, however, an expert on bears, and I know that makes Smokey sad. Fire will certainly do the trick, but save it for the cleaning. Acid would work better, so long as it's really strong and in a sufficient quantity, but acid is notoriously hard to work with and tends to splash. Better stay away from that too.

As far as other methods go, it might be possible to poison a zombie, but there's no guarantee that the zombie's heart is pumping, or that its blood is even flowing, so if you're using a poison, you'll probably have to apply it directly into the brain. I doubt it matters what poison it is, just so long as it kills human tissue. Still, be aware that you can't rely on muscle relaxants or other chemicals that cause death due to some variation on organ failure, because zombies' organs don't really work anyway. Which really brings me to even yet another point.

How Does Zombiism Spread?

Given that the cause of zombiism is certainly unknown, as I mentioned above, and will probably not be expected, it is difficult to judge how it will spread. There is a small chance, albeit so small it's hardly worth considering, that the zombiism will not spread from zombie to human contact, like blood in the mouth or saliva in wounded skin. In this slim bit of possibility, the zombiism may be spread two ways: One is that all dead automatically become zombies, in which case there will immediately be millions of zombies as the dead simultaneously claw out of their graves to roam the earth. For this case, the spread of zombiism is clear and unpreventable; all dead humans, killed by any cause, will need to be dispatched properly as defined by some federally mandated protocol to prevent their imminent return. The second way is that zombiism will spread through specific potions, incantations, or other sources of magic and science, in which case the zombiism would be spread by wizard to human or scientist to human contact. Then the curse of being a zombie would be delivered by an intelligent, and presumably controlling, individual who is most likely up to no good, if not downright evil. Fortunately for us people who do not like evil, this is a negligible possibility. As such, we can spend a negligible amount of time worrying about it and a majority of our time worrying about the senseless evil of most causes of zombiism.

Most likely, indeed I say most certainly, the zombiism will be spread by zombie to human contact, via the exchange of bodily fluids, an airborne substance, cooties, or some dark aura. Such exchanges might be as simple as an infectious yawn or as nasty as a bath in bloody vomit, as innocent as using a dirty napkin or as kinky as a necrophilic romp with an infected corpse. Any open wounds, such as scratches, bites, or even love nips, will provide a direct pathway for complete, invasive, absolute infection. Bingo, zombie.

As you can tell, there are many ways, in such cases as these, in which the infection could spread from body to body, a fact that requires absolute vigilance over the status of your skin and its natural barriers. Be paranoid-serious about this unless you want to become infected through a hangnail or some other means equally as lame and depressing. Note that this contact would also include contact with soon-to-be zombies; just because an infected individual is not yet trying to eat you does not mean the bastard can't infect you. This is all just to say that you can't trust any contact with anyone without at least a three-day quarantine. Otherwise, the risk is yours.

Now, with the aid of sophisticated simulation software, Geoffrey and I have been able to study this most likely scenario of zombiism outbreaks and have concluded that its ability to spread defies all logical reasoning. Rationally speaking, a disease that inhibits the motion of the infected body, reduces motor coordination, and effectively eliminates intelligence should not be able to spread quickly; alas, that is where human stupidity, panic, and blind desperation kick in. That's also where I kick ass at kicking zombie ass. (Geoffrey also kicks the zombie pooper, in a big way.)

Furthermore, in our most scholarly tone of voice, it is our educated opinion that, in most cases, however the invasion begins, via whatever method or combination of methods, zombiism will be incredibly difficult to contain. This is primarily for three reasons: First, once infected, an individual will likely remain human for some time while his or her health steadily declines, and the illness takes control of their wasted body. During this interim period, the individual can unknowingly infect others as well as breach containment boundaries under the guise of a fleeing refugee. Unfortunately, depending on the person and the seriousness of the infection, the interim period may last several days and is hard to predict. This is important to understand, unless you're Miss Cleo and can see that sort of thing in advance.

The second reason is that not all humans who are faced with their own destruction, who stare into the face of an endless darkness and hear only the echo of eternal hunger, react in the way most benefiting mankind. People who realize they have been infected *should* do a lot of things, but a lot will do bullshit and pretend not to be infected, or feel that somehow they can keep it secret until a cure crops up, at which time they'll wave their hand up in the air, confessing the infection, and laugh nervously while they are injected with a vaccine, all the while acting as if they had been completely responsible. Those Trojan horse sons of bitches, damning humanity to a ceaseless battle against stupidity and death. Problem is, the cure will never come, not unless you count my golden gun as a cure. Those people will keep their illness a secret, for one reason or another, until they turn and unexpectedly become a threat to not only all *your* friends and the people you love, especially the people you love, but also some people you probably don't care very much about.

The last reason is the worst of all. Now, I'm not sure if you knew this or not, but it came as a surprise to me. Apparently, and this is what I hear from my sources on the street, there are some people who do not believe in zombies. I don't want to name any names or anything, but I think those people should be ashamed for the danger they put us all in. Because some people are not prepared for a zombie invasion, because they do not believe such a threat exists, society itself will be unprepared for any sort of strategic response or retaliation in a timely manner, not even timely enough to stop the slowest of zombiism from spreading. Some people will be struck dumb, confused, incapable of coherent thought or action, and it is this inability to react that will cause the downfall of humanity.

The solution? Education. Preparation. Responsible governmental oversight. And above all, constant vigilance. The solution is this book, the awareness that it will bring, the new ways of thinking about the world that will make it safer to live in. If you're having second thoughts about spending a wad of cash on a few pounds of paper, relax. This is an investment, one that could save your life. Kind of like a diet book, except easier because we won't make you feel bad about yourself just because you like to eat. Instead, we'll make you feel bad about yourself because you risk the lives of everyone you know every single moment of your nigh worthless existence. But you can fix that by reading this book, so you've already taken the first steps. See? An investment. So read on, my friends, so that when the invasion comes and your friends freak out, you will be able to take action. You will be able to save lives, hopefully even ones worth saving. You, alone, will be a hero—because you bought this book.

Types of Zombies

In order to understand what humanity is up against, it is important to understand what possible threats might exist and what types of zombies might be encountered. It is important to understand how these variations work, what their strengths and weaknesses are, how they think, what they feel, who tucks them in at night. It's important to get inside their head. I can't help you don the suit of a living-dead guy so you can attain practical experience, and I wouldn't want to, and I will never recommend it, but if it helps you better understand what your chances are, what you're fighting, then find someone who *will* recommend it and then continue from there. If you want a more socially acceptable way of gaining knowledge, continue honing your reading skills and read on.

Animal Zombies

You might be thinking that animals can't turn into zombies, and you'd be partly right. But you'd also be partly wrong, and that's wrong enough to pay the price. Sure, for some causes of zombiism, animals are likely unaffected. However, there are a number of causes that have led directly to animals becoming infected with zombiism, at least in simulations, Geoffrey's prophetic dreams, and memories of my childhood. This could happen for reasons, including, but not limited to, radiation from meteorites, erectile dysfunction, and certain types of diseases like rabies and rage.

Zombie animals are perhaps the most terrifying of zombies for a whole crap-load of reasons. They will actually require you to shovel crap out of your pants barehanded. For one, the head on most animals is not in an upright, easy-to-hit position. Instead, it's lower to the ground and can only be hit from the front. Indeed, some animals have much stronger skulls than humans, so a single bullet might not be enough to penetrate the brain. Now that's tricky. Also, there's no telling how fast these animal zombies might be. It could be that they stagger about like typical zombies, but it might also be that they can run as fast as tigers on a great savanna, sprinting after fresh human sausage. Think about a zombie dog that can run three times as fast as you can, even when you're shitting your pants from adrenaline? Yikes.

Another reason zombie animals make me grip my favorite shotgun till I bleed from my fingernails is that there are so many kinds of animals that it's almost impossible to plan against them all. Think about it, human zombies are generally afraid of water, but zombie fish? Or what about zombie bats that can fly around and kill you in the dark when you're hiding in a tree? If whatever causes zombiism affects animals, it's safe to say that we are screwed. Royally. Screwed. There would be no safe harbor, no animal that wouldn't want to lap up our blood, no gun that could fend them all off but perhaps a multidirectional superheated fusion powered plasma laser. And those don't come cheap, my friends. No, zombie animals are scary, so let's hope we don't have to fight them off. The last reason animal zombies keep me up at night is because animals are already dumb, so they don't lose much of anything when they turn. They just get thirsty.

If you do enter into a duel with one, though, I'd say forget trying to snipe the brain and just destroy the animal's mobility by taking out the legs or cutting the body in half. Once the animal has been rendered primarily helpless and immobile, then deliver the finishing blow. If the animal is a rhino or an elephant, you'll have a tough time trying to immobilize it. The best tactic would be to use explosives or perhaps dig a pit filled with heavy-duty spikes and trap it. If you want to slow it down, use a high-powered rifle and shoot it in the knee so that it trips up. It'll buy you a few seconds to escape or for you to cook off a grenade. Either that or shoot it through the eye, and I wouldn't hold my breath for that one.

Stumbling Zombies (Walkers)

The stumbling zombies are the most common type of zombies, which is a good sign for those of us that want to live. The stumblers, or more commonly known as Walkers and less commonly as bumblers, shanties, and tuberculosis Ted, were typical humans that turned into stupid zombies exhibiting nearly senseless, lethargic motion similar to that of most of my aunts. Their slow movement makes them easy targets for practically every weapon, and they only pose a serious threat when they arrive in large numbers. Numbers like three thousand or so. Basically, if you're in the stadium of a football game with thirty thousand other people all around you, you might consider yourself screwed if they all suddenly turned into zombies; that is, unless you discover some dormant running ability every coach would literally orgasm over.

Walkers are attracted to activity, lights, the smell of living people, and any loud noises. They are afraid of nothing, but should be afraid of bears, and they like long walks on the beach. I made that last one up just to break the tension, but the rest of this is serious. Avoiding this kind of zombie is easy: just walk around the damn thing and stay a step ahead. Watch out for sneaky ones that hide immediately around corners or in the dark; they walk, slowly, but that also means they are quiet, so line of sight is your only reliable sense of detection. You can optionally push them over if they get too close, beat them on the head with a bat, or dominate their face with whatever gun is in your hand at the time. Really, Walkers are retarded, and they have slow reflexes, so don't sweat too much about them. If you'll keep your cool, you'll keep your life. Someone would have to be hysterical to the point of paralysis to be caught by one of these bastards. Exceptions apply if there are exceptionally many of these zombies, especially if they are on your neck.

Fast Zombies (Runners)

There might exist some zombies, among all that might exist, that move quite a bit faster than the average. I like to call these zombies flapjacks because they are fast and quite a bit more violent, but most people call them Runners. You can tell the difference between a Runner and a Walker by noticing how quickly their legs are moving as they approach you. If the legs are moving speedily, perhaps even running, you might call that a Runner. Also, Runners tend to leave Walkers behind, mostly because Walkers don't run. This means that if Walkers and Runners are mixed into the crowd of ravenous undead, Walkers generally have to clean up the scraps the Runners leave behind (unless they get impossibly lucky and someone incidentally falls into the middle of the herd from above). The fact that Runners always get the freshest cut has been cause for no small amount of envy and jealousy, not to mention conflict, between Walkers and Runners. They mostly do nothing about it.

If there are Runners, or if there are only Runners, things get quite a bit more ugly than if there were only Walkers. With Walkers, we get the freedom to move about, knowing that our intelligence and normal speed will prove sufficient to get away from even the closest of encounters (excluding unlucky surprises). However, that's not so with Runners. Runners might look like Walkers for a time, then suddenly sprint with the speed of an Olympic runner until they tackle you to the ground and rip your face off. Even our intelligence can fail us, as an onrush of zombies might make us panic so that we lose our wits and end up just running blindly, wetting our pants so that our shoes squeak when we step. That would be a bad sign.

No, we have to be careful around Runners, because they might surprise us, because they are more frightening and vicious, and because we might not be able to outrun them. I bet you didn't think of that, did you? Sure, every movement a zombie makes might tear their remaining flesh a little bit more, and a little bit more, and a little bit more, until their muscles have deteriorated and can no longer function, but in the meantime those damn muscles don't feel a thing. That means they don't feel pain, and they don't feel tired. I'm not sure when the last time you ran from your house out to the city limits was, but when I did it yesterday I threw up three times and had to start walking the rest of the way. That was at the end of the block, and I live on the corner. Sure, I think that I might be able to beat some Runners over a short distance, but they would take me to the ground just as soon as I slowed up for an instant, and don't even bother wondering what would happen if I tripped.

I think that the best way to handle Runners would be the same way as one would handle zombie animals: carpet bombs, gigantic lasers, and trip mines everywhere. If all you have is a gun, first take out their legs or pelvis, which we can all agree is an easier target, and then take out their brains. Zombies might not feel pain, but they can't move very quickly on two broken legs, and that's a fact that won't let you down. Once you take away their speed, they become mostly harmless, but it's always best to finish what you start, which is to say that you should squeeze off a round into their eyehole. Of course, if you can hit their heads, then by all means go ahead and do it, but realize before you waste the bullets that when a zombie is running, its head is going to be bouncing all over the damn place. Take a minute to think about that while I go use the restroom. Oh, and by the way, my toilet is rigged to explode, just in case the world goes south before I get done.

Grabbing Zombies (Stickers)

Stickers aren't really anything special except as a special case of another kind of zombie; they can just catch you off guard if you're not sure what zombies are capable of. These are basically just croaks of any flavor that don't seem to die very well, but instead keep coming at you like tomorrow will never come. I like to picture them as holding on for dear undead life with both cold, nail-broken hands. Seriously holding on. These zombies have a tendency to grab on to things, especially whatever vehicle you might be driving or whatever legs you might be walking on, and once they grab on they hardly ever let go unless you completely cut off every last godforsaken finger. For example, you might run over some stupid zombie walking haplessly in the middle of the road, and you might laugh with your buddies about it while you open a bottle of beer with your teeth, but if it's a sticker, you won't be laughing when you step out of your monster truck and find that same zombie waiting for your ankle. They catch rides, you see, and you always have to be careful about those. Periodically sweep underneath your car, and consider using a mirror to check the underside before stepping out. It's really a good practice to get into anyway, and I've been doing it for the past nine years without any reportable mishaps thus far.

Sickly Zombies (Spitters)

There have been, from time to time, mythical stories of people so insanely ill that they do projectile vomiting across the room, usually from the toilet. I don't mention this so much because sick people will turn into a Spitter (not that they won't); I'm just proving that it's possible for even a normal lad down on his luck to achieve ungodly results. You see, a Spitter is a zombie whose cup runneth over with a force and pressure not typically seen outside the municipal sewer industry, and the volume is such that distance and spread are both equally achieved. This vomit, while not necessarily any more harmful than normal vomit, carries in it the plague of undead unborn children, the plague that will turn you into lifeless target practice, an inescapable curse on the soul of your mother and your father, with a crushing weight pushing you into everlasting despair and unrelenting darkness. You'll become a "zook," for lack of a better term, in an almost-complete certainty. If hit in the face or any open wounds, whatever it is that makes a human become a zombie will sneak into any opening that your body was weak enough to have. When that happens, there's nothing left for you.

Why all this dread and gloom? To make you remember. There's not going to be a great sign that a zombie is going to be a Spitter. They won't all have to be fat and bulging, or covered in vomit from the hour before. They won't walk up to you, gag a little, then put their hands on their knees, and yak on your shoes. These zombies will blend in with other zombies, and you'll think you're safe, zigzagging back and forth between the dumb bastards, and suddenly you'll be hit, blinded from five feet by an unsuspicious midget. Then who will the asshole be? So you have to remember that something like this could happen, and you have to take precautions, or at least give it some thought before you make the heroic but fruitless run through the crowd to get that lucky lad or lass a handful of daisies.

Mutant Zombies

Some zombiism has been suspected of causing some humans to turn into some sort of zombie mutants just because of some genetic glitch or something. Maybe there were some bad vibes when the human was turned, or maybe the human had high blood pressure and the zombiism went to town on it, I just can't say for sure, but I do know that when a zombie starts to mutate, it can turn into almost anything. For most, these zombies look about the same, like normal humans, but become incredibly strong. You wouldn't think those weak, insignificant flabbo fat guy arms on a fat guy body would be able to pick you up and rip you in half, but you would die surprised. These strong zombies would have the strength of some mythical beast that had Hulk Hogan for one arm, Arnold Schwarzenegger for the other, and a pair of Chuck Norris legs clad in exquisitely tight jeans. It's some crazy shit.

Other mutant zombies might turn into more of a skinless reptile with a long tongue or into a gargantuan retarded beast, or they might mutate into a helpless piece of crap you could step on and later wipe off your boots. It's pretty hard to say what kind of mutant zombies you might face, but you can generally bet they will be stronger and faster and maybe look less human than other zombies, and that makes them freakier. But like I always say, the bigger they are, the easier they are to hollow out and make a canoe out of. Or was it, "The faster they are, the more beneficial the target practice"? I forget what I always say now, so just watch out for mutant zombies and try to be prepared for whatever they might throw at you. Like barrels or cars or mailboxes, that sort of thing.

Smart Zombies

These don't really exist. Anything or anyone who says these exist is either trying to play a joke on you or is being ridiculous. There's just no such thing; it's impossible, like a Smurf orgy. If you see a so-called smart zombie in a movie, realize that it's just the exquisitely failed imagination of some writer or director, and that they should be blamed for misleading you and otherwise disgracing all who prepare for the true zombie invasion. Which is coming, and soon. If you see, with your own eyes, what you think looks like a smart zombie, it's probably, actually, in all reality, a normal human that was lost in the woods as an infant and ended up being raised by real zombies on blood-soaked T-shirts and bone marrow. The mistake is understandable, I guess, but don't let it be your doom.

Zombies Do Not Talk

Seriously, they don't. I assume I've mentioned this before, but I don't even care; I'm going to mention it again. Zombies? They don't talk. Period. Zombies don't talk, they don't form words and run around providing witty and humorous dictation, they don't hold conversation with foreign diplomats, they don't do anything. They might grunt, but it won't sound like anything except a fart from the mouth. You can argue with this book all you want, but zombies don't talk. Fuck 'em all anyway.

How does this work to your advantage? The universal zombie litmus test, or UZLT. Don't know what litmus is? Doesn't matter, all you need to know is that the universal zombie litmus test is the fastest and most effective way to determine if someone is a zombie. I've read studies of up to 98 percent accuracy, and that's accurate like a pregnancy test. So how does it go? Simply ask the potential zombie to speak. Say, "Hey, are you a zombie?!" If they answer with what you might consider words, then they are not a zombie (yet); if not, I think you know what to do. Don't be afraid to take it to the next level by learning this phrase in multiple languages so you can make sure you give the person a good chance before you goo their mind. For instance, in Spanish, "Oye, eres un zombie?!" Or in French, "Hé, vous êtes un zombie?!" Or in Dutch, "He, ben je een zombie?!" Anyway I'm sure you get the idea.

You might all recall the classic work *Night of the Living Dead*, and I don't want to give away the ending, but that whole little mishap could have been avoided if everyone knew the simple universal zombie litmus test. This is why it's important for you to make sure you tell everyone you know about the UZLT so there's no confusion when the world goes all to hell and people start feeling like they need to shoot their way out of a paper bag.

Still, no one has asked the question, why can't zombies talk? That's probably because I already mentioned it, but I'll briefly readdress that issue now. The brain gets fucked up. Done. Speaking takes a massive level of memory, comprehension, planning, understanding, and coordination. It eventually comes naturally to all of us, but that's just because the brain does so damn much for us. You think a zombie, barely standing on two legs, has the coordination to quote Shakespeare? If so, you can go straight to hell.

Now that we agree on this most basic matter, we can begin to realize that the old stereotype of zombies mumbling "BRAINS!" is just a theatrical device used to tell the audience sitting in the back that certain stage characters are supposed to be zombies while it tells the audience sitting in the front that these stage characters are not, in fact, actually zombies. Please try to understand this when you see zombies saying stupid shit like that, and don't make the mistake of basing your whole identification system on a lie. Lies, like knives, make an ass out of you and me. Actually, they just kill you.

Zombies' Organs Do Not Work

So let's all imagine for a second that we see a zombie feasting on a human body. Let's say the body was a man, and he was a fatty, so there's a lot of body for that zombie to eat. Well, the zombie doesn't have anywhere to be or any appointments to keep, and it is dumb, so it doesn't know when to stop, so the zombie keeps eating and eating. After a while, that zombie's stomach will be bloated and full, bursting even. Since zombie organs don't work, its stomach won't digest, and the food won't move throughout the digestive tract. This means that the stomach will either explode or the zombie will eat so much that the food will fill its throat and fall back out of its mouth.

Is this a problem for the zombie? No, not particularly. It's probably happy enough to be sitting and playing in that very messy rot. So long as another living person doesn't run by, the zombie might stay there as long as the body does, assuming the body doesn't get up and walk off. The point of all this is that zombies eat, but it doesn't do anything for them. They can't digest what they've eaten, so they can't metabolize new energy. Instead, zombie bodies live off of themselves, somehow creating energy by consuming their own cells. This is called starvation, and it will happen to every zombie eventually. It's all really just a matter of time. Probably, unless the zombiism is caused by your typical magic or evil powers, in which case you should take this book with a grain of salt. (Yeah, it doesn't make any damn sense, but that's how it is, I'm pretty sure.)

You know the saying that a light that burns twice as bright burns half as long? It applies here, which might be why zombies are usually so slow. Imagine a zombie that runs. Running takes a lot of energy (*we* should know), so their bodies will be consumed rapidly to serve up that energy. It won't be very long before a runner just doesn't have what it takes to run anymore, at which point they either become a walker or just sit down entirely, forever. Now, take a walking zombie instead, and you'll see it sticking around for a lot longer due to its shuffling technique. This style of movement is really quite conservative since the movement originates entirely from rotating the hips and not from powering the legs.

Another thing that's interesting about zombie anatomy is that most or all of their body's systems shut down. There is no immune system on a zombie, there is no excretory system to remove waste, and there is no healing ability. This means that if you have to take a massive dump, and then get turned into a zombie, the bacteria in that shit will multiply and create gases that will eventually cause your anus to explode, expelling rank and foul feces all over your zombie pants. That, assuming it doesn't release itself slowly over time, in which case nothing would really happen, and it would turn out to be pretty boring.

The lack of a healing ability, however, is much more important. Every time we move, we damage our body just a little bit. If we go lift something heavy, we damage it quite a bit more, especially if we lift something too heavy or stretch too far. That's why we feel sore the next morning, because our bodies did something that hurt them quite a bit, and they are trying to heal before you hurt them again. Well, zombies can't heal. They can take a bullet, but the wound will never close. They might be able to run really fast, but their muscles will rip and tear and never heal until they just snap in two and leave the zombie unable to move at all. Some zombies might be incredibly strong, but they won't be ripping people in half for very long.

Even if zombies don't starve to real death first, their bodies will eventually give out on them, and they'll be left helpless and immobile on the ground. Either way, if a zombie invasion does break out, all you have to do is wait. Zombies won't be a permanent fixture, just a passing crisis. That is, unless I'm wrong, and zombies get energy through some infernal incantation, and their bodies become much more resilient to minor damage than I can anticipate, which is something that could happen if the zombies were brought back by spells or something. Since this is a possibility, which it is, I hope you've read this far so that you can keep it in mind later on when you start preparing for the invasion. If you didn't read this, then I don't know why I wrote these words and instead could have filled in these pages with random letters and pictures of puppies. I hope you die.

Are Zombies Human?

No. One thing to always keep in mind about zombies is that they are not human, at least not anymore, so don't feel bad about erasing the very semblance of humanity from their faces, the very history of their time on earth completely and absolutely, with whatever is at hand. Sure, maybe in other dimensions there is some way to reverse the damage, make everything okay again, maybe even live a normal life. And maybe there is a way for you to stop surfing on rainbows and get the goddamn stars out of your eyes. Even if there is a cure, which you probably won't know about ever in your whole freaking life, that's no excuse for you to roll over and die or give up without a fight.

As for zombies that used to be humans and that you used to know, I have one bit of advice: no mercy. Nothing pisses me off like those dumb bitches that always look at *ex-humans* with big sentimental walrus tears in their eyes and misplaced, retarded looks of puppy-dog love on their faces, refusing to pull the trigger. Did they even see *Old Yeller*? That kid pulled the trigger like a real champ, even if doing so forced him to see his beloved yellow Labrador retriever's brain splash the walls of its cage. He probably didn't even turn down the job of cleaning said walls with gasoline and setting the cage aflame to purge it of the rabies infection, even though deep down he knew he was about to torch the last remains and memories of his honey-sweet childhood. I would have loved to have been there so I could hand him a beer and tell him, "Childhood is over. Go now and be a man." Champ.

Moral of the story? If I see someone on my team of survivors refusing to pull the trigger just because some zombie has the appearance of a person they used to know, I would be forced to completely destroy the zombie on their behalf, sodomizing and defiling the rotten, stinking corpse with enough lead to kill an orphanage. Then I'd shoot that person in the knee and use them as a distraction; I don't need someone on my team who can't be trusted to do their job, and neither can you.

What do you do if you see your neighbor all pale and cold, stumbling toward you? What do you do if you wake up and find your best pal knocking on your door with a hand that's no longer hot and sweaty? What do you do if you find your mother-in-law inside your house, nagging at you in such a way that your mind starts to splinter into a thousand pieces and every part of you that still claims sanity wants to commit suicide by drowning in the pot of hot coffee sitting on the table? Take it from me and do everyone a favor: shoot them right through the center of their brain like you were Jesse James hopped up on crack and wielding three pairs of six-shooters. You'd probably be doing that poor zombie bastard a favor too, by releasing what's left of its soul from the icy clutches of hell. That soul might go back to hell right after that, but that's not really up to you. That's up to them … and Jesus.

Zombies of Popular Culture

No book about zombies would be complete without a section briefly examining the presence of zombies in popular culture. It might surprise everyone to know that zombies have been in the movies for quite some time, pretty much ever since movies were around. Back then, though, zombies were mostly harmless and nonthreatening, which just means that zombies were poorly characterized until ole George Romero made his orgasm-of-the-decade documentary *Night of the Living Dead*. Since then, zombies in the media have been more accurately portrayed, which is a good thing for those of us who use such movies for class material. Imagine the harm that would be rendered upon our great nation if zombies were still depicted as harmless, fun-loving creatures that always managed to get into problematic, but comical, situations. When the invasion came, we would all go looking for a hug or some good laughs, but instead we would only find a whole mob of bumbling meanies. And death, of course. That's why it's so important that we have zombie games, like *Resident Evil* or *Left 4 Dead*, to give us practical knowledge on how to combat the bastard zombies and to teach us how to really hate those undead monsters ... I guess that's all I have to say about this topic.

My advice? Go to the movie store, rent a dozen movies, watch them consecutively, get drunk, figure it out. Done, that's popular culture.

Chapter 3   Is This a Zombie?
(As inscribed into stone by Geoffrey)

—

"Hey, man, is that thing a zombie over there?"

"Say what? Don't make me go upside your head again! She my hoe, man."

"Sorry, I didn't know is all. I heard that zombies could attack at any moment, and she kinda reminded me of what zombies might be like, from the movies and all."

"Wow, dude. You are an idiot. With each word that passes through your lips, I feel like going upside your head more and more. In fact, let me get my bitch-whip out and pistol-whip some sense into that spine of yours."

"My spine? Why there?"

"Damn it, man, now you're getting one busted to your head, and I didn't want to have to do that. I mean, honestly, you were my friend, being my brother and all. Now I think it's over for us. And by *us*, I mean *you*, because I am going to—damn it, woman, I'm about to administer a skull-busting on this guy's aaahraghhrraah gurgle-crack-splunkerdoodle!"

"Dude. Your hoe just bit right into your neck, which totally killed you. I wonder why she did that. It really doesn't make sense, since she isn't a zombie or anyt—aaahraghhrraah gurgle-crack-splunkerdoodle!"

Zombie says what?

"Urgg ..."

Now, I know that this hasn't happened to anyone out there yet, and the reason I know is because I haven't killed them, as far as I know, but this is a very real problem that most people are unaware of. Nobody seems to know how to spot a zombie in a quick, precise manner in time to prevent accidental terminations or premature infections. Each and every day, I come within a snout's length of killing a few hundred people. But I don't. I don't end up destroying their brains because I know, without a shadow of a doubt, that they are not zombies. How do I know this?

Like all great things in life, it is very simple. I simply follow a guideline that is easy to abide by and makes for lovely dinner conversation with my neighbor's dog. While I know that each potential humanoid contact I encounter could result in the termination of a zombie, thus eliminating the zombie threat, I also know without a doubt that every previous humanoid contact I have had was just with some guy on the street or some girl on the bus. No zombies. And how can I be so sure? Again, the guidelines make it simple.

"What magical guidelines do you speak of, oh Great Zombie Slayer?"

A tingling in my spine told me you would ask that. It also told me there was an arrow sticking out of my spine, but I put a Band-Aid on it and will get to that later. To best sum up the guidelines that will ensure the survival of man in a nonzombie form, for many years, I will present them one at a time and illustrate them with personal stories from Matthew's dreams, my own actual life, ones we just made up, and some people that I made up too. By following these simple, practical lessons with each and every contact you make with the outside world, safety can be achieved for you, your children, your neighbors, and your neighbor's dog, but not their children because those little brats are out of control.

The Ultimate Zombie Hunter's Handbook

Lesson 1: Step 1

One sunny day, I was walking around on top of a mountain. This mountain was not particularly special in that it did not have rainbows of blood or prancing goat-gnomes running around, getting their dirty little hooves all over my clean blankets. It didn't even have a golden star waiting at the top. I was pretty disappointed about that because, let's face it, why would I have gone up there anyway?

Forget about it. I was just up there, and I decided to enjoy the splendid view of the valley. It sure was splendid. In fact, it was so splendid that I felt sure that nobody had ever seen anything so splendid. Just knowing that I was the only person to ever see such wondrous splendor gave me power. It gave me more power than anyone in the world had ever known. I declared to the world my newfound power with a very powerful laugh, worthy of notice. I began to realize that I was better than everyone else and that they should be my servants and be happy about it because serving someone so mighty and powerful was a good thing, especially in those days. But before I could realize this vision, something clouded it. Actually, something had clouded all my vision because a bird had crapped in my eyes. And then my power was gone, and only my little friends, the tears, remained. Plus that shit stung pretty bad. Even worse than an arrow in the spine. But seriously, I was on top of a mountain! What the *fuck* is a bird doing up there in the first place?

Well, to make a long story short, I sat there crying to myself because I was ashamed and hurt and I had bird crap in my eyes. Suddenly a bolt of lightning shot from the sun and scorched the rock next to me. When the dust and smoke and sparks all cleared, I found three stone tablets at my feet with eight life lessons for identifying and surviving zombies. On them were the keys to a long, righteous life without guilt or zombies. What a day.

Almost immediately, I began to preach these newfound principles. Over the years since, I amassed a following who found enlightenment from my principles in stone, and they shared their stories with me. Now, I will share those stories with all of you, who are probably not worthy of such great stories but get to hear them anyway because you earned that right by buying this book. (You had better have, dammit!) If you feel mentally up to the challenge, try to comprehend the moral of each story before I spell it out in all its gory detail. If you can grasp the reasons for these parables before their end, then you can truly say you are a worthy pupil of our teachings.

Tablet 1 had the first three principles on it. The first principle, known as step 1, is best summarized by the story of Gary. Gary was a kind soul who loved to talk to new people, animals, objects, and basically anything that appeared to listen. Most of the people in Gary's life had long ago lost the ability to listen to him anymore because he talked so much that they stopped loving him. But they kept feeding him and providing for him, so he kept on talking.

Eventually, it got so bad that Gary could only talk to animals because none of the people around him would even respond. At first he would talk to his pets, but soon they, too, lost interest, stopped eating, and died. Luckily for Gary, he didn't feel sad or alone because he could still talk with them, even if they weren't alive anymore. Over time, these animals would decay and become one with the earth again, and then Gary would have to find a new friend to listen to him.

Once Gary realized that certain plants, like trees, lasted longer than animals, he quit talking to animals altogether and began talking to the trees. It wasn't long before Gary quit interacting with humans and animals completely, because these trees of his would always listen and never run away or die. Years went by and still the trees remained, ever attentive and always polite.

But there is a saying in this part of the woods that goes, "Good things don't last." This was true for Gary as well. One night while he was asleep, talking to the tree friends of his dream world, a storm came into town. With this storm came lightning and with, this lightning came fire. The largest forest fire of the town's history took place that night and burned every tree within a hundred-mile radius of Gary's house. Luckily for Gary, his house did not burn down, nor did any of his close neighbors. There is no good reason for this.

When Gary awoke the next morning, he was devastated. All his best tree friends were gone. And unlike animals, they do not easily get replaced. Gary vowed to never make that same mistake again. Now, instead of ignoring humans and animals, he ignored humans, animals, and every other living thing in the world. Gary became friends with the rocks. The rocks would never be able to leave him. They did not move. They did not desire. They did not burn. The rocks would be his friends forever, and nobody was going to be able to take that away from him. Or so he thought.

One fateful day, a man came up to Gary, pleading for help. Gary had grown accustomed to being ignored and figured the man was talking to someone else. Gary did not bother to look around at whom the man might be talking to, because he ignored all people equally, and it did not concern him. He just happily continued his conversation with his rock, which he named Hamlet. It was a private joke of theirs because Gary loved omelets with ham in them and called them hamlets. He also said that hamlets rocked.

While Gary talked to Hamlet, the guy behind him died from a wound in his neck that had previously been bleeding, profusely. Gary did not notice. Gary did not notice the dead guy behind him stand up after several minutes of being dead. He did not notice the dead guy come up behind him, and he did not notice that this dead guy was still dead. He was now a zombie, and Gary was completely vulnerable. The zombie did what zombies do and bit Gary in the neck, really hard. Gary became a zombie.

Step 1 is simple. When being confronted with a possible enemy target, determine whether or not it could ever be alive. Do not ignore anything. Be ever vigilant. Gary's story illustrates what being ignorant of your surroundings can mean for your life. He spent too much time on nonliving objects and completely ignoring the rest of the world. Don't make the same mistake by putting too little emphasis on living creatures. Qualify everything. If you determine that it was never alive and could never become alive, then, and only then, can you dismiss it as safe. Remember, step 1 is about determining if your target could have ever been or could ever become alive. Is it organic or inorganic? I cannot stress the importance of this enough. It is the foundation of safety. If organic, move to lesson 2. Otherwise, move along, sir.

Lesson 2: Is He Dead, Ma?

Rusty had lived in a small town outside of New Orleans, Louisiana, his entire life. He hadn't known any roads but those that ran past Main Street, where it went around that one corner, down by the fishing pond. Oh, how he loved that little pond, especially during the hot summer months of July and August (or was it January? Rusty never got the hang of all that "months" business). He would make regular trips down to the pond just to jump in at full speed to escape the hot, muggy day. You know that kind of hot. The kind where you piss on yourself to cool off, and your clothes feel like an old woman's skin wrapped tightly around you, trying to suffocate you from heat and stink and old age and bitterness and Bengay. The kind of hot where you pay your neighbor's kid to get into your car, start it, turn on the air conditioner, and then wait until it starts to cool off before getting out so you can get into a pleasantly cooled atmosphere. And if he passes out from the heat, you just drag him back over into his yard and drive off, but only after the car has cooled sufficiently.

Well, one day Rusty was running merrily toward the pond on a particularly hot November afternoon. He wasn't thinking of cars in the street, just the feeling of the cool water against his dry, sunburned skin. He wasn't thinking about the large ice cream truck speeding down First Street after the driver ran the stop sign because he was too busy digging for another handful of pork rinds and beef jerky while simultaneously reaching for the built-in cigarette lighter to light up another home-rolled smoke stick. Rusty's normally excellent hearing failed to register the trademark ice cream jingle, "Da da da da da-da da-da, da-da-da da-da-da da da-da da." He didn't even hear the speakers over at the public pool, a place Rusty had never been allowed to go, playing the soft words of Anthony Armstrong Jones in "Everybody's Talkin'." Maybe, if he had heard that song, he would have stopped to see if he could get a free treat from one of the kids inside. But he didn't.

Luckily for Rusty, the driver never even saw him. By not hitting the brakes, Rusty died instantly on impact and didn't have to suffer from a long, drawn-out, painful death. Fortunately, Rusty was just a dog (but what a dog!). He was the longtime friend and family member of Jeb Fontain, local boy and private hero who at that instant had just witnessed his two favorite things in the whole world collide. He ran up to Rusty and yelled, "Is he dead, Ma?" Unfortunately, Jeb's mother was not present, so his question went unanswered. He was forced to assume the worst: Rusty had died from his wounds. Too bad, Jeb.

Walking away, head hanging, Jeb cried for his loss. He was all but consumed with grief for his poor friend, the only living creature who gave a shit. You see, Jeb was used to either being ignored or being slapped around by his parents. They didn't see him as a precious child, but just another slippery maggot that wiggled his way into their lives and boosted the welfare checks. He wasn't very good at hunting. He was terrible at belittling women. He couldn't even deep fat fry a turkey for Thanksgiving. Down in the South, he was as worthless as "a miskwuito witut enee turst fer blood." He was practically "a dag wit no tix on dem errs; it ain't natrall." To everyone in his life, Jeb was like a lip without dip, a truck without rust, or even a fish without fillet. "Ain't wurt shee-it."

But to Rusty, Jeb was the world. That poor dog loved that little boy as much as any dog loved any little boy. They spent all their time together because they were both purple spots on a white dress, and that was why Jeb was crying. Because of the crying, Jeb missed the twitch in Rusty's leg. He missed Rusty's body jerk and wiggle on the pavement behind him. He missed Rusty get up to his feet and saunter toward the boy. Because of all the crying, like a baby with a cut lip, mind you, he did not prepare himself for Rusty's bite. All he did was turn around and say, "Heya, Rusty. I thinked ya wur a goner. I missed you." Rusty, on the other hand, was a zombie and did what zombies do: bite shit that likes being alive. Nobody really knows how Rusty became a zombie, but the retention ponds at the nearby power plant might have had something to do with it.

Jeb made two fatal errors in his short life. The first error he made was not learning to read, which means he could never have read *The Ultimate Zombie Hunter's Handbook*. The reason that this is the worst kind of error is because nobody liked him, and he couldn't count on someone else to read him the book, let alone tell him the truth about what it was saying. Plus we all know that the welfare check his parents got was used on cigarettes and beer; he couldn't just go get the audiotape. They probably wanted him dead anyway. His parents probably would have lied to his face and used him as bait so he would become a zombie, just so they could shoot him in the face without any moral or spiritual repercussions. Sadly, he was screwed from the very beginning on that one.

The second error, ironically, was not learning the second lesson: determine if the object in question is or is not alive. The protocol varies in each case. (Strangely, the protocol again converges from several paths, but I'm still getting to that part.) There are a couple of options to explore. If the object is alive, you need to check to see if it is healthy or wounded. If the object is dead, then you need to decide whether it is dead for good or if it is undead. Appropriate action follows each discovery.

The easiest way to decide if something is alive or dead, without getting too close and jeopardizing the entire human race, is to throw a rock at it. If you hit the damn thing with a rock and it doesn't move, chances are it is dead. If you hit it with a rock and it does move or it makes a sound or does something else that could suggest that it is alive, then it might be alive. If this is the case, then further exploration is needed.

One time, I came across a highly suspicious-looking raccoon. I promptly threw a rock at it while releasing a grunt of joy. Shortly after, the raccoon released a scream of pain because it was a pretty huge rock, and I nailed it in the pelvis, disabling its hindquarters. As it lay there, writhing in pain and crying into the wind, I realized that this could still be a zombie raccoon. Just because it appears to be alive does not mean that it is. Humans who aren't zombies still talk. Raccoons don't. Plus it was wounded, and I have a rule for wounded animals: always shoot 'em in the head, because the wound could have been zombie inflicted, and there is no way to find out. Ever. Don't worry, I buried him beneath some leaves and grass next to the highway, under that speed limit sign that says thirty-five, but everyone knows means fifty. You know the one.

Wait, son-of-a-bitch, where was I going with that? Well, shit. I hate when I get really fired up about something and then I forget why I was talking. Let me recap what I wanted to say. If you are dealing with a healthy living organism, then forget what Yoko tells you and let it be. If it is wounded, the best rule of thumb is to put it down. If it was zombie related, then you saved the world. If it was natural, then that was God's plan anyway.

Now, let's get back to the important stuff. If that lump of flesh is dead, then you have to be really careful. I always start by throwing a rock at it. That way I can make sure it is still dead, and it hasn't become a zombie yet—just because it doesn't move around when you throw the rock at it does not yet mean that it is definitely not a zombie, so be careful. Then, for good measure, I shoot it in the head. Usually, if it's a zombie already, the rock business will piss it off, and then you just have to wait for it to approach you, waiting as the target gets bigger and bigger. Don't wait until it gets too big though, because that might be a problem.

Final recap: alive and healthy, let it be. Alive and wounded, death to the infidel. Dead and dead, huge rock to the skull and a shot in the brain. Dead and undead, shoot at will but at least once in the head.

Lesson 3: Grandma Oslo, Is That You?

I remember one time, long ago, but not more than two years ago, I was out at Oslo's house. She was a kind old lady who always wanted me to call her Grandma because she didn't have any kids on account of her being a lesbian during the more intolerant past. Well, anyway, I liked to humor her and visited her regularly because she liked to make me cookies that were pretty damn tasty. That broad had class, even if she was morbidly old.

One thing Grandma Oslo had going for her was her ability to drive a Segway. She drove that thing all the time. Neither I, nor Matthew, had ever seen her when she wasn't burning rubber on that beautiful little machine. I swear she never got off her enviro beast for anything, not even to take a shit. You see, Grandma Oslo wore those adult diapers that let you dump it all in your pants without suffering any of the consequences. I think she paid a neighborhood kid to change her every other week. That's how long it took to get her off the Segway. She even had it fitted with a little plastic can holder, which she used to hold a cold beer, all day everyday. Like I said, that broad had class.

Anyway, there I was, at Grandma Oslo's house. I had grown tired of her jarful of hard candies, which were almost completely butterscotch and peppermint. Once, I saw what I thought was a cherry candy, but when I ate it, it turned out to be a dried-up tomato paste. Needless to say, I didn't touch anything different again. Anyway, Grandma Oslo did not even have a fresh batch of cookies for me. This left me with only one option: leave. Matthew was with me, and we thought it would be best if we just went to Wendy's and got a baked potato. As we got up to leave, Grandma Oslo, desperate with loneliness, did something we could not have expected. She went out to her garden to get us some fresh strawberries.

Neither of us knew about this secret garden she kept. To be fair, it was in her backyard all those years, but who snoops around an old woman's backyard? Nobody. Well, she was out there a long time, and we started to get worried, but mostly for the strawberries we were promised. A decision was needed to be made, and I made one that opened my eyes to the world for the first time.

Thus began an epic quest to save the strawberries from the clutches of a dead old woman. But Grandma Oslo was not dead. She wasn't even alive. Apparently, while she was out in the back getting some deliciously ripe strawberries for Matthew and me, she was attacked by a zombie. The zombie didn't leave alone the loving old woman that we both knew, but a ravaged, flesh-eating zombie of death. As she stepped off the Segway, she transformed into a zombie right in front of us. Closer and closer Zombie Oslo came toward us, taunting us with the strawberries just so she could get a bite of the delicate young skin around our necks. Mine wasn't as delicate though; she was heading toward Matthew, the poor bastard.

Without pausing, we both pulled our shotguns out of nature's pocket and blasted Zombie Oslo into pieces. We didn't stop firing until the lumps quit quivering, which is the best way to kill a zombie if you believe in what you are doing. When the smoke cleared and the strawberries hit the ground, horror came upon us. Zombie Oslo wasn't a zombie after all, but Grandma Oslo in disguise. When she stepped off the Segway, she became so zombielike that it was impossible to distinguish her from the blood-gargling fiends of hell. Unfortunately for her, the training was working, and she never stood a chance.

The moral of the story is simple, like always. Determine the age of the object, if you can. If it is a human or other animal, determine if it is simply an arthritic old beast moments from heaven or a zombie bent on destroying the world. The necessary action dictated by this glorious guide changes based on the answer to that question. If it is a hell-infested zombie, blow away the brains, and any other part, but always the brain, of whoever it is. I don't care if your son is infected; he has to be put down, Collins style. Now, if your son is just oddly decrepit and arthritic, flip a coin on that one, though I feel that it's better to be safe than to be sorry. In any case, those eroded beaches we call old people get mistaken for zombies all the time, which is why this step is important. The screamers tend to flip their lids when that happens, but as far as I'm concerned, it's just saving time.

Lesson 4: The Plight of Daniel Sea

Thus began tablet 2. This tablet was pretty sweet because it had the next two lessons inscribed upon it. For those of you who cannot count, that is the fourth and fifth lesson. Now that I think about it, though, if you cannot count, then none of that really means anything to you. Even now, as I explain myself, you are still confused and reaching for the remote while the rest of the world understood my point two sentences ago and has now moved on. I do not really know what is going on, but I feel the need to get some microwave popcorn. That would be perfect right now.

Daniel Sea was a tall man with dark hair, a rugged exterior, and a beautiful handlebar mustache. He was a man with a plan, and he had a friend named Stan who drove a van and was a huge Bono fan. Daniel never found out why, but his friend always claimed it was because Bono was what some might call a philanthropist. Everyone knows that that is bullshit.

Nobody likes Bono simply because he helps poor people. Not only is that notion bullshit, but it is also almost as insane as bloody diarrhea. Bono, a greasy ultrarich rock star son-of-a-bitch, gets credit for helping poor Africans while he wears his full leather getup, including those badass sunglasses. Yeah yeah yeah. No, that doesn't sound right. How about, he helps poor people because he is so incredibly rich; he goes on vacation by hanging out with poor people just to see something different than his everyday five-star shit basket. By seeing how bad off some people are, he feels that much better about himself and his life on top of a golden mountain with waterfalls of cocaine and tits. Bono is an asshole, and so is Stan.

But all that aside, Daniel does have a plan. He is going to take all his money and gamble in the casinos of Las Vegas. You see, the other day, Daniel heard from his cousin's best friend's sister-in-law that there is a new game in town that pays out every time. Essentially, you play a game of blackjack. If you win, good times. If you lose, you are offered a second hand of double or nothing. This method of play continues until one of two outcomes occurs. If you end up winning big, then cash your chips in, and go live the dollar-menuaire lifestyle you've always dreamed of. If you keep losing and keep losing until you eventually run out of money, then that sucks for you. But Daniel had a plan to beat the system.

He had amassed a savings of just over one million dollars. It gave Daniel the opportunity to play ten consecutive losing hands of blackjack. The odds of not winning at least one hand while climbing this pyramid were so minute that Daniel knew he had a sure thing going. He was so sure of the riches to come that he bought a salty pretzel for every child in Detroit. You see, like Bono, Daniel could take vast amounts of money and do something pointless for people who will still be incredibly poor and without help once he leaves. It really was something to see the smiles on those poor children's faces when he drove up in the salty pretzel van, throwing golden goodness by the handfuls out into the garbage-covered streets. (I'm not crying; I'm just tearing up from the metal shavings in my eye—but, *dammit*, Daniel, why did you do it? *Why*?!)

Oh God, you can do this, Geoffrey, you little girl. Jesus Christ, you make me sick sometimes. Where's my whiskey suicide? Oh yeah, that's better. Now what was I saying? That's right, Daniel had just finished his pretzel run, which he put on credit so that he wouldn't use up his savings and then headed out to Vegas. Instead of driving a car, which is slow and pollutes the environment, he flew on a plane. It pollutes less because it takes less time, and lots of people use the same plane. That made Daniel happy, because white people love that kind of thing, which gave him the confidence to strut through the airport like a pimp. He even got a hooker to pay for his cab to the casino. That was tight.

Once there, he sat and started his quest for millions. He picked the table with the cute dealer because after he was done, she might want to join him in his room for a little private lesson on awesome. He picked what looked to be the most comfortable chair, and when he sat down, it was amazing. Not only was it incredibly comfortable, but it was also the only seat where he didn't have a light shining in his face. He decided to order a drink before he got started and caught the eye of the prettiest cocktail waitress in the place. Things were looking great.

Hand 1

Buy-in for this hand was just one thousand dollars. Chump change for people like Daniel. He was hoping he wouldn't win on the first few hands because the profit from such a victory would be nothing. He pulled a jack and a seven. Deciding to keep it in case of a busted dealer, he sat. Dealer pulled a king and a nine. Daniel lost, but his smile got wider. It was going to be a good night.

Hand 2

Without even pausing, two burgundy chips were on the table. Daniel was here to play, not pussyfoot around all evening. Nine/nine.

Pretty solid hand, but pretty solid doesn't mean shit in blackjack. Next card was a five. Daniel was bust, and those two burgundy chips went to the other side of the table. Everything was going according to plan, and Daniel couldn't wait long enough for the next hand. He was shaking with anticipation like a teenager preparing for some awkward sex.

Hand 3

Two light blue chips into the pot from Daniel. If his luck holds, he won't win this hand either, making it a good payday for numero uno. Jack, 9. Damn it. Queen, 10. Nice!

Hand 4

Eight thousand dollars is what it takes to play this next hand. Daniel feels luckier and luckier because he knows how good it's going to feel when he bones this casino for all that cash. One more hand should do it before he takes home all the bacon. He eagerly awaits the cards he is dealt. The first card is a two. The second card is a three. Naturally, Daniel does not want to be too smug, so he takes a hit. Five this time. Another hit and another five. Daniel calls for a third hit and receives a third five. This puts him at twenty, and he decides to hold. The dealer pulls an ace first. Daniel is pretty pissed off about that, considering that would have put him at 21, and he would have won, but since he needs another hand or two before the big bucks, he is okay with it. Next card for the dealer is four. Another hit for the dealer and another four pops out. Daniel starts to feel uneasy. Things seem to be going too perfect for everyone else at this table. He knows a two will be the next card, and he'll lose this pot too. The dealer takes another hit and gets a seven. That puts the dealer at sixteen, and Daniel feels triumphant. The odds of a twenty-one are slim, and Daniel is ready to roll. He promptly orders another drink and lays on some charm. Then the dealer deals the next card, and Daniel couldn't believe his eyes. The fourth five rears its ugly face, and it happens. Daniel Sea realizes a few things he didn't before.

Hand 5

Bust. The seat has a hole in the back, which allows a spring to reach out and poke him in the back. He didn't notice it at first because his weight hadn't settled onto the foam.

Hand 6

Bust. There aren't any lights shining in his eyes, but he noticed that all the cigarette smoke in the room seemed to funnel into the one space his face was currently located in. He was going to be sick.

Hand 7

Bust. The pretty cocktail waitress walked past and ripped ass right there in front of him. Daniel feels even sicker now and wonders if she farted in his drinks.

Hand 8

Bust. The cute dealer isn't really that cute after all. She has a mole on her upper lip that was nice and small at first, but has seemed to grow in size since the first hand. Also, her teeth are a little bit yellow, and her hair is a bit stringy. Oh yeah, she is also a dude with a penis and balls, the whole package.

Hand 9

BUST! What the *fuck* is going on here. The odds of busting so many times are so close to impossible that a baby in Detroit has a better chance of pooping a golden nugget the size of a coconut. Daniel is not smiling anymore, nor is he feeling confident. Even worse, he has a serious case of swamp ass going on because he is sweating like a fat hooker in Miami during July. All in one moment, he realizes how horrible this game really is. There are no millions to win, just millions to lose. The first hand is for a thousand dollars. If you lose, you can double the amount and play again. The casino is now betting a thousand bucks from your pocket with the original thousand it offered the first time. If you lose that hand, you double the wager, and the casino just bets more of your money. Each round is the same risk for the casino, one thousand dollars, but the player is risking ever more money. Daniel has now lost half of his savings and has nothing to show for it. If he wagers the rest, he could win all his money back and make one thousand dollars. Is it worth $512,000 more dollars just to get the other $512,000 back plus one more thousand?

Hand 10

This is it for Daniel. He has to win this hand if he is going to walk home with any remnant of his wrecked pride and pension. Why, oh why, did he ever listen to that little prat Stan? All he has to do is play the odds, and he can beat this bitch of a dealer into the ground and walk out with an extra grand. First card is an … ace. Booya, aces are great because they complete the blackjack, but they also double as a one, so it's harder to bust. All he needs now is a ten—jack, queen, or king. The second card is a … three. Daniel is crushed by his expectations, but it ain't over yet. Daniel takes a hit and strikes gold. Six. That put him up to twenty, and the only way he can lose is if the "prancifance twink" across the table can score a blackjack. The dealer's first card was flipped over, and it was a jack. That isn't good. The second card that flips over is a king. Tie ball game. And the dealer takes a hit!? There are rules against this! Why would they ever do tha—a freaking *ace*! Daniel's heart stops, and the world goes dark.

A few months go by, and the world hasn't heard anything from Daniel Sea. All his friends wonder where he is, and his employer has already replaced him. His family mourns the loss of their beloved Daniel Sea. They know not where he went or why he hasn't called to let someone know that he is alive, but they feel a sense of loss so deep, it can mean only one thing. You can't go into debt with someone from Detroit. You just can't come back from that.

Daniel Sea made a mistake. He gambled and lost. That is one mistake that I hope you won't make after reading his story. The fourth lesson demonstrated here is to determine the probability of zombiness of everything you come across. Do not guess and gamble your life away. When you gamble on whether a zombie is or is not a zombie, you always lose. There is a way to determine the probability that someone is a zombie. It is called statistics. Luckily for all of us nonzombies, statistics give us the upper hand. Matthew firmly believes that because we are dealing with animals and people, using the standards of biology is appropriate, and in biology, everything is done with a statistical p value of 0.01 or lower. Matthew also believes that if the p value of a zombie probability test is higher than 0.01, then "you gotta blow that motha away." We like to joke around and call it your "Z score." Don't gamble and work with maybes. Use science and give yourself a 99 percent chance for success. You won't find yourself jonesing for human blood if you do, unless you like that stuff for some weird and gross reason.

Lesson 5: Damn It, Bobby

Robert Hubert Ruckenich, a.k.a. Bobby, was and is a man of many concerns. He had a lot of bills to pay, including his two-hundred-thousand-dollar home mortgage, forty-thousand-dollar car payment, six-thousand-dollar Home Depot card, thirty-thousand-dollar school loan, fourteen-thousand-dollar credit card bill, forty-three-thousand-dollar bar tab, and his fifty-dollar Sam's Club membership. His dog, Barney, died a month ago, after living with him for sixteen years. His parents were both unexpectedly diagnosed with cancer of the lips and throat, probably due to the oversized dip of Copenhagen that they each have tucked under their lips all day, every day. Plus, they are both chain-smokers. Oh yeah, I forgot to mention that a meteor came down from the sky and hit his house, destroyed his car that sat in his garage, and burned everything he owned to the ground, including his furniture, tools, appliances, his diploma, and even his Sam's Club membership card. Plus that's how Barney died, valiantly barking at the intruding flames until he could no longer see the orange glow of the fire. Too bad it was smoke inhalation and not victory that made the lights go out. To add insult to injury, the insurance company says he didn't have insurance for meteor damage and would not cover any of the losses.

And it was winter.

It was about time for a change. Bobby sat on the curb, at the feet of his burned-down house, in disbelief. Long ago, when Bobby was eating dinner with his parents at Ku Phun's Chinese Platterfest, he opened up a fortune cookie. The message inside the cookie predicted that his life would change when a meteor came down from the sky and hit his house, destroyed his car that sat in the garage, and burned everything he owned to the ground, including his furniture, tools, appliances, his diploma, and even his Sam's Club membership card. Bobby chuckled to himself at the time because of how incredible this all sounded, but now only the neighbors are laughing. After a few hours of sulking, crying, and beer drinking, he got a ticket for public intoxication and a Tasering to the ribs for being a bitch. His life really did suck. Really, really, bad.

Right then and there, Bobby made a decision to do something about his crappy life. He didn't need any new things: no new house, no new car, no new Sam's Club membership, no new booze, and no new debt. He just needed two things to improve the life he had: a woman in his life and religion. Maybe some booze. If he could find the companionship of a woman and the arrow of religion to point him toward happiness, everything else would work itself out in time. But where and how would he take care of these two needs?

He thought about it for a few days, and all he could come up with was to go down to the grocery store, wait out in the parking lot until an attractive woman walked out with her arms overflowing with bags, and then follow her around in his white van to see what she liked to do. Luckily, his van didn't have any words on it anywhere, so the odds of her remembering it from one day to the next was minimal, which was ideal. Plus, Bobby kept lots of candy in the back to seem like a nice guy. That, too, was ideal.

Day in and day out, he followed her around, watching her every chore. After nearly a week of following this woman around town and watching her shadow through the curtains of her house, Bobby decided that he needed to get organized. If he was to win this woman's affection, he had to learn all he could while he was still under the radar, and to do that he needed to take notes. And make graphs. But these wouldn't be your average, boring graphs of one color. These graphs would be filled with all the colors of the rainbow, except for yellow since yellow is too weak. No woman can appreciate weakness.

The first graph, and his most glorious, was his affection graph. He decided that a bar graph would best summarize the feelings he felt for this woman. It offered the most color and thick, solid bars running up and down the page. Up and down. The first day he charted his affection, it was after she had spent the day at the spa in town. His affection was low that day because she didn't appear to work much, but spas cost a lot of money. Soon, it would be his money that she was spending. The next day, however, his affection shot through the roof. He drew an extralong, extrathick bar with his black marker to show how much he felt for her. That was the day she went to the gym to work on her figure. Every fifteen minutes, the bar got bigger and bigger. Finally, after nearly two hours, she reemerged. She looked exhausted, sweaty, and hungry. In Bobby's opinion, pretty freaking hot.

On one fateful afternoon, she was working a fairly good day on the affectionate graph Bobby kept pinned under the visor of his hat, which he now wore all the time to keep the sun out of his eyes without overheating his head because of said sun. When she walked into the local Wendy's, Bobby realized that he didn't feel the way he thought he felt about her. He didn't just merely like her, he loved her. It was finally time to meet the woman who had stolen his heart, and there was no better way to meet than over the rim of her Frosty's cup. Just before he turned his van off to head inside, he thought he heard something on the radio about … zombies. On second listen, it was just an ad for listening to the radio. What is up with that crap anyway? He was already sold on the idea.

"Go, go, GOOO!"

Out of nowhere, like lightning dressed in a sharp suit, several agents surrounded the van and pointed their guns in Bobby's direction. He figured they weren't loaded because it was a prank by one of those guys he used to know at work, even though they hadn't spoken to him since he quit showing up. Three seconds, a karate chop to the arm and a bullet to the leg later, Bobby was crying and squirming on the ground. Nothing in his life made sense anymore. The love of his life was less than twenty feet away from him with nothing but a thin piece of glass between them, and he was stuck on the concrete, bleeding and sobbing and shitting his pants. What had he done to deserve this?

Stalking. Bobby was being charged with stalking the woman of his dreams, who also happened to be the woman of an FBI agent's dreams. And that agent happened to be a woman, despite the sturdy jaw and shaved head. Apparently this woman had noticed a suspicious-looking van tailing her for several days in a row, and it began to worry her. She told her life partner about it and asked if someone could keep an eye on her just to see if it was all in her head or if someone was actually following her. Her life partner called in a favor and found out that Bobby was actually following her around town, then parking outside of her house at night for hours before finally moving to a nearby alley. On top of that, they ran the plates on the van and found that it belonged to a convicted sex offender who had reported it stolen three weeks prior. The evidence quickly mounted up in favor of Bobby going to jail. And to jail he went. He wrote a letter to his lover at the end of his first day in jail, explaining how he felt. He did not want her to feel bad about how things ended between them.

"Well, at least I have some time for religion now. And free meals and a place to sleep," Bobby said.

Okay, now we all know how Bobby's tragic story ended, but what in the Sam hell does this have to do with zombies? Duh. It has nothing to do with zombies, *and* it has everything to do with zombies. Obviously, there are some readers out there who haven't caught on yet, but each story illustrates a point and a lesson. Just because zombies aren't running amok and the world isn't crazy with chaos doesn't mean squat. Think of it this way: If you are hungry, then you eat food. If you don't have any food to eat, then what do you do? You work. Working has little to do with eating food, but you can get something from work that applies to eating food. Money. Now, money can be used for all sorts of things, but it can also be used for buying food. These stories are kind of like that. The information can be used several ways, but it can also be used to fight zombie ignorance. Personally, I believe that everything can be used in many different ways, but if it can be used to prepare for the zombie invasion, that is what I use it for. No exceptions.

Now that we have that settled, what lesson is this story representing? Can anyone figure it out? Probably not, so I'll spoon-feed it to you like what your school teachers did; qualify the type of zombie you are dealing with. That is the fifth lesson, and one that is very important to master. If you need to review the different types of lessons, reread the rest of the book until you find the right chapter. You could use the practice.

In Bobby's story, he did not qualify what type of woman he was dealing with. He just randomly picked a woman and decided that she was single, available, and willing to be his soul mate. He did not find out if she had a husband, boyfriend, or lover. He didn't even check to make sure she was straight. The importance of this mistake cannot be overlooked. It was a mistake any guy could make because coming across a lesbian is pretty rare, and most of the time guys completely ignore the possibility of a woman being a lesbian, skipping that part of the qualification process. But what if you come across a sticker and you just assume it is a stumbling zombie? Probably ninety-nine out of one hundred zombies you come across are going to be the stumbling zombies, but for that one out of a hundred that is a sticker, you need to properly qualify and prepare for it. Otherwise, you're just another target at the other end of my scope.

Lesson 6: Marv, You're Lost Again

The final tablet has the final three lessons carved into the stone. The first of these lessons features the story of Marv and Marge. It was written upon the stone in a comically large type, leaving little room for the final two lessons. Unfortunately, only three tablets were available for the lightning, and the final two lessons were forced, in a comically small type, onto the bottom edge of the third tablet. What's up with that anyway?

"Damn it, Marv. You took a wrong turn back there, I just know it. Why don't you ever listen to me when I tell you to turn left, and I know where to go, and you don't know a damned thing about where we are going? This town doesn't look familiar to me, and now it's getting dark. Why didn't you just listen to me back there? We need to turn around."

"I didn't miss any turn back anywhere. Besides, we've gone too far to turn around and waste a bunch of time just to prove that I know where to go. Just let it be, Marge."

"I knew we should have stopped and asked directions at that last town. That town looked familiar, but I've never seen this one before. I just know we should have turned back at that left back there when I told you to turn. We are never going to make it to the church in time, if we make it there at all. Everyone is going to stare when we show up late, and the ceremony has already started. Pull over at the next gas station so I can get directions."

"We aren't lost, Marge. We'll be there too early if you ask me."

"Never in my sixty-three years have I ever—"

"Sixty-three? Shit."

"Have I ever met a man so thick-skulled. I swear, by the time you finally admit that we are lost, I am going to have a heart attack from anxiety. We are never going to make it to the church in time."

"Why, God, did I agree to this?"

"Marv, you better behave yourself when we get there. This is going to be very emotional for Olga. I swear, if you say one mean word to her—"

"What are you going to do? Not make that cardboard crap you call dinner or not put too much starch in my work shirts? You know that crap rubs my neck raw all day long, and you still put too much on my shirts."

"You just be civil for one day. That's all I ask of you, and you better not make her day any worse than it already is, poor thing. I wonder how she is coping with her loss."

"She is burying a cat. I can't believe I agreed to go to a funeral for a cat. Did you ask me while I was drunk? You must have because I'm always drunk when I am at home."

"Oh, dear, we are lost for sure. Why do you always think you know where you are going when you always get us lost? There is no way we will make it in time, and Olga will never forgive me. I am going to look like a rat when we show up late, if we make it at all. Marv, why do you always do this to me? I swear, you want me to have a heart attack."

"Jesus Christ. I should have gone to Hooters and got some hot wings."

"None of these buildings look familiar. You got us lost again, and now we are going to be late. Marv, slow down. You know the speed limit is only thirty-five through here."

"How would I know that? We've never been here, remember?"

"There was a sign back there just a ways. I swear, you never pay attention to anything but your stupid games. Sometimes it feels like I am talking to a brick. A brick sitting in your chair. I don't even know why I ever talk to you in the first place. Just five minutes ago I told you to turn left, and you just drove right on by."

"That was only five minutes ago? Felt like longer."

"Marv, you never say anything nice to me anymore. I don't even know why I talk to you anymore. Hey, look, a Walgreens. I heard that Ann went to one of those once, and she hated it. There were too many people buying too much stuff for her. She said it was terrifying and that there was no room to even breathe. I wonder why people go to places like that when they don't even have time to shop around the store. I tell you, these days everything is so hurry-hurry that nobody ever takes the time to enjoy the beautiful weather or take a picnic at the park. That's what's wrong with the world these days. Nobody ever takes the time."

"Could have been sitting in my chair, watching the game and drinking a beer."

"It will mean a lot of Olga when she sees that we came all this way to pay our respects for her loss. I hope the poor dear is fairing well. She is going to be left all alone in that big old house now with nobody to talk to. Maybe I'll invite her over for dinner some night so she has someone to be with for a while. She will need that during such a dark time in her life, and everyone knows there's no point talking to you. I don't know why I even started—"

"It is just a goddamned cat for crying-out-loud!"

"You'd better behave yourself here. I don't want to hear any sighing out of you during the service, if we ever make it to the church. I just know that we should have taken that left turn back there. You need to stop at the next gas station so we can get directions and find out how lost you got us. I just know we are going to be late, and everyone is going to be staring at us, and Olga won't even be able to look at me after this. I swear, you want me to have a heart attack."

Marv and Marge never made it to that poor cat's funeral (the cat's name was Sergeant Flufficans). They continued on their drive for the rest of their unfortunate lives. Marge eventually died of a heart attack, brought upon by one of Marv's thickheaded certainties that sent her into a fit. Marv didn't mind because he was finally able to enjoy some peace and quiet. Unfortunately for Marv, he didn't get to enjoy it long. He had long been a victim of asthma, and about five minutes after Marge went into the great beyond, Marv followed. He suffered a particularly mild attack when he struck someone's pet cat, which sent him swerving into a nearby billboard. There were no survivors.

Their mistake? They both failed to come up with an action plan. They simply did not determine the correct course of action. They didn't decide anything. Some of you might argue that Marge sent an action plan Marv's way when she told him to pull over at the next gas station to get directions. Some of you might be blundering idiots who don't know the difference between a solar eclipse and a lunar eclipse. Marge never set up a real action plan because she never did anything. It was always the *next* gas station. Even as they drove past a Walgreens, Marge just kept on yapping away while Marv slipped into a Marge-induced coma. She never told him to stop at *this* gas station, and he never did. Marv, on the other hand, just kept driving. He never stopped or turned around. He didn't care and didn't want to even go to a dumb cat's funeral. He didn't even turn the radio up. For God's sake, man, at least turn up the radio to an obnoxious level and get the point across.

When zombies inherit the earth, have a plan of action. Do not make a plan of reaction and only ever decide what to do next. Have a plan that decides what to do now. I'm not saying don't plan for the future, because that would be dumb and contradict the entire point of this book. Planning for the future is essential, but only if there are steps that come before then, which would be now. Don't start working out tomorrow, start today. Don't get the ammo over the weekend, get it now. Shoot it over the weekend. Do you see how this works? If you plan to get the ammo this weekend, something can and will always come up. Then you can just get it the next weekend. Fuck that shit and write up a plan to get it done now. That is lesson 6.

Lesson 7: Killing a Zombie Is Not a Hate Crime

A few years ago, I was still in school, and I was watching this film about Martin Luther King Jr. It was in black and white, and I knew it was boring because I was watching it during history class, and it was in black and white. I didn't really pay attention for too long because my teacher told us that it wouldn't be on the test, and let's be honest, I am doing good if I pay attention to half of what *is* going to be on the test.

After about twenty minutes of the movie, five minutes of class had gone by. There was this guy talking in front of all these other people, and I think the film was burned or too old because most of the screen was blotted out, but the sound was still okay. He was talking and talking, and this is similar to what he said:

"I say to you today, my friends, so even though we face the difficulties of today and tomorrow, I still have a dream. It is a dream deeply rooted in the American dream to end the zombie threat.

"I have a dream that one day this nation will rise up and live out the true meaning of its creed: 'We hold these truths to be self-evident: that all men are created equal to terminate zombies.'

"I have a dream that one day on the red hills of Georgia, the sons of former slaves and the sons of former slave owners will be able to stand side by side and shoot zombies in the face.

"I have a dream that one day, even the state of Mississippi, a state sweltering with the heat of zombiness, sweltering with the heat of the feasting, will be transformed into an oasis of human babies and zombie corpse fires.

"I have a dream that my four little children will one day live in a nation where they will not be attacked by zombies, but by the content of their dinner.

"I have a dream today …"

Sometime in or around that speech, I fell asleep and had a dream of my own. Like all dreams, it started with a harmless orgy filled with beautiful women that I've never seen before. Where do all those beautiful women come from anyway? I have seen plenty of beautiful women in my life, and none of them ever show up in my dreams, but the beautiful women my brain makes up are always feeling nasty. Either way, orgies are sweet as long as everyone is clean.

Unfortunately, like all orgy dreams, this one came to a crashing halt. The town's zombie siren went off, screaming its warning of terror throughout the surrounding neighborhoods. They had come, and all my preparation was going to pay off. I was going to be able to save the world. I was going to be a hero.

Before I knew what had happened, I was standing outside of the building with all my clothes on and none of my money. A smile slowly crept its way across my face. The training was working. I knew what to do, and I knew where to go. I had to walk my way toward the zombie infection and completely annihilate anyone who I reasoned was plausibly a zombie. (Based on the eight lessons to determine a zombie.) Luckily, if I ever got into a bind and forgot the eight lessons, I had them tattooed all over my body in places that I can read. That way they are always with me, like my gun, for my zombie-killing convenience.

Instead of walking to the carnage like your average Mr. Rogers smoking a hash pipe, I dedicated a little something special to all the children back in the orphanarium. I decided to use just one continuous Liu Kang kick to fly across the parking lot in a flash, with one razor-sharp foot leading the way and a guttural Asian battle cry bursting from my throat. It's easier than walking or running, it's faster, and it is a heck of a lot more fun. At some point during the kick, I picked up a couple of beers and dominated them. When I flew by a television store, I noticed a completely bitch'n' movie trailer for the new *Rambo* film with an amazing punch line, "Heroes don't die ... They just reload." I also picked up a Whopper, but it was smothered in tomato juices, and the bun was all soggy, so I couldn't eat it. That made me sad, and I hate being sad. Being sad makes me angry. It makes me so angry that I feel bad because I will undoubtedly kill someone nearby during the ensuing diatribe that pours like fiery filth from my mouth. Feeling bad makes me sad, and the circle of life repeats itself like always. It's a beautiful thing to behold.

And then I was there, surrounded by zombies and no longer Liu Kang kicking. For some reason, they didn't seem to notice that I was standing there. They really weren't doing anything except standing around, possessing the greatest potential threat to humanity. They weren't acting like I thought they would. There was no sauntering. There was no feasting on human flesh. There was nothing but standing. Zombies as far as I could see, but no mayhem, just silence. And a dancing six-foot-tall taco in the background, which was nice.

Then, seemingly out of nowhere, I became the kid who lets out a ripe old fart during reading time in history class. It wasn't even the usual ho-hum flatulence. This baby would be legendary to the crew from *The Goonies*, because it was not only the wettest, longest, loudest fart I've ever heard, but it smelled like an old Italian man had just ripped ass on a plate of burnt cheese, in a sauna. Just like the ones you let in the shower and immediately regret because the steam somehow amplifies the smell to a level that even you cannot appreciate. Those are special.

Special enough to wake all the zombies, thus beginning the havoc and mayhem promised by the elders at the end of the world.

All at once, the zombie horde went from being as innocent as a little puppy sitting in a basket with a fluffy blanket and a ribbon to being as dangerous and disgusting as a dirty, stinking zombie. Seemingly in unison, they all turned my direction, staring at me with those lifeless, beady eyes. Then they attacked.

My tattoos were all gone. My gun was missing from its usual spot, and all I had in my hand was a drumstick from KFC. All the training, all the planning, all the work were gone. I didn't panic, and I didn't black out. I just stood there. It was a bit frustrating because I knew what I needed to do, and I had a plan to get it done, but for some reason, I just stood there, staring at the encroaching zombie mass. Seconds ticked by, and feet melted away as they approached, but still I did nothing. There I stood, dumbstruck, as the zombies began to rip through my flesh with their teeth of disease. My worst nightmare was realized as they gnawed on my bones, and everything went black.

Suddenly, I was awake and screaming, thrashing about on the floor. All the kids around me looked frightened, and the teacher looked worried. I felt an odd sensation on my cheek and reached up to find it covered in blood. Apparently the stress had given me a nosebleed that bled from the core. I knew exactly what had happened because there were clues, all along. The fact that I could Liu Kang kick for blocks was a clue that I was dreaming. But I should have known when I saw the movie trailer that I had fallen into a nightmare that I could not escape. Only in a true nightmare could I have ever failed to act in a hostile zombie situation. Even if I had blacked out, zombie destruction would have occurred in real life, due to the training, to a thing I call IZRM. And the training would not have let me go toward the zombie horde, like I did in the nightmare. I would have gone the opposite way and followed my predetermined game plan that helps ensure my survival.

But a very important lesson can be learned from the nightmare. Action is necessary, in all situations. Lesson 6, determining the proper actions for the situation, is not enough. Having the plan is nothing if it is not implemented. In the nightmare, I knew what I had to do, but I did not act. I just stood there, like that tree in my front yard that always had the ants all over it, completely worthless to anyone but the creatures that are destroying it. That thing didn't even have leaves.

If you have a plan and you do not act on it, it is worse than not having a plan in the first place. Think of it this way. Two men are driving their cars down a four-lane street. They are side by side and enjoy a friendly wave to each other as they head to work. Soon, they come upon a T intersection that ends in a huge concrete wall. One man realizes that his brakes have been cut by his brother, and he cannot stop, so he crashes into the wall and dies instantly. The other man has brakes that work, but he fails to use them. He just sits there until he completely obliterates his face on the brick wall. He dies very slowly. Now, they both died the same way, but the man with the brakes is considered a freaking idiot who didn't use the tools he had to save his life. The other guy just got dicked by his brother. A plan is like brakes. If you have them and don't use them, you are a freaking moron and deserve to die. If you don't have them, that sucks to be you.

Now, let's add a third driver and another lane of traffic. He has brakes, uses them, and stops before he runs into the wall. He had brakes, he used his brakes, and he lived to tell other people to make sure they have and use brakes. He knew the value of having a plan and then acting upon it. Action is essential. Otherwise, you're just another storage vessel for my bullets.

Lesson 8: Worst Decision Ever

The previous night was just ending when the morning came running up and gave me the finger. I had closed the store that night and didn't get to sleep till about 4:20 AM; I was now awake again at 9:20 AM. It wasn't much time to sleep, but it would have to do. I took a quick shower because I was meeting someone at nine forty-five in the McDonald's parking lot and couldn't be late. As I was riding my bike with renewed vigor, I noticed how gray the morning was and how freaking cold it was outside. A solid cloud cover was overhead, and the sun was nowhere to be seen, just like the five dollars I lent Matthew two summers ago. My friend and I were supposed to go paintballing today, and he was my ride to get down to the fields. Teamster's Paintball is a pretty nice place at a pretty reasonable price, but it's located about ten miles away from town—seven south and two or three west. It is also surrounded by nothing … nothing but trees and fields as far as the human eye can see. And it has one dirt road leading past it. I had it all planned out that I was going to leave at about 2:00 PM so that I could ride my bike back to town and watch a soccer game.

After about four hours of some hard-core paintballing, I decided it was time to go. The time was now 2:10 PM, and I had waited a little too long, but I expected I would still get to the game in decent time. I got my stuff all together, grabbed my bike out of the truck, and left Teamsters', but when I got on the road I couldn't remember exactly what direction we had came from. I was pretty sure we came in from the south, so I decided to go ahead with that and took a right. After what seemed like fifty miles of gravel road, I finally came upon the road I needed—a small, but paved, east-west road that would lead me to the main highway and on my way back to town. After a few minutes, I started to doubt my choice of direction, but still kept going, positive that the highway would come up at any second. When it didn't, and twenty minutes had gone by, and it still didn't, I knew something wasn't right. So I kept going, knowing I would find it pretty soon since every road in the area eventually led to the highway. Another ten or fifteen minutes went by, and I found myself pretty pissed off that I had gone this way, but I reassured myself that I would be where I needed to be in no time.

Time passed slowly, slower than a one-legged dog, and so did the miles, before I finally found what I was looking for. The highway was right in front of me, and I couldn't wait to get on it and head home. As I got closer, I saw a green highway sign and knew that I was in the right place, until I realized that the sign said, "Now Entering Macon County." I wasn't sure what had happened, but I knew that Macon County was not the county I lived in. This fact was incredibly unawesome. I got to the T intersection and *BAM*, another east-west road. I starting thinking and realized that two east-west roads can't come to a T intersection. I had actually been going the wrong direction the entire time without realizing it. Although this was pretty depressing and very upsetting, it got worse. The green sign that I had been relieved to see was a devil in disguise: it was advertising the next town down the road from mine, which is fifteen miles away. At this time, I still had five miles to get to *that* town, plus another fifteen to get back to mine. What the fuck happened? I was already pretty freaking tired after a twelve-mile bike ride in the wrong direction, and I had another twenty miles left in the trip.

I hit the road again, but with less force or drive. I was a beaten man, and I wasn't even halfway home. To make matters worse, the wind was in my face the entire time. I couldn't even relax on the downhills.

Did I mention it was cold? On my way home, I basically froze to death. The wind wasn't fierce, but it was bitter. I was sweating under all my clothing, but freezing at the same time. My legs were beyond Jell-O, more like Jell-O before it sits in the fridge. It was hell on earth, and I had plenty of time to enjoy it. I had two really vivid depressing thoughts that I kept obsessing over in my mind. The first occurred every time I saw a dead animal on the road. I wanted to be that animal. I wanted to be dead. The second was slightly more sophisticated. I saw a milk jug on the ground, and it had some rainwater in it. I was pretty thirsty, so I had a thought about drinking it. Then I wondered what would happen if it had crystal meth mixed in with the water. At this, I had a torture-induced hallucination about swerving up and down the road and getting hit by a semitruck. That was pretty cool at the time. It made me want the water, need it, but my legs wouldn't stop their torturous pedaling, and I moved on.

The only way I could gauge my progress was by the "Adopt a Highway" signs that said, "The Next 2.7 Miles Belong to Somebody Important." Then the next time I saw a sign, I would know that I just traveled 2.7 miles. This sucked since it seemed to be forever before the next sign would come up. My legs were shit. I was now using my arms to pump my legs to keep me going. It was a pain in the ass to do, but it gave my legs a chance to rest, which was needed.

My hometown's city limit sign was a magnificent sight to behold, especially given my terminally fatigued condition. I was pretty pleased with the thought of being home. Pretty. Damned. Pleased. I kept on going, and about a mile away, I saw one of the rare green signs with cities and distances. That bastard sign let me in on the joke, three more miles to get home. If you doubt me, go look for yourself. Inside the city limits is a sign saying, "Hey, You Poor Son of a Bitch, You Ain't Home Yet. Keep Truck'n', You Got Tmiles to Go, Bub." I say, "Fuck you, sign. Fuck you and your dirty lies."

The signs don't lie, though. It was three miles, and I was finally going to die. My heart was going to explode, and my brain was ready to shut down for the night. The next thing I knew, I was at the soccer field, it was four thirty, and I was eating a hot dog. It was finally over. The worst decision of my life had finally run its course.

But it doesn't end there. There is always a lesson to be learned, especially from the darkest, most horrible events in our lives. I had a plan, and I acted on that plan. I got results, and I ended up in the destination that I desired. But how successful were my actions? Not very. Reflection is a very important process in every sequence of events. Without reflection to determine if your actions were successful, things may not improve, and you may not live long to worry about it. Sure, I got to my destination, but my condition was unfavorable. If a zombie invasion was waiting for me, I lacked the strength to fight them off. Adjustments would have to be made before another trip like that, absolutely. This rule of reflection applies to any situation, including zombie attacks. If you lose a lot of soldiers but survive, then you met your goal of not dying but you lost a lot of good men. That is not a favorable outcome, and you need to reassess your tactics. Lesson 8 is one of the most crucial: reflect upon your actions and make improvements. Do not forget it.

For those of you who can't remember the reason you got up to go to the fridge by the time you arrive there, fret not. I will assist you in remembering these lessons, even though I know you have forgotten what they mean to your survival. Following is a list summarizing the lessons I have provided you. Use them well. Write them down in your little pocketbook or smartphone, or tattoo them onto your body like I did. Make sure you can read the tattoos. Then, get a taco to celebrate.

1. Run toward the zombies.
2. Lie on the ground in the fetal position so that the zombie horde just goes over top.
3. Do not stop yelling if they begin to attack you. It will scare them off.
4. Advertise your wounds. Zombies hate the sight of blood.
5. Never carry a loaded gun. Guns kill people, you know?

6. If a zombie cannot be outrun, stop and close your eyes. Count to ten. It will be gone when you open your eyes back up.
7. Carry a spotlight. That way the helicopters can spot you.
8. Stop reading now and forget about this book.

For the rest of you, follow the abridged version that follows. You have a grasp on the main details and need reminding only of the finer points.

1. Determine if the object could ever be alive.
2. Determine if the object is or is not alive.
    a. If alive, is it wounded or healthy?
    b. If dead, is it moving or still?
3. Determine the age of the object, if possible.
4. Determine the probability of zombieness.
5. Determine type of zombie.
6. Determine which course of action.
7. Act.
8. Determine if actions were successful and adjust.

Chapter 4   Typical Human Responses

(As dictated by Matthew)

—

If you ever find yourself trapped in an elevator with five other people, descending from the top of some skyscraper at incredible speeds, you might look around to check out who is crowding your space. It is quite possible, from that instant in time, that each person you see could be undead within the next fifteen seconds. They all could be five hungry tummies, searching for some delicacy to feast upon, and that would probably be you.

There certainly is some cause for distress, but let me assure you, you have every right to be distressed. If it were me in the elevator, I would probably say, "Holy crap! I don't want you to eat me!" Then I would get out my sawed-off shotgun and wave it about menacingly. Sure, they all might try to plead a case about how they aren't zombies, and they aren't hungry, and that zombies don't exist. My response? I know they don't exist. *Yet.* Then some of them will start crying or praying for the sweet mercy of God, but others might get angry and try to take your gun. If there's one thing I know about zombies, it's that they like to try to take your gun, so this sort of behavior will be a clear indication, even a first sign, of zombiism, and it's up to you to defend yourself and save the world. Of course, that's pretty easy when you have a shotgun in an elevator, but what if you only had a pistol?

You might be wondering where I'm going with this, and I was wondering myself when I started, but after a few drinks it all started to make sense. This elevator scenario illustrates an important point about other people around you: there is no telling how they will respond in a crisis situation under a lot of pressure. I'm not one to jump to conclusions, but I think a massive, all-out zombie invasion might be considered by some to be a crisis, and for those who are unprepared, there would certainly be a lot of stress. How will people weather this kind of mental atmosphere? Personally, I have a gun, all the time, which eases my mind and helps me relax.

Well, I'm certain that when the zombies come, I'm going to have an opening ceremony and a field day, but how will others react? Will they loot abandoned liquor stores to find tequila and whiskey for the party of the century, or will they run screaming, flailing aimlessly like a poor drowning kid with polio? What kinds of people can you count on, and what kinds of people could ruin your every chance for survival? Perhaps more important is, who is worth risking your life to save, even if he or she is being chased by a horde of undead? Read on to find these answers and more. So much more.

The Gunslinger

Motto: I know what's happening and how to handle it—with at least two smoking guns.

AKA: Bad-Ass Mamma Jamma, Mr. Tuxedo, Samurai Warrior, or Chuck Norris.

Memo: This kind of reaction has been glorified by James Bond, *Die Hard*, *Lethal Weapon*, almost every Western movie ever created, and pretty much any action movie with a good guy. This kind of person sees everything that's happening and realizes it for what it is, even if it isn't. No matter who they are, what they're doing, what their plans were, what day their birthday party was supposed to be, or what was for dinner, they adapt almost instantly to the new situation. Lock and load. And I'm not talking about someone who'll be somebody in a year or two, but someone who has combat woven into the very sinews of their core being. Like the sweat of sex, they've got battle all over them.

Most importantly, they see what's going on and become a survivor: they want to survive, they know at least vaguely how to do it, and they don't do too much wishful thinking that will distract them from accomplishing it. The gunslingers won't crack when the dusk of the world comes, and they won't slow you down when it's time to head for the hills. They might not know what to do, but if they realize you do, they will listen to you until the end, or until the end of their respect for you. Speaking of which, they also have a good sense of respect for other gunslingers.

If there's anyone to save, it'd be this kind of person. Remember that they lock and load, so saving them is not usually necessary. You're really just gathering them into the fold of your survivor death riders. If zombies are chasing someone, you'll know they are a gunslinger if they have empty guns in each hand and look pissed that they have to be running. Now that kind of imagery is something I can really appreciate. The gunslinger is the kind of person you can count on and should be the majority of any survival team.

There are other ways you can tell whether someone is a John Wayne or GI Jane. If they look out to the street and see someone get taken down by a zombie linebacker, with the blood and gore and whole nine yards, but they don't freak their shit out, it's a good chance you've found a winner. Granted, for those who aren't expecting it, there will be some amount of shock or fist pumping; nonetheless, a real gunslinger won't falter for long. Now, if instead the person immediately curls up into a ball and goes to sleep, you probably did not find a winner. If they leap up with guns that apparently came out of nowhere and start scanning the room for exits, I'd say keep that one close because they might just save your ass a hundred times before the day is out.

Another way to perform a test is to get an attack dog and hide a package of hot dogs in the person's coat; then watch how they react to the sudden and unexpected situation. If they stand and fight, you've either got one crazy motherfucker or a solid Spartan on your hands. Awesome. If they run or piss their pants, make sure they didn't think it was a zombie dog before you make up your mind; then make up your mind. One last way to tell would be to observe the reaction when someone goes bebopping around a corner and is suddenly ambushed by some zombie attack that comes out of the dark. If he or she instinctively "resolves the situation," perhaps by cutting off zombie heads with a couple judo chops, busting some brains with a karate kick, or whatever, and then they turn to you and say, "The situation has been resolved," that person is probably a goddamn machine hell-bent on destruction!

Keep in mind that some people you might think would be survival types might not be. For instance, a football player might be a muscle train and take a lot of physical abuse every Friday night, but they might not be that amazing at fighting off toothy corpses. They might just freak out and piss their pants, and we shouldn't blame them for that, those crybabies. However, if we invite them on our team and then they piss their pants while they let someone awesome die, then we have every right to blame them, but only so much as we blame ourselves for not making better choices, which should be a lot. All in all, it's like the old saying: "You can't judge a book by its cover." Some people just seem to be born like battle-hardened veterans, and others seem to be more like a bowl of Jell-O that looks really good but tastes like stale cigarettes: a life-changing disappointment.

It ultimately all comes down to what they are made of on the inside, not what they look like on the outside. Whether they can handle the stress or handle a gun has little to do with how much they can bench or how fast they can run. Ask yourself what you're made of, then look inside, and see. Is it gold, silver, or baby shit? Take me, for instance. I'm at least 50 percent terminator (my father's side), with an ultragold-platinum-tungsten alloy for bones. I once traded a pinky toe in exchange for an entire country, but I got bored, in like, an hour, so I "traded back." Still, it was a good hour.

It is important to realize some things about these tough guys. One is that you might sometimes have disputes over authority with them. Traditionally, a lot of these people have been largely independent, so they might not instantly accept the idea that you're head honcho. If a gunslinger sees that you have a weakness, or that you seem to be failing as team leader, they might want to circumvent, undermine, or replace. This is a direct result of their loss of trust and respect in you, and it should not be taken personally. If they start to disobey you, and with good reason, it's not so much that they don't like you but that you suck as a leader. Then they stop liking you. When it comes down to it, they just want to live, and if they think they know how to accomplish that better than you, then they aren't going to let you make decisions for them.

The best way to avoid this occurrence is to be the most prepared of anyone, and to command authority and respect. Sometimes you might find yourself in a situation where people simply follow you by default, but most times you'll have to earn that leadership, and in the end, that's how it should be. Ignore the fact that I would never follow anyone so I can tell it to you straight. I probably won't follow you unless I agree with you, and if your decisions result in the loss of a few team members, I'm probably going to be pissed and try to take over the job that should have been mine all along. If you get all personal about it, I might judge that you've become a hindrance for the team and have you abandoned. Again, it's nothing personal; it's just survival.

Another thing to realize is that these gunslingers might have ulterior motives, and if these motives are of an undesirable nature, then you might not have found a gunslinger after all. You might have found a bandit, which is something of a snake in your bed. This should come as no surprise, but both those who would help you and those who would hurt you can wield a gun and hold their shit together, and sometimes it's hard to tell who's who until you know their motive. Survival is one thing, but acting in a way that destroys the almost negligible amount of life left to save is something else. Basically, I don't want to die, and if I'm being a great person, high-fiving people, shooting dead folks, and someone comes along and stabs me in the back, what's a man to do? You tell me, what's a man to do? (Look below for more information about the bandits.)

The point is, though, that the gunslingers might have their own agenda, and that isn't something you want to have to worry about while you're trying to survive. If you find that someone on your team keeps disobeying your excellent, best-possible orders and instead opts for dangerous, risky, naive, or otherwise ridiculous courses of action, you might have to leave them behind. The team should never be compromised as a result of the actions of a single individual. It's certainly a mournful occasion to lose a possibly good team member, but as the wolverines know, survival isn't a walk in the park where everyone gets to ride the merry-go-round without ever having to push, which is to say don't take any fucking catnaps when you should be watching my ass.

The Screamer

Motto: I know what's happening, but I really wish I didn't.

AKA: the Liability, Most Children, Zombie Alarm, Banshee, or Dumb Bitch.

Memo: Women in popular media have typically portrayed this kind of response, such as by Julia Roberts or George Costanza, but that's just the stereotype and should not be a guide to who you save. Let me reiterate. Just because some guy has biceps the size of your head and a gun strapped to his back doesn't mean he's a good team member, especially if all he's doing is sitting on his ass and loudly crying great big tears out of his big dumb face. It may be that this response is more typical in women, but do not assume it only affects women, because that would almost certainly be the primary reason for your annihilation, somehow, somewhere.

The screamers have a tendency to look outside and understand that the zombies have finally come just like, deep down inside, they always knew they would, but they refuse to make the best of the situation. Take note that this is quite different from denying the existence of zombies altogether; these people know the zombies are there, and that's why they can't stop blubbering in hysterics. Some might hyperventilate, and if they pass out, they will likely be the lucky ones. Either way it happens, these people won't be scrambling for a weapon any time soon, and that makes them defenseless and useless.

Why are they crying, you might ask? It could be a lot of things. Maybe they just had a bad day, and seeing their waiter being consumed by a legless corpse might just have been the straw that broke their back. They might be crying for society, asking why they didn't see this coming and prepare so the world could be better protected (I ask myself that every day). Maybe they're crying for themselves because they read this book and then didn't prepare or take it seriously, and now they feel so stupid that they can't think of any reason they should live, and that makes them sad. Maybe they just wish everything was like it used to be, and they think fondly of the happier times of yesterday, all the while comparing those happy times to the horrifying slow dance of death unfolding before them. I can't say I know exactly why they might be shrieking uncontrollably, and it probably wouldn't help to ask, but I'm sure they all have their reasons that don't make any sense to the rest of us.

Now, let's say you've got your doubly warmed-up smoking shotgun in hand, and you're cruising down the street. On the corner you see a person, man or woman, screaming their eyeballs out at a duo of zombies strolling their direction. Do you slam on the brakes and smoke some croaks, or do you let the dead bury the dead? It's really a tough question unless you're a bleeding-heart humanitarian, and your decision depends on how much help you think you might need and how much you can spare additional supplies to feed an extra person.

The problem, you see, is that this screaming bitch (man or woman) might be useless for a day or week or so, but eventually they might grow a backbone and become a real asset to your team. There is no telling what they know or how useful you might find them, and for that reason you might consider stopping to save their life. For instance, they could be a doctor, and even though zombies blow their medical minds, you could hide them away from the unseemly sights and use them to treat your cuts and scrapes (but not bites, you treat that yourself). Of course, that person might also be a wimpy leech that sucks up your spare food, doesn't do their part, and steals your shiny things; it's always hard to say, but if that's the case, the individual can be easily dispatched. (He's coming right at us!)

The Disbeliever

Motto: I'm calm and collected, because the world is still just a ray of sunshine on a rainbow: ~~there's nothing wrong~~.

AKA: the Decoy, Gopher, Helen Keller, or That Guy from "the Company."

Memo: If the screamer's response didn't make much sense to you, then the disbeliever certainly won't. These people adamantly refuse to grasp the concept of zombies. They see the zombies, but somewhere between their bloodshot eyeballs and their brain, the zombies get deleted out of the picture, and their minds are completely oblivious to the fact that the world has taken a turn for the worse. Then these people start sweating without reason and feel like drinking something hard. If you asked them why they wanted Jack Daniel's so early in the morning, or why they were moistening your floor with a spray of sweat, they wouldn't have a good answer for you because they couldn't tell you anything was wrong. And that's how they'll die: unaware that anything is wrong, just like babies.

This kind of response is perhaps the most infuriating response of all, because no matter how hard you try, you cannot force them to come to terms with reality. It's almost as if they were living their lives just fine until one day they saw zombies feasting on a coworker, in his pressed white business shirt, crisp but with an odd splotch of red near the missing arm, and their mind just crapped an electric load right on top of their senses. From then on out, they will never see anything undead or act the least bit aware of the sudden turmoil around them. Because, you see, nothing has changed since last week, when there were more people alive and certainly many more people actually dead. "I don't see anything wrong. You might be pointing a gun at me and telling me to run, but let's not get into a fight because I'll call my lawyer, and he'll call the police and have you arrested, and then I'll sue you for assault. Yeah, you just walk away. Bitch, no one messes with me. Whooooouch! Holy *shit*! Something just *bit* me! Bears, bears are eating me! Ahh …" You get the idea, those poor dumb bastards.

Should you save a disbeliever? Probably not. In fact, I would go so far as to say it would be detrimental to your mission if you did acquire a disbeliever. Think of it: can you count on a disbeliever to watch your back when zombies are invisible to them? As far as they're concerned, you just kidnapped them with your guns, and they're going to try to escape as soon as they can so they can get back to their old life. That means that they might be a direct threat to you, because they will want to disarm or disable you in order to "free" themselves for imminent consumption by the wolves. If they aren't a direct threat, they are probably an indirect threat because they will escape when you're not looking and leave a huge hole in the security of your fortress, a hole you might not detect until the zombies come pouring in with a mysteriously revitalized thirst for blood. Either way, the risk and threat are overwhelming, so much so that the disbelievers should clearly be left behind. It's a sad, cold, hard world. Then the zombies will come, and all bets will be off. Gnashing of teeth anyone? Huh? Huh?

Now, if you're a bleeding-heart humanist or you find that your best friend, whom you absolutely cannot live without, happens to be a disbeliever, then there are some things you can do. First off, there is a splash of cold water to the face and a slap across the cheek (forehand or backhand, it makes little difference). The sudden shock of such an action might jolt the individual back into clarity, though I've never seen it happen. Another idea is to knock his or her lights out, either with a tasty knuckle sandwich, frying pan, or other blunt instrument. Once they have been knocked out, you can carry them to safety (a real pain in the ass, let me tell you), and then maybe you'll have a chance to work with them on comprehending the current state of affairs. If they continue to refuse the existence of zombies, even after proof, instructional videos, and a pop quiz, you might consider tying them to a chair and locking them up. It's for their own good, of course, and you should let them know that's the case. Maybe after a few weeks of thought, they might come to a consensus on the subject of the undead, one that cures them of their disbelieving status. It's a long shot, but it might work.

Now, if it wasn't difficult enough to deal with the disbelievers, it just so happens they are by far the most likely of any other type to go absolutely shit ass crazy. Sure, the screamers might blow their sanity to smithereens with some resounding shriek. Sure, the gunslingers might just see some sort of paradox that blows their mind, like a man biting a zombie biting the very same man, or like watching the impossibility of a pair of undead mating and subsequently conceiving a child in less than an hour. But, barring impossibilities and unaccountably high improbabilities, the gunslingers are pretty much good to go on the sanity front, and the screamers aren't too far behind as their wailing is a sort of self-therapy.

The disbelievers, however, have no sense of a need for therapy since nothing is wrong and are therefore already clearly flawed in their mental foundations. There is likely some part of their brain that understands everything just so that it can take extreme care in censoring the senses, and maybe it provides the individual with some subconscious idea that the world has gone to the crappers. However, there are other parts of the brain that evaluate what information they receive rationally and look for connections. Now, when people suddenly start disappearing from view, that rational side might have the sense of something being wrong, and before long the disbeliever is edgy without reason. This all starts a slow chain reaction, from edginess to uneasiness, to anxiety to hysterics, to outright fear and terror. The fact that there appears to be no reason for such feelings tends to exaggerate them even more, and before long you have to be very touchy with such an individual else they will crack like a dried-out hollow egg.

The Bandit

Motto: I know what's happening, and I'm going to take everything that isn't bolted down.

AKA: Judas, Rasputin, Slimy Shit, Pirate, Shredder, or Ming the Merciless.

Memo: There are some people who put on an act as if they are good citizens contributing to society and working to solve cancer, but deep down inside they are just another person bloated with envy and desire, and all they really want is everything you have. Sure, they might already have it, but if they have two, one can break, and they still have another one, or they can brag about having two, or they can sell one for free money and then blow the proceeds on hookers and beer. These people could be your friends, they could be your coworkers, they could even be your neighbors, and you need to realize that these kinds of people would slit your throat to get your sweet-ass LCD TV if they could do it with impunity. You might be thinking that your best friend wouldn't do something like that to you, but then you have to ask yourself a question: has he or she ever asked you for something? Huh? That's usually all the indication you need to know that that "friend" is a bandit in disguise.

So what happens when the world goes crazy, and most of the cops are zombies and everyone is crying and running and hiding? The bandits throw off their ridiculous "good costumes" and become what they were always meant not to be: a thief and, more likely than not, a generally bad person. As newly declared bandits, these people will loot, kill, murder, steal, kill, and not chew gum with glass in it. They will most likely be mean drunks and also will always be sloppy drunks, but somehow the zombies won't kill them. The bandits will manage to plague society for much longer than they should.

Notoriously hard to kill, the bandits have no lack of ambition for fucking your shit up, no failure of confidence when it comes to eating your sandwich, and competitive spirit? They'd kill their own mother just to jump up for the hobo slam. Really, I think it all comes from a factor I like to call Nasty. These bandits are nasty, and they have a lot of nasty to spread around. Bad guys in movies never seem to die, always coming back when you thought they were dead even though the good guys beat the bejesus out of them, all because the bandits have a lot of nasty in them. The bandits will be like that: resilient, persistent, and throwing steaming piles of their Nasty everywhere.

Will the bandits stop to help you? No, not unless they help themselves by selling you into slavery, you're their "bitch" and they want to protect their property, or you have a bomb strapped to their body and a remote detonator in your hand. They aren't about to stick their necks out for anybody unless they stand to gain, which probably means that all bankers, brokers, and politicians are the bandits incognito. Will they stop to steal your shit while you're distracted fighting the zombies? Yes. Will they fight the zombies off just to steal your organs? It's possible. Will they kill you to steal your guns to kill each other for a good pair of shoes? All signs point to yes. Will they try to kidnap your women and children and throw you to the bears? Most definitely. That's why they all need to die, unless you're a bandit too, and then you need to die.

I'm not sure how many times I can warn you about it, but here's another. The bandits have this uncanny ability to survive even when you would think that they shouldn't. For example, it will be an everyday occasion that they have to fight off a pack of zombies while attempting to run with a three-thousand-dollar entertainment system in their hands. Somehow they make it home every night and get all the richer for it, whatever that means. They'll end up with *all* the shit if you give them enough time. Sure, maybe with the end of civilization there won't be any electricity to run their five-thousand-watt surround sound and high-definition TV, but at least they can say they have it, and that's what they care about. The point is, they survive, despite all your biggest wishes. If you want to make sure you kill a bandit, you don't just nudge them with your toe after they are broken and bloody; they could still get up as soon as you turn around. No, you need to treat them like a zombie and smear their brains across the floor. There's no need to take any chances, and in any case, it's my belief that everyone who dies should get a bullet to the head just by default, perhaps as a part of the whole grieving ceremony.

Sure, I might steal a few things to survive, like extra guns and ammo, some canned food, liquor, etc., but I'm not going to be a bad person about it. Is it really necessary to shoot the manager just to get their goods, or could you instead add them to your team and get their cooperation? Sure, I won't go out of my way to save a disbeliever, but I wouldn't outright shoot them in the leg either. And I'd never force the living to fight unarmed against the undead for sport or pleasure. That's just goddamn sick. Sure, I may burn down some houses too risky to sanitize or that are obstructing the view from my fortress. However, destroying things without reason is a waste of time and serves no purpose but to remove from the world things that might someday be useful. Do the bandits destroy things irrationally for fun? Like a box of Twinkies at a weight-loss camp.

Personally, I like to think of myself as more of a hero, spreading a gospel of sorts to those who will listen and a warning to those who think I'm crazy. When the world is falling apart, I think I'll be like Shane from my favorite Western story—a bad-ass, fast-handed, but quiet-good-guy cowboy that stands up for the weak and just wants to live a good life. Except I'll also get drunk sometimes, like I mostly do now, which means I won't be as accurate as Shane, which also means I'll need more bullets and a faster gun. If you're a bandit, I won't say that I'm going to kill you, personally, but I might think that someone ought to. Just a thought. Nobody likes a bandit, especially me.

Don't invite the bandits on your team, and if you find a bandit is on your team, dispose of them in a timely manner as you see fit. These bandits lust for power and control, which explains their constant state of arousal, so you can't trust them not to kill you in your sleep. While aroused.

Another note about the bandits is that, like zombies, they feed off of people. If gathering in a large motorcycle gang helps them better feed off the people, then that's what they are going to do. At first the bandits will be disorganized and alone, but it won't be long before the bandits form mobile armies with enough firepower to battle many small countries—at once. This means that the bandits, who have no scruples in killing someone for what they want, will form an even more formidable force with less than no scruples in killing someone for what they want. Think of the Reavers from *Serenity*, always raping and killing and being all kinds of relentless crazy.

(Two words: *blood orgy*.) If those people break into my fortress, I think I'll fold my hand and make my escape. This, of course, is where the explosives come in (see the chapter on preparation if you don't know what I mean).

The best way to defend against an army of bandits is not to make your own army, which only attracts all kinds of bandits because of your power and influence, but instead to appear sparse and without wealth of any sort. Go underground, perhaps, because like zombies, the bandits are attracted to lights and movement. You might think it a chicken thing to do, that hiding business, but if running in fear from an army of Reavers to survive is cowardly, then yes, Captain Courage, I am a coward. I'm amazing, like Shane, but I think even Shane would run from those freaks. No one should be so dumb as to give up his or her life for so little gain. Remember this: be expensive. If you have to die, make it worth something.

An alternative to hiding underground, of course, is just to build a better fortress with more hidden explosives rigged in the ground, or with some kind of trap for the evil armies. I don't have any uncomfortable feelings about disposing of bad guys with explosives except that I have to clean up after them. Also, if any explosives explode automatically explosively, like land mines, I suggest a fence to help keep out the animals and help save on exploders. The fence would also protect other good guy survivors by keeping them out, because hey, it's dangerous in here.

The Religious Freak

Motto: I know what's happening, and I believe it has something to do with what I believe, and I'll sacrifice myself on its altar. Or not.

AKA: Jesus Freak, Bible Thumper, Zen Samurai, Zealot, or Monkelstiltskin.

Memo: Something very few people know about the religious freaks is that there are two kinds. One kind, when confronted with a zombie, will think that hell is full and has somehow oozed onto earth, and it will be their prerogative to dispatch the forces of evil with heavenly smite while singing hymns. The other kind, though, will see the zombies as a plague brought on from whatever higher power they believe in and will wail aloud and feel sorry for themselves, all the while not lifting a finger to fight. This type probably thinks it's their curse, and that they did something to cause the end of the world, like not throwing up enough after dinner or stepping on a worm or something, and that the end of the world is what they deserve. Really, I think both sides are understandable in the context of religion (if that's understandable). Think Jesus expelling demons versus plague of locusts. Historically, this kind of thinking makes sense; at least it makes sense to me when I'm wearing my raw chicken–sequined hat. Let's think about that for a minute.

So what is there to know about these religious freaks? Depending on the strength of their faith, no matter which kind they are, they might be unstable. For instance, someone who doesn't know what they really believe might wake up one day and realize they don't believe in anything. Then they stop being a religious freak and could suddenly become any of the other types, which is kind of like Russian roulette, especially if their entire moral structure was based on the idea that someone was always watching, someone they now believe does not exist. It would be kind of like leaning against a wall for support, but suddenly you no longer believe the wall exists, so it doesn't, and you fall. And then you see you scraped your knee, and you feel hurt and betrayed, so you go rob a jewelry store. Yeah, it's kind of like that.

Also, another problem with the religious freaks is that they constantly bother you about believing what they believe, and if you don't believe as much as they do, they bother you about that. You might be trying to tell them how you just can't understand where these zombies came from, and they'll go off on a Jesus rant as if it's the answer for every question. Then you'll say how you feel stressed because the zombies are beating on all four sides of your fortress, and they'll try and comfort you by some little-light-of-mine bullshit. Sure, they might be doing their best to reinforce the rigid structure by which they comprehend reality because they feel the entire universe of sanity sliding out from beneath them, and maybe they're just trying to be a good friend and cheer you up with their doomsday talk, but if that's not your cup of tea, it gets old real quicklike. This isn't a big factor that determines their effectiveness or usefulness, just something to keep in mind.

However, aside from these apparent setbacks, there are some benefits to all kinds of these religious freaks, at least to a few religious freaks of all kinds. One is that they can be wise, because they study parables and know a lot of riddles, or they meditate for millions of hours every day, and so they know everything about thinking about everything. That kind of thing can come in handy when you need people who can think rationally on your side, especially when some plans need to be drawn up for the best way to get more booze without attracting too much attention. Another is that some of them have an inner peace, and that gives them confidence, and just being around someone who has inner peace and confidence tends to make you feel better, which also makes the whole team feel better, so they become less jumpy. This fact in itself is very important because people make fewer mistakes when they feel peaceful and confident, and they also fight better and just feel more "okay with the zombie thing" than they would otherwise. A final benefit is that some religions really promote martial arts, and I like that. I can't judo chop my way out of a coffin, but I can really appreciate someone who could.

So what should you do with the religious freaks? You probably won't be able to tell how much faith juice they have in them when you pick them up, but maybe after a little small talk, you could discover whether they are off their rocker and praising Jesus to turkey. That might be a good indication that you should leave that one behind, because their religion didn't save them, and it's not going to save you. On the other hand, if your small talk turns up terms like "smite," "destroying evil," "demon," and "I could really use a drink," you might have found a real winner, a religious gunslinger, if you will. Some probing might be necessary to evaluate their mental situation and whether they have pointlessly devoted their life to a pacifist religion or actually gained some useful skills while reading their sacred texts. We're not looking for a nun who wants to help every drunken man to his feet, because to everybody else that man is just another dumb zombie, and she is going to get bitten in a hurry. Zombie nuns are f-r-e-a-k-y. Freaky. On the other hand, if that nun was Mother Teresa and exuded a brilliant white God Light that could heal wounds, ward off evil, and perhaps, miraculously, reverse zombiism, then she would be one hell of an asset. I'd carry her on my back, and finally, after decades of trying, I would be truly invincible.

The Elderly

Motto: I don't have much time left.
AKA: Geezer, Old Fogey, or Grandma.
Memo: There really isn't that much to say about the elderly, except watch out! For the most part, they will slow you down and won't be of much help in building a new world, but they have knowledge and advice that they might have learned through their years fighting in other similar circumstances. They might also have some pretty dang funny stories, and what else are you going to do around a campfire at night but drink, listen to stories, shoot wildly into the dark, or drink?

Really, I just mention the elderly because you have to watch out for them so that you don't mistake them for zombies, or vice versa. I mean, some of them look like zombies, and if you're the kind of person that would feel bad about killing an old person because you mistook them for a zombie, then maybe you should keep your gun on safety when you're at a casino or a convention or bingo night. Remember to follow the rules to test for zombiism, or use the UZLT as a quick safeguard against improper annihilation. Granted, some old folks don't speak, or even respond, in which case it might, just maybe, be best to take the safest route. I don't want to sound cruel or anything, but they should probably be shot. In the head.

Chapter 5   Weapons

(By Matthew, while oiling his shotgun)

—

Hear me, my readers! Pick up a weapon when you see the dead arise, and beat their lifeless force back to the ends of the earth. Say to yourself, "Self, I hate me some zombies," and prepare for the seemingly unnecessary but endless battles ahead. If you pick a fine weapon and you're smart about it, your greatest dangers come from a severe case of carpal tunnel and careless confidence. If you pick a crummy weapon, then you'd better be a ninja so you can kick zombies' heads off every time you flip out, which you'll do, and often. Either way, your greatest weapon is their stupidity, and your greatest weakness is your own. If readers at home are highlighting these pristine pages, I'd highlight that last sentence because it sounds so majestic and somewhat important. Also, please note that I am awesome. Highlight that, for real.

Lately I've heard rumors flowing like bad water through the grapevine about what weapons are best against zombies and what weapons are inefficient or ineffective. Some of these rumors are tasty, like a sweet Concord wine chased with a shot of spiced rum, and some of them are bitter and taste like poo. For many of the more dedicated readers, I'm sure they have their own opinions about what is best for what and what is most effective in general. Certainly those who have played any quality zombie game will understand the Gatling gun's undeniably fun personality, but will also recognize that ammo can sometimes be in short supply. Furthermore, the general greatness of the shotgun can never be forgotten, and it certainly cannot be bested, unless it's by a bigger, automatic shotgun with lasers and heat-seeking explosive rounds. And who could forget the Magnum, the end-all-be-all of what it means to feel lucky. If you already know, and indeed already own, the weapons you will use during the zombie invasion, then feel free to skip this chapter. For the rest who want a nonprofessional's professional opinion on what is best, read on.

Nontraditional Weapons

First, let me say to myself that I hate me some zombies. No matter if I am armed with a rock, a knife, or a drunken stupor, I'll go out of my way to destroy any evil zombies that I see. This one time I was on the sidewalk, and I saw a runner coming straight at me with a big strand of drool spilling from his mouth, and I swore it was a zombie. I blacked out, as I have been known to do, and it wasn't till after I'd smashed the poor soul's head through a car window and peed my pants that I came to, and only hours later did I realize he wasn't a zombie after all but a normal fitness freak. All that story is true except about the part where I peed my pants; my bladder is like a steel trap and hasn't lost my trust since the day I let go of my cloth diapers ... really. This just illustrates how you have to be constantly prepared for battle, armed and ready at a moment's notice, because you never quite know when or how they are going to come crawling after you. Some people might call you too prepared, perhaps even "offensive," but pay no attention to them and their silly restraining orders. One day you'll be right, and then you can make them all feel bad about how they hated you so much for no reason.

Here's the bottom line: sometimes when you really need a gun to do something, like shoot a zombie or open a beer, you don't always have one. Maybe you do have one, and it's empty, or maybe you had to pawn it so you could buy porn. Who knows, and who am I to judge? But what are you supposed to do in such situations? Well, whenever I need to open a beer, I could get up and walk to the kitchen and grab a knife, but then what would be the point of asking someone else to get me the beer in the first place? Instead, I generally opt for plan B, which is to grab anything within arm's reach and use it as a sophisticated prying device.

Sure, I could go to the "hardware store" and get a gun to kill those zombies, but then what would be the point of having a hideout? Generally, anyone who is in danger and in need of some means of defense doesn't wait around for the perfect weapon, but instead grabs anything and uses *that* as a weapon. In my earlier story, I used a car window. Was it meant to be a weapon? No, and engineers have probably even tried to design it so that it can't be used as such. Is it a very good weapon? Probably not, but maybe it'll do the trick, and most likely it will do better than your bare hands (exception for kung fu masters, see elsewhere).

If you're wondering what I'm trying to say here, it's this: feel free to plan the perfect arsenal against the ultimately heinous enemy, but don't forget that there are great weapons lying around everywhere you go. You might be asking, "Can a tyrant be thrown down with only a pen?" Sure, but skip writing the novel about your awful existence under their reign in an attempt to gain public support for your cause over a period of years; instead, jab it through the eye. Through the squishy eye. "Can a chair be used as a bludgeoning device?" Have you learned nothing from watching prowrestling 24/7 on cable and pay-per-view? I haven't either, but I saw this once in a bar fight, and it looked pretty cool. Whatever, you can find weapons anywhere, and it is a recommended practice, as recommended by these very words, that you scan your surroundings constantly for anything that could be used as a weapon.

Of course, if I were you, I'd buy a gun the next time I took a trip to the hardware store. That is, if I were you, which I'm not. Still, I'm just saying ... I would, and I'd get a matching holster too. And I'd etch my name into all my bullets. Not that I actually do that, but if I were you, I might.

Traditional, as in Middle Ages, Weapons

What weapons are so traditional they were used in the Middle Ages? Stuff like knives, swords, maces, axes, war hammers, staffs, nun chucks, boards with nails in them, and other craps like that. Almost all of them, certainly all I've listed, are meant for close combat. As the astute might guess, this means the zombies have to be close before you can break their face or cut them in half. Around here we have a little saying, and that is to keep your friends close and your enemies closer. I think it's dumb. I want my enemies to be as far away from me as I can get them, and only there, from a safe location a great distance away, with a good tripod, will I make the kill. If my enemies are close enough to feel my awesomeness like a man heat on their skin, they're getting a free ride to the gun show, and I hate free riders. I want to keep zombies not only like my enemies, because they are, but also because the closer they get, the greater the chance of infection. Usually a guy munching on your leg isn't going to kill you so long as you take control of things, but this just isn't so with zombies.

I advise that, like me and my enemy, a distance be put between such weapons and yourself, if at all possible. Sure, if you have nothing else but a Buster sword with which to smite the evil in a massive way, go for it. This basically follows the rules above concerning nontraditional weapons. And don't get me wrong, I totally understand the appeal of the sword or the skull-crushing power of the mace, especially in the hands of a master. I just don't want to risk the chance of having a severed head nip my toe. How lame would that be, to die from being bitten on the toe from a head you'd already severed? I also don't want flying heads to land on my shoulder, or have chunks of skull some how or other get in my mouth. I also don't want blood in my face, because that's really gross and extremely unsound. If you're a nameless mystical ninja pimp and can repel arrows and armies and armies of arrows with your sword, then you're probably A+ and don't need my advice. Heck, after all that training it would be a pretty big waste not to use it. Still, watch out for those chompers.

Nonetheless, if one of these antique killers is all you've got, then you'd best learn to use it as well as you can. Really, the class of traditional weapons is so broad that it would be hard to master all of them, but there are a few strategies I've developed for some general types of weapons. For instance, if the weapon is a pole axe or other similarly long stick, one option would be to spin like a top. You heard me, spin like a top. You might say to yourself that this idea is the most ridiculous idea ever, but do you really want to risk being right? Do you? So, like I said, spin like you're a malnourished Russian ballerina obsessively pirouetting to avoid being discarded into the frozen vodka fields of the mother country. It will provide 360 degrees of protection as long as you're still on your feet. Avoid swinging high at the head level because kids can be zombies too. Instead, try to cut 'em down at the knees to further slow the zombie advance. Granted, a lot of force will be involved in this maneuver, so try to get some rotational speed built up first. For more ideas, watch the second *Matrix*, particularly the scene between Neo and the Agent Smith.

If the weapon is a mace or club or other blunt instrument, the above method would still work but for the fact that the weapon's reach is generally much shorter. Instead, hope there isn't a crowd and go bonkers for gophers. That is, smash their heads in. It should be easy enough because most of those weapons were designed to smash heads through armor helmets, and zombies don't typically wear armor helmets. Avoid spending too long smashing any single zombie's head; also avoid getting your weapon stuck in a head because that would really suck. If too many zombies attack all at once, the weapon should do a fair job of knocking them back with a few swings, but I would recommend running to string them out. Then turn about-face to bludgeon the crap out of the shuffling line of zombulators.

Finally, for swords and smaller knifey objects, I give only a few suggestions. With all of them, do not poke or stab. It's useless unless you hit a brain, and even then it isn't very efficient. Instead, always slash and hope your blade is sharp enough to cut bone. A traditional samurai sword, for instance, was historically tested (sometimes) at the executioner's block some couple hundred years ago. The quality of the blade was based on what part of the body the sword could cut through. If a sword could cut diagonally through the torso, then it was granted highest quality, but if it could only sever a limb, it was granted shit. Of course, it would suck to be the test dummy for any of these tests, which is why some convicts swallowed rocks before walking that last mile. To me, this means you could probably cut a zombie in half with a good sword. Sadly, most swords you see in stores are crap, so don't expect much. In any case, avoid getting in close with shorter blades like knives and knives. If you do have to get in close, hopefully there is only one zombie and hopefully you jab the knife through the eye. Otherwise, I recommend trying to throw the knife, then running. Running is a good weapon.

Therefore, and in no certain conclusion, don't bet your life on glorified sticks and whips. Just because you think it's cool, your friends think it's cool, it looks cool, it makes you feel really cool, and you get ogled by the opposite sex, it doesn't mean it won't get you killed. Zombies don't know what cool looks like. They also don't have a sense of humor, so don't even bother trying.

Handguns

There are few things in life that make you feel as powerful as shredding a hand-caught raw trout with your teeth, which I do for breakfast every day, but one of those things would undeniably be a weighty six-shooter smoking in each hand. Let us take, as example, some of the greatest men of all time: Dirty Harry, Doc Holliday, Billy the Kid, Robocop, and Shane. Why take them as example? Well, let me tell you. One, they're awesome. Put together, they would boil down to some sort of superconcentrated man juice that would almost rival my own. Second, they managed to accomplish a hard feat: nigh-perfect accuracy and deadliness with a pistol (or two). Sure, one of them is part robot, and all the rest have their problems, but we can surely overlook such minor details considering the fact that shooting a pistol is extremely hard for most people. If I could piss as straight as those legends could shoot, I wouldn't soak the leg of the guy next to me, and being out-of-my-mind Irish blitzed is no excuse, thanks to Holliday and Munny being drunken aces. Damn alcoholics and their iron.

If I could assemble a team of fictional or dead characters, on one list I would most certainly choose a number of those guys, because in a tight spot with a horde of zombies they would be able to work some magic. Pistols, whether they are Colts or Glocks, are ideal at short-range and against a number of somewhat spread-out enemies. Their deadly force and infrequent jamming, combined with reasonable clip sizes, makes the pistol a trustworthy weapon and a staple of any assaulting force. The results of the pistol are clean, with few holes in the corpses and few bullets wasted, and the ability to travel (run) with them is unparalleled. To be certain, the most mobile and effective weapon of all would be a pistol.

The warning here is the foil of our legends. The pistol is only a great weapon in the hands of someone who can use it well. In the hands of a newblet who has never fired a weapon before, they might be better off just throwing the bullets and hoping for God to explode them. Pistols, with their kickback and short barrels, are hard to use effectively without a good deal of practice, so if the inexperienced is ever given the choice of a pistol and a shotgun, the shotgun should always forever be chosen. Still, Shane's pistol would put a shotgun to shame any day.

My recommendation? Practice some with the pistol, preferably one with a clip of fifteen or more, but don't break your wallet buying one and becoming Annie Oakley on steroids unless you just love it that much. The idea is that when the zombies come, you'll be able to pick up pistol shooting quickly, and using the pistol is something that should be considered most necessary. Like I said, it is mobile, and it is effective. Other benefits include an abundance of ammunition, large clip sizes, and a quick firing rate. Also, you look badass when you use it. I would sleep with a pair of pistols instead of a shotgun except for the fact that I can barely see when I first wake up. Also, the shotgun is a jealous lover.

Strategies using the pistol are really quite simple. Actually, I can only think of two that are worth mentioning. Shooting apples off heads is a good parlor trick, but one that zombies find lacking in any serious entertaining value, so I'm not going to discuss it further. The first good strategy is the obvious one: shoot them in the head. Really, after that you're done. I guess you could shoot them twice in the head just to make sure, but if it looks messy to you, it looks successful to me. Shooting a zombie in the neck or heart or anything dumb like that isn't going to help at all, so don't. Other than that simple idea, the only other idea is this: if you get a running zombie or undead animal chasing you, the head will be bobbing and weaving and won't give you a very good shot. The way to handle such a situation is not to fire blindly and empty your clip. That would actually be the worst way to handle such a situation. No, the better idea would be to aim at the legs or the hips, more likely the hips since the legs are moving at least as much as the head. The goal is to hit bone with enough force to stop, or temporarily slow, the oncoming annoyance. Upon a successful hit, the opponent should stall long enough to provide an opportunity to hit the head, and then you're done again. Nice.

There are other handguns that don't quite fall into what I've described thus far, like Uzis or automatic pistols, but the only real difference is that they are much harder to control and are inherently much less likely to be accurate. Consequently, the strategy is a little different; there is the extra requirement of carrying additional ammo, and these weapons would best be used with a partner who has a pistol or rifle of some sort. If a number of zombies are quickly (or slowly) approaching, the above strategy of aiming for bone would work quite well with an automatic weapon to slow or stop a bunch of the zombies. You might even hit some brains with the stray bullets. Once the monsters are down or whatever, cleanup is significantly easier. That's all I really have to say about this topic. Ask someone else if you want more information.

Long-Barrel Guns

Long-barreled guns would include many of the staples we all would consider staples, like shotguns, rifles, assault shotguns, assault rifles, and other kinds of shotguns, and rifles. Now, as you know, I have quite the soft spot in my big heart for an aneurysm, but also for my favorite shotty, of which I love more dearly than the children I don't have. Some of my most enjoyable memories are of my shotgun and I ... shooting things ... I wasn't supposed to. Many of my Friday and Saturday evenings are spent polishing and oiling and cleaning my shotgun, which I affectionately call shotgun, or sometimes shotty, and boy, do we have a hootin', hollerin' good time. Sometimes I even cruise for babes with my shotgun, but I think most women are put off by the size of my barrel and run away crying and screaming, except for that one time when things got pretty freaky. Needless to say, my shotgun is the one I sleep with every night, but not in the freaky way.

Well, enough about my shotgun, the one that gives me reassuring glances and comforts me after the nightmares where I'm kicking so much ass I blow up the world and fly out into empty space, the one that is always there for me, loaded and at the ready, the one that never gets angry or leaves me for another man. Yes, enough about *that* shotgun and back to the topic at hand, which is long-barreled weapons in general. I guess I think they are all right, but I don't know if I'd bet my life on one. It just seems kind of like a pretty big commitment. Maybe it's one of those decisions everyone will just have to make for him or herself.

Seriously though, aside from sex, shotguns are pretty sweet weapons in that they are extremely powerful and can be fired effectively from the hip. The beauty of the shotgun is the spread of the buckshot, because this spread is what really does the damage against a mob of the undead. I mentioned previously that pistols are great against somewhat spread out zombies; well, the shotgun is great against very closely packed zombies, like those you would find stuffed in an elevator or a hallway. A shotgun of sufficient power would cut those zombies in half, and if you aim at their head, you won't be seeing it for very long.

Of course, to the veteran fans of *Resident Evil* and similar such games, this is all old news. Everyone knows why the shotgun is awesome, so I don't really need to say much else about it. It is kind of a pain to reload sometimes, especially if you pull a Sarah Connor and only have one arm. Also, the bullets are pretty big, so it can be hard to carry a large stockpile with you at any given point in time. You might be able to just live off the boxes of bullets you find hidden in pots or left absent-mindedly on shelves, but if you're in the kind of neighborhood that doesn't have pots or shelves, you might have to hump the shells with you.

Another thing about shotguns is the difference between the normal shotgun and the sawed-off shotgun. You can really do battle either way, but they each have some benefits. For instance, a normal shotgun will do damage at a farther distance, and the damage inflicted will be more concentrated and, consequently, more awesome. The flip side is that the spread is limited, especially at close range, which is where the sawed-off shotgun comes in. Basically, take everything I said about the normal shotgun and reverse it. The closer the zombies are, the better the sawed-off works, whereas the normal shotgun works better if the zombies are just a little farther off.

Personally, if I were you, which I'm not, but if I were, I would take a pistol for those zombies just a little farther off and a sawed-off shotgun for the zombies that get a little too close for comfort. That is, if I were you. I'd also aim at the shoulders, not the head or stomach like you might imagine. Since you can count on the spread, aiming for the shoulders will help maximize the damage done, with some buckshot hitting the head, the shoulders, and the stomach. Really, the stomach part is just for effect and satisfaction since it doesn't do much in and of itself. Also, as always, keep in mind that a zombie cut in half from a shotgun blast is still a dangerous zombie so long as the arms keep pulling the head around.

Now, one last thing about shotguns is that there are those that are double-barreled only, which usually means you load the shell into the barrel yourself, and there are the semiautomatic and automatic shotguns. I personally am a big fan of the semiauto, but some of the biggest shotguns are of the double-barreled variety. It's a question of power and speed, but I'd take speed and safety in exchange for a few extra rounds. There are probably more exotic shotguns out in the world, hiding in the hands of some government or other, that are even more freaking fantastic than my shotgun, but it might be hard to get one of those. Hard, or expensive, which to me still means hard because I'd have to steal it. Just ask yourself, how much money *do* you need to spend to feel safe again?

For rifles, on the other side of the moon, there are yet even more options. There are plenty of rifles that are automatic, semiautomatic, or single shot. There are also the options of attaching laser pointers or grenade launchers or scopes. Rifles are pretty sweet if you're in the position to use them. I think everyone can agree that a sniper rifle isn't something you'd use to rob a bank, and I think it just follows that it isn't a gun one would use in a crowd of zombies. Really, a sniper rifle doesn't have much of a place in a zombie world except for in two occasions. One, it could be the tool to an interesting game I like to call Struggle. The point of the game is to place in an empty field one zombie for each player. Then a referee acts as bait so that all the zombies bum-rush him. Each player's goal is to shoot their zombie in select places so as to slow, but not stop, their attack. The player whose zombie arrives last is the winner. Of course, any player who intentionally or otherwise hits or kills another player's zombie is automatically disqualified and made fun of by his peers.

The second occasion in which a sniper rifle is useful is to offer protection from a distance. The sniper rifle could provide cover, clear a path to safety, or create a well-timed distraction, all without putting the shooter in any danger. However, against a gaggle of undead, this rifle is practically useless.

Other rifles, however, can serve as a much greater asset in general. Automatic and semiautomatic rifles can be effectively used against zombie masses, especially in controlled-burst modes. Since rifles fire high-velocity projectiles in rapid succession, they can be used to eliminate crowds at a distance, before they become a real threat. The weight of the bullets and the possibility for armor piercing rounds (among other things) means that one bullet could easily rip through two or fifteen zombies, possibly laying them down, finally, for the long orgy with death. This makes rifles an attractive option when it comes to maintaining a perimeter, defending a position, or advancing to attack in an open area, especially when there are a number of riflemen in the operation.

Aside from the add-ons you can use with rifles, like the aforementioned grenade launcher or the bayonet, rifles are pretty straightforward in their techniques. In general, you'd prefer to aim at head level with controlled bursts of fire. Whether you know it or not, the average man is six feet tall. This means that, on average, a volley of lead aimed six feet above ground into a crowd of undead will destroy the brains of half the men. No one knows what the average height of women is, but if you aimed at that level, you would certainly get half the women and probably some dudes too. Undead dudes.

Note that while shotguns are very good in tight quarters, they have a minimal level of penetration into crowds. The first few layers of a crowd may be decimated by a shotgun blast, but the rest of the zombies behind will be unhurt. Rifles, on the other hand, may not immediately decimate any layer of a crowd, but the deep level of penetration would best be summarized in a very offensive mom joke, one I'm too dignified to put down in writing. Keep this in mind if there are a number of rifles and a number of people using them. Semiautomatic and automatic rifles can rip through crowds, even at a distance, killing or immobilizing them quickly.

Explosives

There is a certain class of weaponry characterized by ticking clocks, burning fuses, trip wires, shrapnel, and fiery explosions. They are often called explosives, less frequently exploders, and you have to be careful with them because they can be quite explodey. In fact, it is your goal to make explosives as explodey as possible, so the more successful you are, the more careful you need to be. As much as you wouldn't want to be caught outside during a firestorm, you wouldn't want to fall on your own explosive and be exploded, so make sure your shoes are tied and your hands are dry before trying to handle any of these bombshells. Personally, I like to use them as my bulletproof vest, not because I'm afraid of bullets, but because I'm not afraid *enough* of bullets. I wouldn't recommend this to most people though, especially not for people who want to live forever and are allergic to metal and fire.

Some explosives are camouflaged to look like something else, something you wouldn't normally consider dangerous, something not generally considered an exploder. For instance, some bombs, if you will, might look like cats, but in all actuality they are time bombs of everlasting death. Key points here? One, it looks like a cat, which doesn't usually explode. Two, it's not actually a cat, but a bomb, so it's camouflaged. Three, when the cat does explode, it would be unexpected, because you don't expect cats to do something they normally don't, which is to explode. Four, this is why I don't kick cats, not because I expect it to explode, but because I don't know what to expect. I know it's complicated, but bear with me, because this is important. Watch out for bombs that are hidden, not just so you can use them for yourself, but so that they are not used on *you* when they were meant for dumb zombies. Also, watch out for bears.

Warnings aside, there are several kinds of explosives you might see in the wild, ranging from small grenades and baseball-sized nuclear weapons to large missiles and truck-sized propane tanks. Some classical examples include mines, grenades, missiles, gas leaks, time bombs, booby traps, fireworks, and dynamites. Then, for each of those types, there are subtypes. For grenades, there are smoke grenades, flash grenades, fragmentation grenades, spike grenades, incendiary grenades, sticky grenades, and even plasma grenades. For propane tanks, there are some for grills, which are small, and there are a little bit bigger ones, still for grills, and then there are those that are bigger than fat horses that attach to houses; lastly, there are propane tanks for moving propane on trucks, which are basically the truck-sized propane tanks I mentioned earlier. Talk about a lot of bad gas. Or is it good gas … really good gas?

This madness of size and shape continues with missiles, where there are some that are smaller than small children and others that are bigger than a group of large children. (Read fat.) Some missiles can be carried around in briefcases and are light enough that one could run from the cops, or even the government, with one in hand. Others can be fired from portable tubes at people or vehicles and are what some might call "rocket launchers." Still more, there are missiles bigger than a man and other missiles even bigger than that. A lot of missiles cause a lot of destruction, with a small class of nuclear missiles causing enough destruction to poke the moon in its little eye. In most cases, unless you're the government trying to contain a zombie outbreak or conspiracy, nuclear missiles should be considered overkill and off bounds. This will keep *you* safe and the *bad guys* frustrated.

When it comes to strategy, explosives are extremely flexible and easy to use. Unlike bullets, which have to be fired accurately so that their linear trajectory will intersect with a critical target, thereby causing maximal damage and achieving the highest grade of effectiveness, explosives aren't like that. They blow shit up, by which I mean that you just have to get kind of close. If you put one near a zombie, it will blow up the zombie, easy as cake pie. The only thing you have to worry about is timing and distance. If you blow the mojo when the zombie is a hundred yards away, you'll probably find that you suck at life. If you set the explosives too far out of the way, when they explode you'll only find you're wasting your time, and you've only made Dragg angry. Of course, this is only the case if you're using explosives that can't incinerate a football field and are bound by the usual constraints of space and time, but most of us won't be running from zombies with something that could.

Now, here's the kicker. You'll probably never lay your bright blue gunslinger's eyes on most of the explosives that exist on the market. For one, maybe they are too expensive for someone of your means, and you're afraid of robbing someone who sells explosives, or the dealers are too black-market shady for your reputable, upstanding career as an American citizen. It might also be that there just aren't any manufactured munitions in your area, by which I mean your city, state, or backyard. And, to be honest, this poses a problem, because we all know that real explosives are dependable and pretty well foolproof, something we can bet the lives of our friends, family, and small pets on. They might not come with explicit instructions, and maybe you won't know what kind of power you're dealing with, but surely you could figure something out. However, since there are none to be found, and there probably won't ever be, people who want the offensive force and defensive backup plan must resort to making their own. They (we) are forced to gamble with their lives in order to improve the odds of survival during the later, greater zombie-filled gamble with their lives, and let me tell you, there won't be any fuzzy pink dice in this Great Gamble to cheer you up or make your friends laugh at you. There will only be death and survival and, occasionally, a homemade bomb.

As it turns out, there are actually a lot of ways to kill one's self while making homemade explosives, mostly because there are a lot of ways to screw up but also because there are a lot of ways to make homemade explosives, period. Exclamation mark. I'm not going to cover those techniques here because I don't want to be listed as a terrorist and have trouble not being starved and beaten, but don't think those techniques aren't important just because I'm afraid of disappearing forever. You'll be glad if you have some knowledge of such techniques when zero day hits, even if that knowledge isn't from experience or doesn't come from this book. Do you know how to prepare for the zombie invasion? If you do, or did, you would know that preparing takes a lot of explosives, and I mean a lot. By the time you finish preparing, you would have a lot of experience. You could probably join the bomb squad as captain, which is better than being attacked by the bomb squad or even being beaten by a bomb squad captain, and I think that's a good thing.

My only tips, as far as thinking about homemade explosives in a purely hypothetical manner, is to stay away from dynamite and other explosives that could crater your house in a pure form. If you appreciated my use of "crater" as a verb, then you might also appreciate this second piece of advice: don't let your family know until you're done. It's a lot harder to stop a man who has rigged your house and car to explode than a man who hasn't but intends to. Finally, and this is my last thing to say about explosives or weapons in general, be constantly ready and leave the safety off. There's a reason why the police don't have safeties on their guns, and it's not so that they can let criminals get away.

Final Warnings

Unless you choose one of the hand-to-hand types I previously warned you not to use (if you can help it), you need to understand that there are dangers in using a weapon. Other than fighting zombies in a school for the deaf and blind, you need to be aware that the sound and light expelled from a fired weapon or detonated explosion can, and probably will, attract zombies. In some cases, this is a great thing, because it means that zombies will do all the legwork and save you the trouble of getting off your ass to kill things.

However, in most cases, this is a bad thing, as you'll find yourself attracting zombies from all sides. When on the move or in search of supplies, the problems are obvious: you may not have a place you can hide, or you may not have enough ammunition to hold your position until the zombies in earshot are piled at your doorstep. This occurrence should be expected as often as you can expect it, which should be often. Or always, whichever happens more frequently.

Sadly, this implies that there may occasionally be instances in which your best weapon is stealth and silence. Getting in and out without drawing attention will often be the best way to avoid hairy situations or undue danger. I'll grant that it's about as satisfying as Tabasco sauce when you're parched, but at least you'll be able to fight another day, a day in which you'll have more canned dog food and enough bullets to survive the week on top of your well-positioned roof.

Nonetheless, no matter what, never waste your ammunition and engage in an orgy of risk. Don't shoot your gun up in the air and shout unless it's the Fourth of July or you just lost your virginity. Any other reason and I'll probably punch you—right in the mouth.

Chapter 6 When to Throw in the Towel
(Wildly penned by Geoffrey one late night)

―

Before we get started, I want to make a few things crystal clear so that we are all on the same page, which is 78. First of all, I wanted to put a definition of "throwing in the towel" so that nobody is confused on what we are talking about. To "throw in the towel," you have to give up on life and kill yourself. This does not include letting yourself die by passive actions such as starving to death or dying of dehydration. That is called being a badass that is dedicated to being human. Throwing in the towel means that you purposely end your life in an effort to keep yourself from becoming a zombie. Considering the fact that zombies are overtaking the earth, and you obviously survived that somehow, do not take this decision lightly. There are specific guidelines in the following chapter that will help clear up this dilemma. Are there times to throw in the towel? Yes. Are there times to not throw in the towel? If you are legitimately curious to the answer of this question, then you probably won't get the choice anyway, so go play with an outlet. For the rest of you, read on because it could mean the fate of the human race.

When is the time right to throw in the towel? Well, if you're like Cassius Marcellus Clay Jr., you won't know until it's too late, so read carefully because this could be the only thing that keeps you from spending the rest of eternity wondering where all the salsa is. I fully realize that some people live in this world not to contribute to the social environment of the earth, but to muck it up. These are the first victims, and the last victims, of zombies. They don't know what's happening, and they don't know when to quit, even when they are tainted with zombieness they still struggle to retain any shred of humanity they mistakenly thought they once had.

If you had half a brain in between those skin flaps I call ears, you'd see where I am going with this. These people get bitten and try to hide it as long as possible, not understanding the last great towel needs to be thrown. Meanwhile, they manage to get inside the barrier between zombie and nonzombie worlds just to eventually turn and wreak havoc from the inside out. Not only would this be slightly problematic for the humans, but it's also going to be pretty annoying. When the new history books are written, Mr. Iscariot will long be forgotten; Brutus and Cassius will be but a small entry of great duos next to Siegfried and Roy and Batman and Robin. Hitler will still be remembered as bad, but not the same kind of bad. He'd be about as bad as Mom walking in when you are having your special time with the silk panties of that one hot chick from across the street. These people would be as bad as his mom walking in while he is eating the hot chick's dog from across the street. Raw. Yes, all the books would remember the ultimate traitor, the one that almost forsook the entire human race in the name of dumbassness. This would be the guy everyone remembered to hate. It would be this one person who resides in the ninth circle of hell, waiting for eternity to end just so he could scratch that itch on his arm. And guess what? Nobody wants to be that person because that itch won't get scratched.

So again I ask, "When is the time right to throw in the towel?" It is not a simple answer, like most of you are thinking. I know that the first thing that popped into your heads was, "When I got bitten. Duh." Wrong. Being bitten isn't necessarily the end of the world. Now, since I haven't come across a real, live, undead zombie, except in my dreams of course and maybe that one time in Chicago, I haven't been able to discover the secret of the infection. I do know, however, that it is transmitted when you are bitten. Naturally, I can make a few assumptions about how the infection spreads from there: (1) The infection either spreads through the bloodstream, flesh, muscle, bone, or any other possible body substance. The reason I say this is because the transformation takes time. It does not always happen instantly, so I can deduce that it does, in fact, spread. (2) The infection takes different amounts of time for different people. This implies that there is no set amount of time for complete zombie infection. So there is a small window of opportunity to prevent the full-blown zombie. (3) If it can be prevented, it has to happen near the source of the wound. I know this sounds trivial and obvious, but I am pretty sure some of you are having this book read to you, so I want to spell it out clearly so you can understand too.

Now that we have our assumptions laid out, however weak and oversimplified they may seem, let's save the world. When you get bit, what is the first thing you do? Correct, pull out your huge knife and cut off the limb at the nearest joint. I don't care if you get bit half a centimeter above your elbow, take the whole arm at the shoulder. Nobody knows how long this window may be, and it may not be long. So we aren't going to mess around trying to cut through bone; it's too slow. Cut the joints. I want that damn arm off immediately. If the zombie isn't chewing on it anymore, then you waited too long. Now, get out a tourniquet and do what needs to be done. And if you haven't figured out how to run while doing this, then don't run. You need to get the bleeding to stop fast so that you have the energy to get away and hide somewhere safe. I say hide, because you aren't going to go back to the safe zone. You hide out for a while, at least a couple of hours, just to be sure you won't turn once you're inside. You don't want to be that guy, and I don't want to be the guy you eat. If you start to feel a certain distaste for cheeseburgers and a sudden like for blood, human blood, then throw in the towel and kill yourself however you feel fit.

If you don't crave human blood, but you do start craving swine blood, then you have to give the benefit of the doubt to the human race and kill yourself. Swine meat doesn't count ... mmmm, bacon. I've heard, on the street of course and not in my own thoughts because that would be crazy and gross and crazy, that pig blood is very similar to human blood. In fact, once upon a time, say pre-1983, doctors used to bleed their patients and replace their blood with pig blood. So this proves swine blood is pretty much the same as human blood, and you should kill yourself if you have an insatiable thirst for it. If you don't feel any such urges and you can still speak and do math, then everything should be okay, and you can go back to safety—assuming you can still make it back. Have someone keep an eye on you for a couple of weeks, just to be double extra sure.

When you get bitten, make sure it's something that can be cut off. If they get you in the neck, back, stomach, or anything else important, you're done. Throw in the towel right then and there. The best thing to do would be to arm some explosives in the general area of your body, thus eliminating yourself and the zombie bastards that bit you. I know Matthew prefers dynamite as a bulletproof vest, which is an option. If this is impossible, then I suppose a knife will do. This time.

Assuming that you take the rest of this book to heart, you shouldn't have to worry about getting bit or infected. Except by Russian water. But there are other problems that might arise, giving you no option but to hand your life back to God. The first one—and arguably the most serious issue we will deal with—would be running out of Reese's Sticks. I am pretty sure, zombies or no zombies, I will kill myself if I ever run out. But seriously, people who make Reese's Sticks, don't ever stop. If you have any self-respect or compassion toward your fellow human being, don't stop making those beautiful peanut-butter-filled wafer sandwiches covered in smooth, rich chocolate. Seriously. But since I won't let that happen, we can move on to more realistic problems, although less serious.

To Men

(No, I'm not being sexist. I just have different advice for women.)

Let's say the second worst thing that could happen happens. All the women die. Well, last time I checked my biology notes, which was awhile back, men need women for one thing: making babies. The kicker is, we can't do it alone. No matter how hard we try, how many guys we bone, no babies. Ever. And this is unacceptable. I just cannot condone straight gay sex without any goddamn results. Uh, I mean ... I ... uh, can't condone stuff like that. There is a simple rule I follow when dealing with matters of the sex. No women = No dice. Ouch.

Let's be honest with ourselves. Life wouldn't be worth living without women anyway. Like all our great problems, the addition of zombies is really just being redundant to the fact that life on earth is actually over. It isn't worth seeing another sunrise without the constant nagging of a woman. Why should we ever breathe in fresh air without the endless supply of commands from a woman? Who would spend all our hard-earned money without women around to do it for us? Life without women would be without joy, without color, without breasts. Just a giant mass of hairy, sweaty, naked, gyrating men having a gigantic gay sex pile. This is not awesome. Add to the fact that zombies are probably eating most of these guys, and not in a good way mind you, it is simply unacceptable. If you have intimate knowledge that the last woman on earth has perished, end your life immediately. End it faster than you would cut off your bitten arm. If you haven't died before the synapses in your brain tell your body to kill itself, then you were too slow. I cannot stress the urgency enough. If ever there were a time to throw in the towel, this would be it.

But don't be too hasty. Just like when you get bitten by a zombie, not all is lost. Take some time to assess the situation unless it is absolutely certain that they are all gone. You must realize the truth from fiction. If someone says that they believe all the women are gone, then it becomes your life's work to find a living woman and make sweet, sweet love to her all night long. But before you can do that, you may have to search for quite a while. You may end up searching for days or weeks or months. You may even search for years, but as long as there is hope, you can keep up the search. Now, I don't want to alarm any of the slower "listeners" that we may have, but you may even have to search outside of the fences, in zombie territory. You will undoubtedly have to search the countryside, mountaintops, cities filled with zombies, wastelands, deserts, and every other landform on earth until you find that last can of tuna, but it will be worth it.

To Women

Women, don't throw in the towel, ever. Seriously, nothing short of being bitten in the neck, head, torso, or back should be considered grounds for throwing in the towel. You are too important to the human race and the survival of our species. Even if Reese's Sticks run out, try to keep it together. I don't envy you because I already know I couldn't do it. But be brave. Life on this planet sucks already, and the addition of billions of zombies will only make it suck more, but sometimes you just have to keep taking the next step. Someone once told me, in the form of writing typed in a large book, that God only gives us what we can handle and nothing more. Remember that, and you might just win the lottery.

Women, if you happen to be the only gender left on this planet, hold off on the celebration for a while before you consider your options. First of all, and I don't need to tell any of you this, you definitely do not need to kill yourself. Just try not to kill yourself from overcelebrating. Also, you don't have to be afraid of useless homosexual tendencies. Instead, you should embrace them and all get together in a big sweaty pile of hot women and go swimming. And I don't mean in the water. There is nothing hotter than a hot group of female on female-on-female action. This act would bring a temporary balance to the universe as a metaphor for the unrelenting hope that mankind keeps in faith of better days. It is okay to spend the rest of your life in ecstasy, experiencing one orgasm after the other. And it's okay for me to watch from heaven.

When I look at all the other possible problems in the world, they all pale to the first two reasons to throw in the towel. Because of this fact, I will be as bold as to say that the towel shouldn't be thrown in for any other reason. As long as you haven't been bitten and there are plenty of women around, the situation is not hopeless or fruitless. Yes, there will be a lot of problems all around you, but things won't be so bad that you have to commit the ultimate sin. Reserve the right to exercise that option for a later date. Don't be a pussy about it and just give up. And for the love of God, don't complain about how completely horrid your life has truly become. People in Africa deal with this very situation daily, so go have a doughnut and get over yourself. That is just what the world needs, a bunch of twelve-year-old girls complaining about how hard their life is when their daddy will only buy them anything they want but wants a hug every now and then in return. I don't need any whining morons going on about how their teachers hate them, and that is why they get bad grades and can't understand the difference between a mixed number and World War II. In fact, behavior like this is considered suicide because you will almost certainly be killed for it, and it is no one's fault but your own. God will not be pleased. Here are a few reasons to not kill yourself, or bitch about.

Running Out of Food

You are never truly out of food. If you happen to be in a place where you can't grow food, you're an idiot, but hope is not lost. There are most certainly animals lying about that can be cooked, plants that can be mashed and eaten, trash to be chewed on. If, for some reason, all these things have been exhausted, then just wait around for a while until one of your fellow humans dies. Hopefully they die of something other than starvation, because that would make it better for you since there is more meat. If they get bit by a zombie but cut their limb off in time and then bleed out, get the fire going and have a feast. If a baby suffers from SIDS, go get some grub. If an old man dies of cancer, go to town but stay away from the cancer. I don't imagine it tastes good. But wouldn't it be fabulously ironic if it *did* taste good? *Really* good? If all these options are exhausted, then go somewhere else. Easy as pie. Pie that you won't be eating.

Hypothetically, if you have yourself barricaded in a corner somewhere and you possibly cannot get out, say on top of a mall for example, then you are definitely in a bit of a pinch. Eventually you are going to run out of food, or if it doesn't rain, out of water. Most people would just assume that the towel is in the process of being thrown, but it isn't. You mustn't give up hope in this situation. As long as you are safe from the zombies, you needn't take your own life. You could be a man about it and kill everyone else in the place for their "mercy," but you should never turn your hand upon yourself simply because you don't have food. Especially since you just gave yourself enough food for months. Don't give up, and maybe something gloriously unexpected will happen. Say... a bird dies and falls on the roof, and you eat it. Or you can hope to get a miracle helicopter rescue from the marines who inform you that the rest of the world is okay, and the outbreak has been secured and quarantined to this area. If nothing happens, at the very least, you starve to death. I know this may seem to be torture, but you'll get over it when you're celebrating a righteous afterlife in heaven for being totally badass. Only then will you find out how great it was to die nobly when you have all the pie in the world at your disposal. Also, heaven doesn't exist.

Personal Zombies

No, I don't mean you get a zombie and carve your name into it and make it jump through hoops and whatnot. That would be silly. But seriously, if you do it, follow Matthew's advice and knock out his teeth. I am talking about a friend and or a family member, namely a spouse or child, who has become a zombie and is trying to eat you. I know you are going to feel depressed and not really know how to cope with life after the apparent loss of a loved one in this manner. And I know it is going to be hard for you to see them, see the longing in their eyes, longing for your sweet, sweet blood. But get a grip. What is done is done, and you really cannot do anything about it except put all your effort and brilliance into cutting off their heads, because that is how you can kill a zombie. And by killing them you set them free again.

If you're in a sad state, pull yourself together and think of nothing else but how to safely destroy the brain of your loved one. Dream about it, day and night. Never wake from the dream until the deed is done. But don't be a damned fool about it. Keep your wits about you and release them without succumbing to the zombie lifestyle yourself. They wouldn't want that, and nobody cares enough about you to set you free. Once you become a zombie, you're like a Japanese chap in a photo full of Chinese people. Nobody can pick you out because you all look the same. So keep your fingers and toes back from those snapping jaws and do the deed. Just don't sit around all day, sulking about how hopeless the situation is because everyone you care about wants to eat you for dinner. It's not that big of a deal anyway. Like I mentioned before, people in Africa deal with this very scenario daily.

One time, my friend Hank had a situation like the one described above. His family was turned into zombies, and he wanted to kill himself because his life was basically over as he saw it. Well, his life wasn't over, but full of more purpose than ever before. For one, he had thirteen children and three wives, because Hank was a Mormon, and he vowed to release them from this hell they were forced to endure. He devoted his life to freeing his family and spent countless years searching for his long-lost family in the hordes of zombies. He secretly hunted them down, one by one, and cut off their heads until their bodies stopped jerking about like a white man on a dance floor (like me). He liked to lure them into his trap with cotton candy, because he discovered in his research that other than human and swine blood, zombies sure do love them some cotton candy, and then used a big pair of scissors, like the kind your mayor used to cut a ribbon at the grand opening of your local fire station (which is where he got it), to cut off their heads and smash their brains, effectively removing them from the zombie registrar. The big scissors provide eneough distance to keep him safe, and since they were occupied with the raspberry-and-watermelon-swirled cotton candy, they put up little fight. Well, Hank was down to his last family member, his first wife, Judy. He loved Judy with all his heart and longed to be with her again. Judy was a lovely woman of fifty when he finally tracked her down. Her beautifully long olive pit red hair had long lost its bounce and shine, and her olive skin had obviously suffered from her affliction, but how he still loved her.

And this love faulted him, for when it came time to cut off her head with the skill and precision of a master butcher, he missed and cut off his own leg. He was like a wounded chicken in the sea, and the sharks immediately began to circle. Guess what, no dolphins in sight. It was Judy who delivered the first blow, because even Strawberry Jubilee, with a twist of grape and walnut, cannot stand up to fresh, alive, human blood. She was on him quicker than you can say, "Tengo una cita con tú madre." In his death throes, Hank managed to cut her head off with the slightly humorous oversized scissors, but fell himself into a fit of zombiism. Don't let this be you. Hank still wanders the earth to this day, forever haunted by the never-ending thirst for human meat. Forever will his thoughts belong to human flesh, tormenting his soul because nobody was left to hunt him down and release him. Why, Hank, WHY!?!

Ammunition and Gas

Running out of the other two staples of the postzombie society are not good excuses for throwing in the towel. QUIT BEING LAZY! While not having gas would be a pretty major inconvenience, you can do without it. Walk, ride a bike, use horses or donkeys, or just bum a ride off of someone else. Big deal. Where are you going anyway? I know that you think you need to go shopping in another fortress for elbow grease or headlight fluid, but you don't. That would be dumb, and you would just be doing your part to spread zombies. Just sit where you are and make your own Prada skin bag. Ammunition is never an issue. Pick up a stick. Problem solved. If you want to throw in the towel for something as stupid as that, then maybe you should have had this book read to you, blended into a paste, fed to you, and spit on you, because you obviously didn't understand anything about what you "read." Put the beef jerky down and pay attention to the next sentence. Don't be dumb, or I'll hate you.

Mono y Mono

If you get trapped in a corner, and a zombie stands in between you and the freedom of open space that isn't in a corner, and you broke rule number one and don't have a weapon, don't panic and will your heart to stop; that wouldn't be very sensible. You will simply have to fight this zombie one-on-one. I know this isn't ideal, but you broke the number one rule, so deal with it without being a pussy. Now, unless you are me, you probably won't be able to pummel the zombie to death with your fists or feet, because zombies aren't like children: they don't die easily. Chances of finding a weapon might be pretty good, but I wouldn't count on it. Have a backup plan. Because I have never fought a zombie, I can only take what I do know and apply it this situation. The closest thing to a zombie to me, right now, would be a spider on my face in the dark. How do you fight an enemy that you don't know, but you know is potentially deadly?

Simple. Fight fire with fire. I know that spiders bite. So if I bite it before it can bite me, then I win, and the spider just dies, like zombies. Now, spiders are full of poison that can kill if swallowed, and zombies are somehow infected, so be careful not to swallow any of the undead blood or flesh. Even if it *does* taste good. Like strawberry jam cotton candy. Make sure you bite all the way through the neck and completely sever the brain from the body, or chew your way through the skull and eat the brain out, which effectively does the same thing. Chewing through an arm or a leg would be as useless and as dangerous as attending an Amy Winehouse concert. It won't kill the zombie, and it opens you up to attack. Go for gold with the throat or brain. (Just to be sure, I want everyone to know that I was kidding about that last part. Biting a zombie is not a good idea, ever. Just kick the poor bastard in the knee, away from arms or teeth, so that you can get around it and escape.)

Don't Be That Guy

Throwing in the towel is the last desperate measure to ensure that you don't become a zombie. Make sure it's the only option because it's the last option. When the time comes, you'll know it, and you'll be dead before you remember what to do, assuming your training is complete. Don't force it. Just like sex or a good poop, it feels better and more natural when it needs to happen.

Chapter 7 Preparing for the Zombie Invasion

(Formulated by Matthew for public use)

—

The world is ending today. If that thought isn't running through your head every time you wake up in the morning, then you are not sufficiently prepared for a full-scale zombie invasion. Those who are truly prepared, wake up standing, eyes wide open, with a fully loaded shotgun in their hands. They wipe the sleep from their eyes with the butt of the gun, and then they make a quick sweep of the house, just to be sure. If you don't want to die in your sleep, you have to be prepared for anything. And, really, how many times has she been almost a zombie? Think about it. It will frighten the hell out of you.

The easiest thing you can do to increase your chances of survival is to practice waking up. Now, we've tested a few different methods, and we generally agree that the best way to practice is to start with an unloaded gun. There have been quite a few instances when someone got a little jumpy and filled an unfortunate wall or chair with buckshot, like the time Geoffrey fell asleep on the couch and let the empty bottle of vodka fall from his hand. He bolted upright and promptly disintegrated my favorite movie poster. Then someone called the cops, and there was a bit of a disagreement and a small amount of scuffling, followed by a fair number of Tasings and jail time and bail and all the bad stuff we don't want to discuss.

The point is, if we're going to overcome the zombies, we can't be going off half-cocked like that. On the other hand, we never know when the zombies might come, so we also want to keep our shotgun loaded with the safety off as much as possible. Therefore, we recommend, without officially recommending any such thing, that you try to become as comfortable with the shotgun as you are at brushing your teeth. Know its curves. Know where it likes to be touched. Know how to squeeze off a round. Just this little thing could make the difference. It could save your life.

The key to the entire trick seems to be quite simple: just practice loving up on the shotgun. Practice all the time, even on lunch breaks or at recess. Set up a cardboard target in the parking lot and devastate it. If you use it enough, and make it your obsession, you won't be able to help but dream about it, in all its beautiful big zombie-destroying glory. It has been said that I've been found clutching my shotgun in my sleep, and that when they took it away from me I cried a little. Of course, I cried big-man tears of alcohol and gunpowder, because hey, that was my favorite shotgun, my sense of security. Still, I like to keep mine underneath my pillow. Some people might complain about this.

A Lover of Lists

Once you've learned the essential skill of waking up ready to rock, you can at least say that at the start of the day you're prepared to face whatever hordes of zombies lie ahead. But how else can you become more prepared? Well, if there's one thing we love about preparing for zombie invasions, it's making lists. What we suggest is a regiment of list making like you've never had before. Make lists, then revise those lists, then make them again. Make lists of food, lists of expiration dates, lists of people to see, people to save, and people to shoot. Make a list of things to do and things to get and things to take with you. Then, when you've made a few dozen lists, organize them based on priority and necessity. Make a list of lists, a table of contents if you will, so that you don't leave any of them out.

When the zombies start lurching and everyone gets a little freaked out, grab a list. Start taking action, ticking off the items on each list as you go. Maybe you could hand one to the screaming bitch and tell her to do something useful. Perhaps you could even create fake lists that just occupy some useless person's time while you actually get something done. In the end, though, the most important reason for making lists is so that you don't forget anything in the heat of the moment. Sure, you might be ready to go smoke some folks that are trying to creep in through your window, but you have to stay calm. You can't get ahead of yourself, or you'll be dead, and if you're dead, then you weren't prepared enough. Here's a bad example of a bad list:

List No. 1121001: A Bad List You Will Die From

1. Kill zombies.
2. Survive.

Whoa there, Shakespeare, you best tame those mad poetry skills before you woo me to your grave. If this list-making regiment is going to work, you had better take it seriously. You might think this is tedious and annoying, that you can just ride off in your blazing saddle with a heavy iron in your hand and a box full of bullets in your pocket, but you'd be wrong. Dead wrong. You can't eat bullets, and you can't procreate with a six-shooter. That is a fact, no matter how weird things get. So that's why we need to make lists, and do it right. Now look at an example of a good list:

List No. 1121002: A Good List You Could Eat to Live Forever

1. Wake up, as described above.
2. Confirm no-zombie status of wife.
3. Sweep house for zombies.
4. Sweep neighbor's house for zombies.
5. Check the neighbor's daughter for zombiism. If not, skip to 7.
6. Shoot the neighbor's zombie daughter in the face instead of being surprised and confused.
7. a. If step 6 is unnecessary, continue sweeping throughout the day.
   b. If step 6 is necessary, forget sweeping, grab master list of lists.

Here's a side note and an idea: if some kid walks into your room and is growling and staring at you, you should probably not wait for them to tear your throat open. Don't stare dumbfounded like some idiot in a bad horror movie. Instead, test them for zombiism by performing the universal zombie litmus test; if they fail for three seconds, cut their hair with a chain saw.

Now, notice that this list starts at the beginning, and then moves step by step over the important activities. It doesn't cover too much information; it's clear and concise and to the point. It has focus, a singular purpose, being what I should do when I wake up every morning. And I do it. Every morning. It's practice, it's safety, it's life. The list also doesn't ask or explain; it commands and expects you to fill in the details. Why? Because details are part of the moment, and for every detail that matters there will be a different list that takes it into consideration.

You make lists so you have direction, order, and a clear head amid the adrenaline and calamity. You make a list so that when the time comes, you don't fart out on yourself and your friends, and you go about surviving like it's any other day of business. If you make a list, you stick to the list, or else you wasted your time making the list and my time demanding that you make a list. Also, at the end of every list, add a reminder to bring along at least 103 proof whiskey. You'll understand if you get that far.

Actually Being Smart and Preparing for Real

So, just speaking hypothetically here, let's say you want to live. Let's say that you don't think being eaten by zombies is a good idea, so you want to really be prepared to stick it out. Well, the best idea would be to find a nice house out in the country and move in. Do you really want to be living in a large city (or even a small one) when the zombies come? It will be ugly, it will be dangerous, it will be a little depressing. No, it's a much better idea to just leave all that behind. Quit your job, sell your house, and move out into the country, miles from anywhere. Don't listen to your neighbors. They will call you crazy, but when they do, take the opportunity to try and persuade them to join you. Tell them about how they need to prepare for the imminent zombie invasion, and that they are risking their lives by staying. They might call the cops on you, but at least you can say you tried, and trying is usually only a crime if Duck Tape is somehow involved. And if they do take that disagreeing tone with you, at least you'll feel a sense of vindication when you liquefy their brains and say, "I told you so, zombie-bitch." That's probably what you'll have to do, you know.

Once you get out into the country, you can't sit and do nothing. You might find a job, but more importantly you should fortify your new home. Perhaps build a moat around the house, or a large crevice filled with spikes. Remember to include a drawbridge so you can get across, and leave enough space in back for a nice garden. It will help you relax. Oh, and you can eat what it grows. If zombies or bandits attempt to siege your fortress, they'll have to cross the dangerous trenches, and that will give you time to take them out. You might also build a few barbed-wire fences, approximately six feet high and very sturdy. If your old neighbors thought you were crazy, your new neighbors definitely will. Granted, if you have neighbors close enough to spy on you, you might need to move again. Either that or scare them away. I guess you could try warning them too, but country cops don't like strangers very much.

So you have your lovely country house, you have some barbed-wire fences, a moat or trench, and a garden area. You also need to fortify the house itself. Reinforce the doors and consider putting bars over the windows. I think a nice trick would be to have spring-loaded bars that can pop up over the window with the push of a button. That would keep the ugly bars hidden until it was time. If you've got the manpower, you might as well plate the outside of your house with stainless steel armor, then disguise it by putting on old flaked paint outside. If you follow that route, make sure the house is sturdy enough to hold the weight. It would be rather pointless if your house caved in and destroyed you ... that's not being prepared at all.

Then there comes the escape route. You're planning for the worst here. You're far from everywhere, but eventually zombies will come after you. Zombies or bandits, and when they come, you might not be able to hold them off. Sure, you'll probably get quite a few of them. Make it a family event, and you might even get most of them, but maybe you just get unlucky, and they make it through the fence and over the moat and somehow breach your door. You have to have an escape plan, and one that is safe. You can't just be running out the back door as they go in the front. They'll still be after you, so you have to lose them. My suggestion: a secret tunnel.

I know what you're thinking. It's going to take awhile to make the tunnel, and you're going to have to be discrete, so it's going to take that much longer. Do it *Shawshank Redemption* style, a little at a time, dropping handfuls of dirt secretly in the garden. Maybe stick one of the family on the task around the clock so you can get it done quickly. Your tunnel is going to have to be pretty long, and it's going to have to go under the moat, so make sure it's reinforced. Make a secret entrance to the tunnel from the cellar of your house, and make a cellar to your house while you're at it. Also, rig the house to explode. Your family will enjoy the fireworks display, and the bad guys will be set on fire. And exploded. Which, I think, is a pretty good idea.

Now you have an armored house, a yard full of obstacles, and a secret exit just to be sure. At the end of the tunnel, when you see the light again, you should have a working car hidden under some brush that has plenty of gas and some extra supplies inside. If you haven't gotten the idea by now, you should rig the tunnel to explode. Just in case. Really, I don't think there is a way to use too many explosives. With all the house and obstacles set up, all that would be left would be to clear the front yard of hiding places and create an arsenal of weapons. Shy away from the dynamite; it's too unstable if you let it sit. Instead, go with the classics if you can. Tommy guns, Uzis, a machine gun of any kind really. Also have plenty of pistols, rifles, and shotguns. You might consider rigging your front yard to explode, just as a last ditch effort to ward off the invaders. Otherwise, for more information about how to build a suitable antizombie arsenal, read the guns chapter. Do it; it's for your safety.

If you ever find a job around your new reclusive home, don't tell them about the zombies until after you've signed the contract. Then, when you're warning them that their life is in peril from the walking undead unless they take precautions, don't tell them what you've done. Sure, these are good ideas, but you don't want to let them know you have a fortress, because you'll never know when your boss will turn into a bloodthirsty bandit. If the boss turned into a zombie, I bet he would make a funny zombie, dressed in his stupid zombie suit. Recommend this book to them if you think they're man enough to read it, but don't let them know your secrets.

Preparing, but Staying in the City

Now, let's say you want to die and stay in the city. I'm not the one who will be calling you a coward because you were too sensitive to negative criticism, you coward, but I might be the one to say I told you so when the zombies are having a buffet of you. If you want to stay in the city, it's probably safe to say that you have no future, so the next advice is probably going to be moot, but here it is. Let's say you want to prepare for a zombie invasion while being a "good, hardworking American." What should you do then? The best advice is to do everything up above, but have that fortress be your second house. Then you have a safe place to escape to, if you do indeed escape, which I doubt you will, because you didn't listen to us. Bastard.

If you don't have that house, I guess I just don't know what I can say. Head for the hills I guess. Make plans about where you think you can be safest, which is probably some city where there aren't any other people, like Idaho. You might discover that you're outracing a zombie invasion, in which case you might be able to stay in a small town far, far away. For a while, at least. It's going to be a slow race, but don't race like the bunny who went home crying because you won't be going home if you lose. And you won't be crying; you'll be dead. I would say that if you don't have an armor house or an armored car or at least a planned destination, then you're not really being prepared, and you should slap yourself silly, because that's what I'd do if I were reading this over your shoulder. Thanks for not heeding my advice and making me feel like a jackass.

However, if you do have a destination in mind, then I suppose that's something to work with. You'll still need to plan an escape route out of the town, one that won't have much traffic but also avoids residential areas. You can skip fortifying your apartment or whatever piece of junk you think is worth risking your life over and just plant bombs inside. Make the bombs remote detonate-able so that you can reduce it to a mushroom cloud if you ever need to. Strangely, I'm sure you'll desperately need to right after you leave. Do the same for your car. It might come in handy. Just replace the lock and unlock buttons on your car's remote with Detonate Car and Detonate House. That seems like a pretty handy idea. It would also be a pretty funny practical joke on one of your friends.

With your car rigged and your escape plan mapped, add supplies to your car like canned food and a few boxes of ammunition. Include guns too, and then be sure to warn the cops about the zombies when they pull you over and search your car. I'm sure that if you'll explain it to them, they will wonder why they hadn't done the same thing already. If nothing else, leave supplies by the door so you can grab them quickly on the way out. Consider putting bulletproof glass on the car too and adding armor to it. Maybe have a really big car that can smash through things and have a huge fuel tank so you don't need to stop for gas very often. Like a tank. That's kind of like a compromise, and who said you could never compromise. It's a mix between having all the guns and having an unstoppable killing machine on two treads. If the cops try to pull you over in this, don't stop. That would be bad.

As far as guns go, don't worry about the rifles until you get out of the city limits. For the most part, cities will be up close action against numerous foes, so you really need weapons that you can easily use close up and are quick to shoot and reload. I like machine guns for this, but for some reason most gun shops don't carry them. That's why I made my own out of plastic, and I always carry it with me. Don't leave home without my plastic machine gun, that's what I always say. I was even going to take it to my meeting with the president to discuss how the government should prepare, but he canceled for some reason. I guess he doesn't want to prepare the country for the invasion. Hey, Mr. President, this country's blood will be on your hands! The lesson you should learn from this? No one is going to prepare for you. Get the country house.

All the Small Things

When the going gets zombies, the zombies get going. No matter where you are or what you're doing, there are a number of things that you can do to be just that much more ready to outrun your coworkers and small children. Here's an idea, especially for you ladies out there: replace all those dumb shoes with combat boots. Think about trying to run in high heels for three miles. It just isn't a pretty image. Sure, you'll look like the classiest fleeing person in the whole hysterical mob, but you'll probably also fall and break your ankle. Do you think anyone is going to stop to help you then? Maybe, but the zombies will just have a two-for-one deal if someone does.

Solution? Combat boots. All combat boots, all day, all the time. Wear them to work, to school, to the playground. Get your whole family a matching set of combat boots, and make them understand the dire importance of being prepared. Tell them anything else will get them killed, especially those risky flip-flops. You could probably get some boots in different colors if you wanted a pair to go with a suit or elegant dress, just so long as they are rugged and up for the challenge of tackling every type of terrain. Running shoes would be a good runner-up. That pun might, or might not, have been intended.

And what about clothing, speaking of suits and dresses? I bet you didn't know this, but the ancient Greeks used to exercise naked because clothing was too restrictive. I think there's something in that, but it doesn't seem to be a very widespread concept anymore, what with all the Tubby McTub-Tubs raising the average weight to elephant. I love food. Instead of sweet, sweet nakedness, there are new alternatives, like spandex, T-shirts, and shorts. The Japanese liked to use the kimono because of the freedom of movement it allowed, and I'm pretty sure all Japanese know kung fu, so they could be a good role model. The Irish liked the kilt because it was flowing, sexy, and conveyed a sense of robustness. The only thing I like more than food is robustness, or maybe sexy food, but robustness is definitely a good thing. Like hot dogs. And tequila ... sexy tequila ... mmm.

There are a lot of choices for clothes, just so long as your wardrobe consists of only movement-allowing ones; you don't want your clothes to limit you in any way, especially since you might be doing a lot of jumping, dodging, crawling, and flipping when the dead starts running after you. You also don't want to be wearing the same clothes for three weeks while you're escaping and then have them fall apart on you, so they need to be of good quality. For instance, consider crafting your own custom clothes out of double-layered carbon fiber, for extra protection on the go. If you have some sort of suicidal, ultrafairy dress code at work, or if your friends don't love the way spandex looks on you, you could put on a disguise that makes you look more unprepared and ignorant. Then, when the shit hits the fan, at a moment's notice and in the sparkly wink of Santa's eye, you can utterly dumbfound your witless and unprepared "friends" with an ear-shattering tear as you rip those stiff-man's clothes off in a swift move that would make Superman fancy your jazz. That would probably be fun. And gratifying.

Now that you have a nice wardrobe, you might as well wear it to bed. Everyone knows how long it takes to get ready in the morning, so it makes sense to get ready at night instead and go to bed fully clothed, boots, and all. Brush your teeth twice in the evening so that you've already got a credit built up for the morning. Of course, that makes sense. Shower in the evening, then put on your morning makeup. You'll never know what hell might break loose while you're sleeping the critical hours away, so when you wake up and find the world in a state of catastrophe, you'll probably need all the time-saving tips you can get. Besides, with the time you saved by going to bed fully dressed and ready to go, you could probably brew a cup of coffee while sweeping the house and still have time to grab it on the way out before you set the house on fire. If you like coffee, that is.

Ideal Transportation

I may have alluded to this before, but I think it might need a bit more stressing. Everyone needs to find the right transportation to get the job done. Sure, you might have the sweetest little red hot-mama on four wheels as your ride, and it might hit sixty in under five seconds, but it might not have much room to carry people or supplies. If you're the kind of person that can scavenge for whatever is needed, and you hate people and would never save another's life by giving them a ride, then by all means have your little red cab of death. Just don't go thinking that you can smash through a crowd of zombies without busting up your windshield, and don't think you'll be making it through any deserted streets littered with cars. You can have your Speed Demon, but you're probably going to die. That's all I'm saying.

But seriously, you probably will die.

Now, there are some better choices out there. First, beware of the various pros and cons of any vehicle. A truck has a bed that you can load lots of crap in, but a lot also have negligible room in the cab for people, and if the zombies are quick, I know at least one person who doesn't want to have to sit in the back. Trucks, Jeeps, and sport-utility vehicles (SUVs, if you didn't know) could all roll if you attempt that heroic sliding turn at forty-five miles an hour, though they might be able to push through cars and handle a lot of abuse before they let you down. Little cars will have better gas mileage (so you have to stop less often to risk refueling), hold more people, could probably speed up quicker, and handle much better, but they have less storage room for survival things and less protection. Being closer to the road might mean you'll never flip your car on a curve, but it also means that you're at a good clawing level for the undead. Don't even get started on a motorcycle; I don't care what anyone else says. Does it feel like a good idea to you? Does it?

If it were up to me, I'd probably choose a roomy SUV with cruise control, automatic locks, a bulletproof sunroof, air-conditioning, and missiles. A CD player would be a pretty good perk too, especially since there probably won't be anything on the radio for a while. An SUV might not get very good gas mileage, but it's tough and can fit a lot of people. I'm a generous guy, especially when I think someone might compliment my skills, so I'm not opposed to giving a ride to the right kind of people. On the other hand, however, I also need plenty of room for the guns and supplies I keep in the car for just the occasion. The SUV provides perhaps the best solution for my needs, and I don't think gas will be much of a problem. It's not like I'd have to pay for it most of the time anyway. However, you have to decide for yourself.

Geoffrey just threw a brick at my head with a note tied to it. It reads something like, "Hey, I'm an asshole. Also, I would choose an extended cab pickup with four-wheel drive. They are beasts and can handle terrain, large animals, sausage zombies, and debris while still holding a lot of people with room for supplies in the back. Plus they have large gas tanks, sit high off the ground, and generally have sturdy tires. SUVs are just pussy truck/minivan hybrids, like a rhino screwing a walrus."

What a jackass.

You might have seen on movies where there are people fleeing on buses or semitrucks or other large trucks, and I would have to admit they are somewhat appealing. However, the bigger the vehicle, the slower it runs, and the harder it is to handle, so there would have to be a good reason for taking one when a smaller vehicle might serve just as well. For instance, what if you absolutely loved and adored every one your neighbors. You might need a bus to save them all, although for some reason zombies can smell a bleeding heart like this for miles. Or what if you found an eighteen-wheeler chock full of canned goods or ammunition. You might want to steal it so you have fewer things to worry about stealing later. And yet again, what if you're driving in a caravan? It might be quite handy to have a bulldozer in front just to clear the path, even if it is slow and prone to stickers. These vehicles all have their place, and it is up to you to decide which one fits you best. However, when you do decide which it'll be, sell off the old trusty car and venture out for the ideal wagon. Tell the husband or wife that it's really just a safety measure, and if they are still in opposition, ask them if they really want to be riding in a box of death. That usually gets them every time. So what's it going to be, the roomy and strong, the fast and stable, or the ultrafast death bicycle (trick option, not a real choice). Or the tank, which is a compromise.

Knowledge Is Power, and Zombies Don't Have It

There are a host of other things you can do to prepare for zero day, and a good many of them require learning new skills. Really, a lot of this comes down to learning, educating yourself. Society doesn't teach zombie Survival 101 in school, worthless school, and last I checked there wasn't even a class for it in college. The media generally does a pretty shitty job of it too, since most of the main characters in films and comics tend to die off in a horribly gruesome and idiotic way. Sure, it's comical. Sure, it's entertaining. Sure, I sometimes masturbate to it. But at the end of the day, there are too many role models who are just asking for some zombie love, and we don't need that.

Instead, what we need is to take it to the books. Learn how to survive in different types of terrain. Learn about what is edible straight from nature, what animals are good to eat, what plants have what uses, and what bugs to swat at. Learn about geography and memorize the area where you'll be escaping. Know the best places to defend from, the best places for clean water or supplies. Know what you can expect when you get there, and know if you'll have the gas to make it at all.

You might think that's enough learning, all that book stuff isn't for you, but you'd be wrong. Dead wrong. After you've learned all that, learn some more. Study survival techniques, worst-case scenarios, and different fighting styles. Read a zombie survival book, even if it isn't mine, and then buy a second copy of mine to make up for it. Then read that second copy to your kids.

Go to the range and do plenty of target practice, enough so that you can take out a zombie with a handgun at fifty yards with one shot. Practice hunting deer with nothing but large rocks and your wits. Learn how to field dress what you kill, how to cook it, and how to make it taste good. Then learn how to make it taste bad again, because the new world is a hard one, and you don't need a spritz of lemon or a sprig of parsley with your steak: you need blood and salt and buckshot. Learn how to swallow buckshot and work through the gastrointestinal pain. Learn how to waste nothing. Then learn basic first aid so you can save yourself from the buckshot accumulating in your spleen, then learn how to stitch up cuts, set broken bones, and how to make sturdy splints. There's nothing you can learn that will hurt you, except bad habits and how to lay down and die.

Learn about various types of guns until you can identify them by year and manufacturer from the sound of the gunshot or the sting of the hit alone. Then learn how to judge distance, where to find gas tanks on every kind of car made in the past two decades, and how to build explosives (it's only illegal while there's a government). Then learn how to siphon gas, how to hot-wire a car, and how to build fortresslike structures. Read *The Art of War*, study ancient philosophy and military tactics, figure out why Napoleon was defeated at Waterloo and make sure not to do that. Learn to never try and invade Russia, especially during the winter, and never, above all, to start a land war in China. Learn how to grow crops and how to eat them. Watch every episode of *MacGyver*, *Man vs. Wild*, *Survivorman*, and *I Shouldn't Be Alive*, and then watch reruns of *Barney* and the *Teletubbies* to hone your rage.

When you think you've learned enough, put yourself to the test. Hire someone to knock you unconscious and leave you in some remote land with nothing but a burned-out car. No matter the terrain, no matter the climate, if you can't get out, then you didn't learn enough. If you do get out, then you can relax for a day and drink a beer. You've done a good job, and you're prepared. Prepared, that is, until the next day when you have to start reviewing everything you've learned. Sometimes it's the small details that get you in the end. The wasp that stung you and made you give away your location, the car whose wires were green instead of red, the three hundred zombie mob bearing down on you without a chance in hell for escape. The small details, you see, can make all the difference in the world.

Dream Lists

There is one list above all that we love to make. Whenever we do, there is much glee. There is some drinking. There is some giggling. There are a few tears. Sometimes, when we finish, we ball up the paper and throw it away, laughing merrily, and then fight over the pen while we make another one.

Sometimes Geoffrey threatens to kill me in my sleep unless I hand it over; sometimes I apparently black out and wake up a minute later holding a knife to his throat. Such good times, such good memories, because this surely is our favorite list.

What list might evoke such a reaction among fellow zombie contingency planners? Well, let me spin a tale. Let's say, hypothetically, that one night you invite five people over to your house for dinner. They might be real, they might even be your friends, but they could be fictional too. They all show up around six, and after some meaty lasagna, you bring out some expensive wine to get trashed on. You're about to pull out the cork when you glance out the window and see zombies running throughout the neighborhood, taking people down like three-hundred-pound football veterans and chowing down on their faces. The worst has happened, you realize, and you need to get to a safe place. The five people sitting at the table suddenly become your teammates, and you all have the same goal of survival. Are you regretting who you invited, or are you feeling relieved enough inside to wet yourself and enjoy it? If you had the chance to invite whoever you wanted, who would it have been? That's the question we ask ourselves every night, or every ten minutes in my case. Who would it be?

There are many ideal characters in the fictional world, and some in the real world, that would be amazing teammates to have on a team. Some of those choices, though, would be just plain cheating. There might be people in the real world who can fight like Beatrix from *Kill Bill*, but there surely aren't people who can pop claws out of their hands like Wolverine. One of the rules, then, is pretty obvious: the people on these lists must not be superheroes (as in, they must not have inherent special abilities or powers). Another rule is that there can only be five people, not four, not six, and not ten. Only five. For a good example, take a gander at one of my lists. (For another example, see Geoffrey's list in appendix A.)

* * *

List No. 8102: Matthew's Dream List—Oops Made a Mess

MacGyver (Dean Anderson) from *MacGyver*
Chuck Norris (himself)
Doogie Howser, MD (Neil Patrick Harris) from *Doogie Howser, MD*
Jules Winnfield (Samuel L. Jackson) from *Pulp Fiction*
Alan "Dutch" Schaefer (Arnold Schwarzenegger) from *Predator*

MacGyver of MacGyver. This guy is a no-brainer. Every list we make starts with MacGyver, and if you don't believe me, just look at Geoffrey's list. If there is one thing I can say about him, this guy is resourceful. That's why he's so important, because you'll never know what supplies you'll have when it comes time for a crisis unless you're completely prepared. I am an expert at preparing, but even *I* feel safer knowing MacGyver is on my side. Geoffrey has wet dreams about him.

Chuck Norris. Now here is a man who practically has superpowers, but for some reason with Chuck Norris, he gets away with it. Looking at him, you see a mere mortal, but Chuck has been endowed with the spirit of God or fairy dust or ninja turtle radioactive ooze or something. He might be a distant relative of Samson, but Chuck Norris draws his power from his perfect beard instead of his untrimmed head. I heard that one time Chuck Norris killed a man by roundhouse-kicking him in the face, then turned him into a zombie just so he could roundhouse-kick him in the face again. Another time, Chuck Norris saved the planet from a zombie invasion by looking at a mob of zombies and saying, "Bam." Saving the planet was an accident. On second thought, maybe Chuck Norris does have superpowers, but I think those tight pants he wears helps keep them in check, if you know what I mean. Do you? Huh? Do you?

Doogie Howser. The man is a genius doctor, and that should be enough for anyone to include him. What happens if you're vaulting a high wall to make an escape over an otherwise dead-end alley, and you sprain your ankle on the other side? Who's going to help you heal fastest, best, and good as new so you can run and live to see another day? Doogie's the man, and Howser's my boy. Best of all, he's still young (forever!) and has a good future to look forward to. A future of killing zombies and making sure the rest of the team stays healthy. Besides, with his scalpel skills, I bet he could field dress a deer in under two minutes. I think that's impressive.

Jules Winnfield of Pulp Fiction. If something can be said about this guy, it's that he's a badass muthafucka. He's also got spirit ... the Holy Spirit, that is. Sure, he might have hung up his hat and handed over his guns when it came to killing people, but surely he couldn't resist smiting the undead by gunning down some lurchers. He's a good shot, and I bet you can count on him not to freak out when things get a little weird. I also think he might have a pretty good sense of humor, if you can get past the fact that he used to kill people every day for money.

Alan "Dutch" Schaefer of Predator. Two words: "Auh-nold"! Did you see those muscles? This man is ripped, so surely he would have the strength to lift an overturned car off me if it came to it. If you saw the movie, you'd also know that not only was he a master of camouflage, but he was also pretty resourceful when it came to making weapons and booby traps. And the guy was a commander or a captain or something like that, so he would already know all about tactics, organization, and weapons. He might freak out I guess, he was getting pretty weird near the end of the movie, but I'm sure Jules would make some little crack about someone's stepmom being a bitch, and everyone would get a good laugh and lighten up. Except Chuck Norris, because he doesn't laugh. Ever.

Now, I've been criticized about this list quite a bit. For one thing, it's a sausage fest (as in there are no women). There are certainly a good deal of women that could be on this list, and I think a lot of them would be amazing at whatever it is that they do, but I think I was drunk and angry at the opposite sex the night I scratched this on the back of a Dixie cup. Also, I would be absolutely pissed if some woman on my team shrieked and got all weepy on us because she realized the world was ending. It's not that I expect them to blitz out any more than a man, but a wailing man just sounds like a dumb walrus; a wailing woman sounds like a migraine. Another thing I've been criticized about for this list ... I can't remember anything else I've been criticized about for this list. I'm pretty awesome.

* * *

What we've generally found about our lists is that they tend to be filled with typical archetypes. There is usually MacGyver, because he's so awesome. There are usually a few tough guys or gals who won't freak out and know how to kill out of the box. There is usually a doctor of some sort. There might be someone else, but usually it's just another gunslinger. I think a good tip about someone to include on your team would be one who sees the end of the world has come and says, "Finally." That's almost the right kind of attitude to have. At least they won't be holding on to the past.

Another good idea for someone to include on your team is anyone you could call on to help you bury a body. Let's say you somehow end up with a dead ex-person on your hands. It might have been an accident, or it might have been the bloody shovel in your hands, I'm not judging here, but you can't clean it up on your own. Who would you call that wouldn't have any other questions but when and where to meet you? If you can think of someone like that, not only do you have a good friend but you also have a good teammate. Siblings are typically a good choice too if you share some sort of subconscious connection, especially if they're stronger than you. And will help you bury a body.

If you ever manage to make a list of people that would actually join your team in the event of a full-scale invasion, you might consider not warning them in advance. For some reason, persistently warning someone about the coming zombie apocalypse seems to break up any friendship held in common bond. I've seen it happen too many times in the past. Words were said, people were harassed, children were temporarily placed into foster care, and certain death threats might or might not have been made. Now there is one less person on my "To Save" list, and they'll be feeling the hurt when they figure out I was right all along. No, learn from me and don't warn them too much ahead of time. Instead, just prepare for them. Then, when they do join your team on that fateful day, they'll see that you've already got a perfectly fitting, matching jumpsuit for them, and you can all have a good laugh and share slaps on the back. Friends for Life—or the Rest of It by Brian Smith

So You're Finally Prepared, Now What?

First off, stop lying to yourself. You might think you're prepared, but you're not really. You'll never be prepared because you can never prepare too much. But for the sake of argument, let's say that you at least think you are prepared, or you're tired of preparing. Whatever. What do you do then? Live your life just like normal. Live life to the fullest, even, out in the country in your fortress. Take chances, find adventure, do something new every day. Just be constantly conscious of the fact that zombies might lurk around every corner, be hidden in every dark room, or be creeping along the bottom of every pool and lake, waiting for you to swim overhead so they can reach out and wrap their decaying fingers around your ankle. You'll have to watch out for those sneaky ones most of all, the ones that don't even seem to be there until you turn around and get a face full of teeth. If you think you're prepared for the invasion, then always be prepared to undertake your preparations, at any moment and in any place. If you're doing that, then I guess you can relax. But not too much, or else you won't be prepared. Death generally follows.

Something else to consider is how you will prepare yourself for the fall of humanity, which is mostly about how to treat your fellow man. You can take one out of a few paths, the way I see it. For one, you could ignore the existence of those some might call humans and instead live as if everyone was already a zombie. This is surely the safest way to live, because you'll never be taken by surprise if someone actually does turn into a zombie, and you'll never have to worry about feeling bad for hacking off the head of one of your late friends because you won't have any. Sure, you might live completely alone and isolated, with a cold heart that would freeze the devil out of the ground and an otherwise poor disposition, but at least those bastards won't take you alive. Besides, when the invasion does happen, you'll probably end up all alone anyway, so you might as well get used to it. Geoffrey likes to live this way, alone and always on guard, a fact that has caused some pretty funny situations, like the time I came to visit, and he shot at me. Fifteen times. Good thing he had started drinking early, or else I wouldn't be able to laugh about it now. For some reason I also laughingly sweat uncontrollably.

However, if living a life of solitude doesn't sound like your bowl of chips, then you could shift toward just the opposite and be a bible thumper. Now, I'm not talking about the Holy Bible, or the bible of some other religion, I'm just talking about a way of life. We've all seen them, those people who stand on street corners shouting about hell and the fate that awaits us unless we find the sweet love of our Gracious Savior, those people who think they love you but deep down inside probably hate everything about you so much they can barely keep from splashing your evil car with a steaming pile of vengeful vomit as you drive past with your selfish eyes on the road.

Well, that person could be you. Instead of a life of one, you could live a life where you see hundreds or thousands of people a day and get promptly ignored, if not downright and openly hated, by all of them. You could even wear the big signs with words like "hell," "suffering," and "you" written on them, or hold a scholarly-looking book and smack it like it holds the truth about which you speak. If, by some chance, you were holding *this* book, it *would* hold the truth of which you speak, and since you're holding it and shouting its message, you might as well recommend other people to buy and read it for themselves. You could also buy a few dozen copies and go house to house, sticking one in the doorway of each person, just hoping someone will pick it up and read it, hoping it will change his or her life forever. I think that if you get down on your knees and close your eyes, it might help you to hope extra hard. Just a thought that occurred to me in-between cupcakes.

Keep in mind that there are some major differences between you and those other street preachers, aside from the name of the book. Instead of trying to convert people to some scheming, not-for-profit-based religion, you're trying to inform them about the day when the zombies will come and reap all who are unprepared, destroying or cursing those fateful souls like some sort of evil beast that has risen from the ground. Tell them that in the zombies' wake, only those who knew the day would come and who had worked constantly to prepare for it will be left, those who had been ever vigilant and ready, with their cars loaded and their boots on.

A lot of people aren't going to want to hear the truth, mostly because it means sacrificing their comfortable lives to follow your message and do what's right, and a lot of those people will also hate you and try to throw rocks at you or give you a good lynching, but if at least one person hears your words and takes them to heart, then maybe it would all be worth it in the end. You would have saved his or her life, someone we might later describe as "saved," and you'll be able to count them as a friend because they would not be filled with disbelief or a heart of stone. Maybe, if you're both lucky, you'll be able to shake that person's hand in the glorious light of survival, the light of life, after the zombies have purged the land of the disbelievers.

Watch out for those hesitant to believe; they need extra work. Some might be willing to listen to you, but before they go home and sell their house to move to the desert, they will want to see a sign, a show of confidence or some bit of proof. They want to believe—they really do—but the world has trained them to investigate and require evidence before they can rationally approve. Therein lies the major problem with warning people about zombies, one that we cannot get around. Zombies don't exist. Yet. So there isn't any proof, and many people will say this and turn their backs on you.

You know they don't exist—yet—because you're not an idiot, but you also know that during the eventual Great Purge zombies *will* exist. You know this because you're not an idiot, you read this book, you became prepared, you believed. People have to believe without evidence, and we shall say that such people have a certain quality about them named "faith," and it is important for people to have faith if they want to avoid being eaten by zombies. If you care for your fellow man, and you have faith, and you believe, and you have this book, then it is your duty to spread the message of warning and hope to all who will listen. Just try to avoid being killed by normal people who call you a radical, or by the government because you're unraveling their conspiracy.

At least if normal people *do* kill you, by lynching or whatever, someone might see how devoted you were to antizombie preparation and would decide to steal everything you had done to save yourself. You might stand as a testament of belief, an icon of faith, so that your grisly and painful death publicizes the message beyond what your life could have done. That's still winning them over in my book. If you *are* about to be lynched, and they ask you for any last words, it would be a funny joke to say, "It wasn't me; it was the fat one who took your cookies!" It might make people realize how hungry they were, and then they would all feel guilty about wanting the lynching to be over so they could go eat cookies and have some milk, then maybe take a nap, or chitchat about the weather.

If the shoot-all-humans-on-sight and the sure-to-be-lynched styles of life don't interest you, then I guess you could pick something more in between, like a bible thumper who randomly shoots people and uses the corpses as proof that zombies exist. You could also just ignore the fact that other people might be in peril or might at anytime turn into a zombie and live life as if these things didn't bother you. You would still be prepared, but you wouldn't show it inside, kind of like how Clark Kent is always Superman but doesn't show it until there's a time of great need.

I don't recommend this style of living because it makes you become needlessly attached to people and things. When the invasion begins, you'll probably respond less quickly than others because you'll at first not believe that the cute chick down the street is actually dead, and then you'll feel like saving everyone you know and the plants you've come to love. Of course, with this style of living you'll also have the chance to meet the cute chick down the street without attempting to take her out from a hundred yards or spraying her with spittle as you preach in her face, and this will probably grant you more luck when it comes to scoring.

All styles of living really have their ups and downs, their pros and cons, so you'll have to decide as you go, as you will with most things. Do what feels natural, just so long as you can claim it was in self-defense. In the end, no matter which way you choose, always remember to always be ready. Never compromise your principles, your gut instincts, or the knowledge you've gained from this book. So long as you do these things and prepare without abandon, you'll be ready to survive the zombpolypse and the wars that follow. Then, when we've survived the night, we'll stand together on a great hill, overlooking the zombie-free landscape, while the sun peeks over the horizon as if for the first time. Then I'll turn to you and lay my worn, calloused hand on your armored shoulder and say, "That'll do."

Chapter 8   Necessary Government Preparations

(Formulated by Matthew for public policy)

—

Elections are coming! Elections are coming! What are we to do? I'll tell you what! We must consider each candidate carefully. We must examine their platforms, their integrity, their service records, and their merit. Then we must find the pros and cons for each, perhaps creating a well-drawn table to organize our data. Finally, after hours of research and examination, we should be prepared to consult with our friends and family. As a group, debate who would best serve us and our community. We need not be afraid that our choice be known or feel that we must keep our choice a secret. To the contrary, we should share our choice and spread it widely, because we would feel confident that we made the right decision.

You might be asking yourself, "Self, what the hell is he talking about?" Well, I'll tell you. (Backup singers chant, "He's going to tell. He's going to tell.") Every election, there are serious issues to consider, ponder, and dwell upon, issues that will have a serious impact on the future of our society. That is, whenever I prepare to vote for some election, I always try to investigate every candidate's plan for avoiding or minimizing the effects of a full-scale, worst-case zombie invasion. Now, it might be surprising to you if you've never tried to get this kind of information, but most candidates do not widely publicize this important characteristic of their platform. It's not even on their Web site, and if you try to ask them about it at a press conference, they will ignore you or have you "gently" escorted out of the building. If that doesn't work, they Taser the resistance out of you until you're limp as a crying noodle that just wet itself. Then they throw you in a trash-filled alley far from the cameras, leaving you with nothing but multiple burn marks and a bad taste in your mouth like you've just been used.

Why is this? One reason is that politicians might want to keep their zombie plans a secret, and if so, I cannot stress enough the level of secrecy shrouding these plans. Let me tell you, politicians are not afraid of using force to keep these plans quiet, and I should know after fighting off so many security guards and political aids. I can't fathom why they would do this *unless* it was a matter of national security. It must be imperative that politicians keep this most-important plan under wraps so that enemy nations will be hopelessly unprepared and unable to successfully avoid wide-scale pandemonium and heavy losses at the time when zombies burst from their cold, hard graves. This makes some strategic sense, I eagerly admit. If a competing nation is collectively busy fighting the dead, playing dead, or otherwise being dead, they can't do very much competing. Then, after our cleverly placed and timely executed plans have been wrapped up, we can put out our minor fires and monopolize the industry of ruling the world. Then step 3. Profit.

However, I think that's all bullshit mailed direct from my wet dreams. No, the more likely reason is that most politicians don't really have a disaster plan or a battle plan or even a health plan, when it comes to zombie invasions. In my view, this is retarded, and I will aggressively advocate, to the very end, that no one support any such candidate. The downside is that no candidate, anywhere, seems to have a zombie-contingency plan (or ZCP), so I have to campaign against *every* candidate. That makes for a lot of fliers, as you might have guessed, but I more or less use the same design on all of them and swap out the names. The hardest part, really, is sticking the fliers under everyone's windshield wipers while he or she is shopping at Wal-Mart for bullets and chicken, especially when he or she comes back and catch you in the act. Over the years, however, I have developed a secret tactic to really maximize my ability to spread the message: use the children. Those little ones just love to run all over the parking lot, in and out of cars, out in lanes and everywhere. They're not even afraid to jump in front of moving traffic just to spread the message. Now that's dedication, and it makes me, so happy I could cry, but in a good way, not like the way they cry when I warn them about zombies waiting to creep out from under their bed every night. As a side note, unlike with me, people don't punch children very often.

Understandably, I quite clearly think having a ZCP is very important for a candidate to have. I want to know that when I vote, I vote for someone who will help me sleep at night, with or without my shotgun. I don't want to vote, like I have the past hundred years, for someone who makes me lose trust in our government's ability to secure us from harm. The Department of Homeland Security had me whooping with joy until I learned they didn't do anything but eat money and spit out useless rhetoric. I think a ZCP is so important, so crucial to the state of our nation, that I'm considering making my own political platform based on it. I'm figuring that in three weeks I'll have most of the nation's popular support, so I don't need to really worry about most of those other smaller issues, like terrorists or torturing terrorists or rooting out corrupt politicians. I think zombies really are the new terrorists anyway. I'm sure that if one happened to be strapped with a bomb, they wouldn't hesitate to saunter over to a busy marketplace and explode themselves on a hot dog stand. That is frightening, like bears, and frightening things make people fearful, which helps them spend money and give power to the government. I'm pretty sure we're going to take over Washington come next election.

Now, since every party needs a name, I think a good one could be something like the Protecting-Innocent-Women-and-Children-from-Endless-Death Party. We could even have our own slogan, such as "Protecting America today so zombies don't devour America's innocent and vulnerable children tomorrow," and we could put it to a little jingle that parents can sing to their kids at night as they fall asleep. We could also start grass roots campaigns with names like Americans Against Zombie Infection, Zombie Abuse Resistance Education, and After-School Zombie Hunt, with Web sites and school assemblies and programs that really talk to the children (that is, future voters). Additionally, we could join forces with groups that already exist, such as the international supergroup Zombie Squad, thereby expanding our otherwise extensive diplomatic efforts with citizens of the world who already have their priorities straight.

Now, I'm not much for all the lights and sound of politics, and I don't really like to get up in front of crowds that could turn into zombies, so I doubt I'll be running for president any time soon. Instead, I see myself more of as party leader, and I have a set of suggestions on how to create a successful ZCP for anyone who wants to run under my platform.

A Model Zombie-Contingency Plan

First off, we need to arm our citizens. All of them, at least all of them old enough, but not too old, to heft a nine-pound rifle and aim it accurately. Think of how many nightmares you have had where you didn't have a gun, and a zombie invasion began, and how that made you piss yourself. Then, when you woke up feeling wet, you realized you really didn't have a gun, and the invasion might have already started, and that made you crap yourself. Well, if it hasn't happened to you, then it's probably happened to someone you know, like me, although my piss can heal flesh wounds and sells for fifty bucks a pint. The problem isn't that I can't get a gun, but that I can't get an automatic assault rifle with depleted uranium-tipped bullets, legally. This problem, the issue of legality, is really a problem that applies to everyone, because everyone will play a part in putting down the rebellion of the dead. Therefore, it makes clear sense that the government should provide such weapons to the public. Consequently, if my party were elected to office, I would press for just such a policy, taking as a great example the Swiss who have been arming their citizens for who knows how long. Surely, with their armed quasi-civilian population they could be deemed one of the safest countries in the whole world.

Which really brings me to my next point. Even if we arm the public, how are we going to be certain that the public won't use it to hold up a liquor store, or that when the zombies do happen along, the public won't freak the shit out and drop their gun just to speed up their retreat? Well, we again bring in the Swiss: require some military service for everyone of age. Sure, two years might be a little unnecessary, even excessive. I don't want to give up two quality years of my inebriated young life to some training that might, with any luck, be unnecessary. We aren't talking about memorizing every strategy of war in the history of man, although that would be a good idea; we're just talking about building a little teamwork, a little sharpshooting skill, and a bit of discipline. Basically, we're looking at boot camp, just for everyone, and maybe without that crazy gas room.

Then, when everyone knows how to handle their weapon, they get to take it home. When my party takes control of Congress, they will quickly draft new laws, disregarding all others till the task has been completed, that regulate how ammunition for such weapons can be procured and used. Such ammunition must be bought at government-authorized dealers, for instance, and every bit of ammunition is recorded, with a minimum purchase of five thousand rounds. Taxed, of course, except when you buy ammo with food stamps. Then there would be spot (i.e., random) and monthly inspections to make sure the ammunition is not being misused and that the weapon is safely stored—loaded and with the safety off. This will be, of course, mandated by law, because for public security's sake, we need to have weapons ready at all times. If it were up to me, I would have each household post shifts at their door 24/7 to monitor the state of affairs constantly, but some candidates that adopt this policy might be described as radical, irrational, or too awesome to be soiled by elected positions.

If there are some parents out there who are still a little apprehensive about this last plan, just keep in mind that by having such weapons at hand, coupled with plenty of ammunition, it's possible to prevent zombies from eating your children. Think about that for a minute, let the imagery sink into your brain, and then vote however your heart tells you. Really, it's a matter barely deserving of consideration. You wouldn't let big corporations brainwash your children so they spend your money impulsively on worthless junk, would you? You wouldn't let doctors use your children for stem cells, even if they might cure the cancer you'll someday have, would you? I didn't think so. Therefore, you must vote with your heart, which is basically me. I'm pumping for you, ol buddy, every day of the week. I'm just here to watch out for you ... from inside your chest; also, to spread propaganda and sell Valentine's Day cards.

Now, not only will my party support our veterans by adding a second Veteran's Day to the calendar, but we'll also increase the amount of money provided for veterans' benefits by freeing up money from the nation's education budget. Additionally, we'll also add a Pre-Veteran's Day, where we celebrate people who will someday become veterans but have not yet come of age, and we'll skim some money from Social Security benefits to pay for the annual nationwide festivities. This day will likely become one in which everyone gives each other presents, and perhaps decorates a Pre-Veteran's Day tree. Since Veteran's Day is in November, we'd probably make Pre-Veteran's Day after that sometime, perhaps near the end of December, because it just makes more sense that way. I feel, as a future behind-the-scenes leader of our nation, that we need to support all our troops—past, present, and future.

Besides, we'll need to celebrate our preveterans all the more because practically everyone that can hold a shield from neck to thigh will be going to boot camp. Heck, I don't see any problem with patting myself on the back once a year, then receiving fun trinkets in my boot camp stocking hung over the fireplace. (Burr, it's cold outside!) Hopefully retail and army surplus stores will catch on and throw great sales that quietly remind us of the future sacrifices that the preveterans will eventually make while also providing the masses with cheap gifts and stocking stuffers. Which reminds me, socks or no socks, boot camp will go beyond just the usual boot camp of today. It will be known as boot-and-ankle camp, and there will have to be a couple of augmentations to the program that train civilians in different aspects of zombie warfare. Obviously, the public should be informed on how to destroy a zombie in a one-on-one duel, perhaps with and without a weapon. Other ideas would be general tactics to defeat mobs of the undead, or how to battle the undead in some common circumstances, such as when one is holding a beer.

Another important facet of such an education would be how to properly dispose of a zombie corpse. It would be a bad idea, for example, if someone who had a cut on his or her hand grabbed the bloody arm of a zombie. They could get infected that way, and that doesn't help the starving white baby seals in Africa one bit. Also, it would likewise be a bad idea to pile up all the zombies and leave them in the trash for someone else to clean up. Animals might feast on that rotting flesh like it was the last delicacy they would ever see with their big sad eyes, and then there might be animal zombies feasting on *our* delicacies. Then we'd all be SOL. Even more likely, animals might become carriers and spread the disease into quarantined areas, creating major complications in containing the infection. Clearly these matters are serious enough to require public discourse and elaboration, ending in clearly defined protocols for handling zombie invasions, sort of like fire codes and smoke detectors. Proper zombie waste disposal should include transportation and containment protocols and should ultimately end with government-run incineration facilities.

Now, with those aforementioned policies and plans in our platform, I think everyone should be convinced that the nation would be much better prepared for a zombie invasion if only my party were elected president and majority in Congress. However, there are additional measures we could take to practically guarantee that the nation has little to fear. One thing I include in any platform I create is the practice of encasing every coffin in cement. This makes sense, and every paranoid mayor would agree that the practice offers benefits worth more than any problems it might cause. Sure, it would be harder to exhume a body, and sure, people buried alive would have an even smaller window of opportunity to escape, but we don't really want the dead to exhume themselves, do we? No, I didn't think so. Vote for the person I support. (Democrats are too liberal! They want everyone to have a cookie! Republicans are too conservative! They ate all the cookies!)

Forgive me, as I don't want to sound too cliché about this next policy, but I think it's a pretty good one. We need to begin fortifying our nation by building tall, sturdy walls around the inner cities. Think back to the castle days. Castles sure were a lot of fun. Remember the horses and playing dress up and being silenced by the church, eating slightly rotten meat and never showering and dying of the black death, and then fighting with shiny swords after dinner for pointless entertainment while wearing those helmets that we always forgot to wash but always regretted not washing? Yeah, those days sure were good times. Well, in those times there were these things called walls, you might remember them, and they went all around the castle. Sometimes they went all around an entire town, or in at least one case, along a whole stretch of a country. These walls kept invaders out, invaders that could have been zombies. These walls are especially useful since zombies mostly can't climb, and they can't really jump to speak of, and they won't be able to chop the walls down with a dull butcher's knife that they somehow managed to be holding. We could probably build watchtowers at the corners too, just for fun, really.

What does all this mean? Safety. Well, safety for the few thousand people who can fit inside the walls, assuming that the zombies don't get inside while the people surge through the gates, and assuming someone didn't bring the infection in with them. Granted, that safety might be short lived as living conditions deteriorate due to a lack of space, poorly designed sanitation systems, and a problematic scarcity of food that would certainly drive even the nicest of men to thievery and, eventually, cannibalism. But ignoring all these unimportant details, I'm pretty sure this is a good idea. Some might point out that we'd just be trapping people, but I would point out that if those people later turn into zombies, we would be successfully containing them. Seems like a win-win situation to me.

Going a step better, we could require all new building plans to add a bright green zombie alarm next to every red fire alarm, and right next to the fire extinguisher will be another break-glass-with-fist compartment full of axes. Also, building plans absolutely must include a zombie panic room near the center of the building. These panic rooms would have to be stocked with zombie survival paraphernalia like candy and bullets, and they would be secured by three-inch-thick steel and a separate air supply. If zombies invaded and were bumbling around the building, survivors could hole up in these panic rooms and regroup; then, after a battle plan was developed, they could burst out and make a break for safety to the sound of Yanni or Bette Midler. If nothing else, these rooms would make a nice private place to make out during lunch breaks, and I think that sounds pretty hot. Of course, like the *Titanic*, it won't be required for everyone to fit in the zombie panic room.

Of course, it's easy to say that every band of survivors will have the competency to generate a solid battle plan, but let's be straight: that's just something for publicity. No, the sad truth is that a lot of people are stupid, and even if there is someone with a good plan, most of the stupid people wouldn't follow that plan even if they tried. So what happens when there are only stupid people locked up in the panic room? They need an escape route, and no matter how much I scream otherwise, we could all use a little help on finding the best way out. This is why buildings have fire-escape routes superimposed on maps of the building. Well, I think that's not a half bad idea, except the route should be a zombie-escape route, and it should be superimposed over the entire city. That way, even stupid people would be able to grab that map off the wall and escape to relative safety, just so long as they can read a map. Better yet, we should coordinate with street gangs nationwide to spray-paint large green arrows on streets and buildings that point toward the nearest safe haven so that even those without maps will be able to find their way out. Sounds like another topic to cover in boot camp.

So, with enforcing mandatory boot camp, checks of ammunition and readiness of weapons, building walls, and otherwise updating building codes, someone needs to be in charge to make sure things run smoothly. Now, I know what you're thinking. Frank and beans. Am I right, or am I right? But no, seriously, someone needs to be responsible for these things, and it's not going to be me because I don't want to be hated by the people. Instead, I think it's up to either the Department of Homeland Security, which is my favorite, or the Department of Defense. To the DOD's credit, they mostly just wage war, so that doesn't particularly help our cause, yet. Really, the

DOHS, the real department of defense, is our best bet since they're already charged with making us "ready" and working to prevent mass tragedy. The fact that they are probably failing has nothing to do with preparing for zombies, which is why I'm particularly enthusiastic that they will succeed at outsmarting the dead.

So the way I see it, all we really need are just a few departments in the executive branch, which means we can do away with those others. If I were president, I would just ignore their opinions anyway, so it's not like it would be a major loss. Imagine how much money could be saved by eliminating so much overhead, how much money could be spent on Pre-Veteran's Day parades, if there were only three departments in the whole of the government. Those lucky three would be the Department of Homeland Security, the Department of Defense, and the Department of Awesome, which would consist of a total of three members: Director Chuck Norris and two lieutenants, Geoffrey and me. In this way we can really extract ourselves from all the complications of modern politics and focus on the basics of kicking cold white zombie ass for oil.

Conclusion

What is the conclusion? I don't know, but I suspect it's something someone made up so they could stop talking. Usually it sums up the points, kind of like a basketball game always ends in who got the most. For me, though, I don't shoot hoops. I shoot the dead, so my points take the shape of bullets and tequila. For politics, support the one who thinks the most about America's safety and provides a sound strategy against zombie invasions. Like I said, though, there isn't one, but if you're an aspiring politician, you can take a hint from the ZCP I just laid out. By arming the public and training them in zombie warfare and by otherwise ensuring the safety of the masses as best as possible, I think America can really whoop the Z in the B. Now, doesn't that scream bald eagle with an American flag bandanna, in one claw a crisp Franklin and a belt of ammunition in the other? Patriotic to a T.

Sample Debate

For those readers who are interested in taking up my antizombie platform, I offer the following fictional debate as an example of how my party would respond to today's most pressing issues. Of course, it would be wholly unreasonable to include every possible question, so the greatest source for pure, honest, noble answers bearing integrity and sureness of heart is this book. Read it twice, then read it to your children, then sleep with it, and make it breakfast in the morning. Toast, with strawberry jam, but not too much. Just enough for a thin layer and a bit of color. Then hold lengthy conversations with it, where you argue a point and it refutes or agrees, for hours on end. Constant practice will show you the road to success and the Oval Office.

Moderator: We now begin our presidential debate with Politician 1, a normal candidate from some party or other, and Politician 2, a candidate with a comprehensive ZCP. The form of the debate will be that someone in the audience will be allowed to ask a question. The question will then be answered by one candidate at a time, where the first to respond will alternate for every question. After the first candidate has spoken, the other candidate will be allowed to give a response. Let us begin with our first question, where Politician 1 will be first to respond.

Question: In view of your enthusiasm for small business, will you institute some sort of special subsidy for small businesses that have been devastated by having owners or key workers called up for military reserve duty?

Politician 1: It is important to our economy and our society that small businesses are given every opportunity to grow and flourish, and this is especially true for those businesses whose members have decided to aid our nation by serving in the military. I know that running a small business can be hard and that people put a lot of their hopes and dreams into their business, so I will take it upon myself to assist such businesses as best I can by providing tax breaks accordingly, and when I press for such legislation, I will focus particularly hard upon small businesses that have workers absent as a consequence of serving America.

Moderator: Politician 2, it is now your chance to respond.

Politician 2: The only reason for a member of the general public to be called up for military reserve duty would be if there were certain opposition forces, namely zombies, that have risen to threaten our way of life and consume our flesh. Now, if you look at it seriously, there are only two possibilities for what might result. Either the world will collapse and small businesses will become irrelevant as the need to survive surmounts all others, or the general public will rise against the undead and eliminate the threat in a timely fashion. In either case, small-business owners and workers have little need to worry about their businesses, because they will either be forgotten, or their workers will return to their normal ways of life shortly. If I were elected, I would work on legislation to increase the probability of the latter possibility.

Moderator: Well then, uh, an ... unconventional response, from our second candidate, ends the first round of questioning. We start the second round by asking another audience member to state their question. This time Politician 2 will respond first.

Question: As president, what would you do specifically, in addition to, or differently, increase the homeland security of the United States than what the current president is doing?

Politician 2: That is a very excellent question, and I hope you're having a lovely evening. Actually, I'm glad you asked this question because it is a major component of my platform, one that I feel very strongly about. As an elected president, I will enact a plan that will prepare our country for the imminent dangers of the future, foreign or internal. This plan, known as a Zombie Contingency Plan, or ZCP, will make our country impervious to practically all threats. For one, we will revolutionize the way buildings are designed, and licenses are granted. Newly constructed buildings will be stronger and will provide safe havens for occupants with the supplies necessary to engage in defensive maneuvers.

Another facet of my ZCP is to work to guarantee that common people, like members of the audience such as yourself, will have the power and the means to protect themselves and their children from harm. I will also campaign to make it a standard feature of local fire codes to require the existence of gas masks, one for each member of a household, that effectively filter out dangerous contagions that might spread unseemliness, just in case. The last thing I will mention about the ZCP, which has many more features than I mention tonight, is that the government will fund and support extensive education for adults and children with the major goal of creating a society that can respond quickly and acutely to unexpected dangers.

Moderator: Am I, am I hearing this right? Are you saying zombie?

Politician 2: Yes, Mr. Moderator, I am.

Moderator: Sure, sure, okay then. Politician 1, do you have a response?

Politician 1: Yes, Mr. Moderator, thank you. In response to your question, member of the audience, I would do many things to augment the efforts of the current administration. I would start by deliberating with the current members of the Department of Homeland Security in order to develop a plan that will provide results immediately and will be sustainable such that current safeguards remain effective while others are developed or improved. For instance, if I determine that the major ports in our great nation are not being adequately protected, that bombs or other dangerous materials are not being detected, I will improve funding to provide additional workers, additional detection equipment, and additional research. On the other hand, if I were to detect that some of our actions were not improving the nation's level of security, I would have them scrutinized and, if need be, eliminated, so that only plans showing results cost taxpayer dollars.

Moderator: This concludes the second round of questioning. We will now take another question from the audience and allow Politician 1 to answer first, followed by Politician 2.

Question: Candidates, on another subject, Communism is so often described as an ideology or a belief that exists somewhere other than in the United States. Let me ask you, sir: just how serious a threat to our national security are these Communist subversive activities in the United States today? How serious a threat is Communism to our foreign affairs?

Politician 1: I think that if we turned a few pages in our history books, we would find that Communism isn't as big a threat as we once thought it was. There were certainly a variety of issues and worries in the years after World War II, ranging from the Iron Curtain to Vietnam, but in the end, these beliefs that Communism would somehow bring about our downfall turned out to be unfounded. In fact, one of the biggest Communist nations right now is also one of our biggest suppliers of imports: China. So to answer your question, I don't think Communism is a very big threat, and I'm not sure what subversive activities you refer to.

However, in that same train of thought, there is a significant threat from certain groups, terrorist cells really, like Al-Qaeda and other similarly minded organizations. For fear of another devastating terrorist attack in our country, we must be constantly vigilant of all subversive activities here and abroad, including those by Americans, that could lead to terrorism. In the name of protection, protecting our friends and families and neighbors, it is imperative that we take these issues seriously, confront them, and work with our legislators and foreign allies to diminish or prevent them. In this cause, it is important that we have the tools, such as means of gathering intelligence, rapid-response teams, cooperation with foreign nations and banks worldwide, as many as possible, to intercept and stop terrorist plots before they hurt innocent civilians. In this regard, I will make it one of my major goals to secure these resources and relationships in the hope that we will be able to save lives.

Moderator: Politician 2, your response?

Politician 2: That was a very good history lesson, Politician 1, and I agree wholeheartedly in respect to Communism and the threat that it poses. No, Communism is not a particular threat these days, yet the idea still holds a sense of foreboding or inescapable terror, the idea that the masses may work together toward some common goal. When I say this, I do not mean to imply that I personally fear, or that there is anything to fear about a peaceful gathering of mothers selling freshly baked cookies as a fund-raiser for their kids' soccer team. However, there is something to fear about mob rule, particularly zombie mob rule, in which no one living is safe. Now, I'm no expert on subversive activity, but you can bet that I consider such cannibalistic group behavior a heinous violation of normal activity, and, America, I promise to do whatever I can, to use as much power as I have at my disposal, to prevent the massacre of your loved ones, your children, at the hands of undead monsters. After I've dealt with this, and America feels safe again, I'll of course come back and handle those Communist activities, just so I don't leave any loose ends.

Moderator: Mr. Politician 2, are you sure that you want to, uh, be here tonight? It appears as if, perhaps, you have a temperature or an illness and that you might not be forming your responses appropriately. Are you sure you want to continue, or perhaps you might take a break?

Politician 2: No, no, Mr. Moderator, a break won't be necessary. I assure you that I feel in top condition, probably on account of the extensive conditioning and training I undertake as part of my daily regime of preparation. I think we should, if it is fine with you, Mr.

Moderator, continue this debate, as I am eager to answer more of our audience members' questions.

Moderator: Okay then, we will continue with our questions from another audience member. This time Politician 2 … will be allowed to answer first.

Question: Now that baby boomers are entering their later stages of life, there will be an increasing reliance upon the government to provide medical aid for those elderly who are too poor to maintain their health adequately. Do you have a plan to cope for these demands? Who will pay for this service, and what kind of aid can the ailing expect?

Politician 2: I suppose that, during the night, there has always been that lurking fear that all the exceedingly old people will simultaneously die and be "born again," if you will, to threaten our lives. The image of slow-moving, saggy, slack-faced, and toothlessly grinning elderly zombies is terrifying, simply terrifying, as I'm sure you'll agree. Nevertheless, like fear, this problem can be managed. There will need to be plans, contingency plans, that will not only restrict the level of danger but also limit the otherwise widespread outbreak into smaller, more manageable areas.

I believe such a plan might include dividing the United States into geographic zones, with an annual lottery held to determine which zones get medical aid and which do not. In this manner we might have finer control over when people die of natural causes; this will allow us to reinforce those zones that missed the lottery while we prepare the general public in those areas for worst-case scenarios. As far as the cost goes, I think this will be a nonissue. What need is there to spend millions of dollars on the health of a group of old people who are shortly about to die no matter what we do? The real money should be spent protecting the group of young people who remain, protecting them from that very *same* group of old people. The next couple of decades will certainly be very intense, perhaps one of the most dangerous times in our nation's history, especially for children, so this, the United States of America, cannot afford to be led by those who are blind to this imminent threat and refuse to instigate preparations.

Moderator: You can't be serious! This is either some outrageous prank, or you have gone completely insane! Old people turning into zombies? Grandmothers? Are you kidding me? At first I thought you were ill, but this—

Politician 1: Mr. Moderator, if you don't mind, I would like to give my answer, perhaps before the time is up for our debate.

Moderator: Yes, I suppose that is required, but I highly advise that this debate end as soon as legitimately possible.

Politician 1: Thank you, Mr. Moderator. Now, it is with certainty that the issue of providing medical aid for those who need it will become increasingly important at the same time as it becomes increasingly difficult to provide. I already know of some people, like eighty-nine-year-old Mitchel Jimbo, an honest American who spent his entire life farming but now suffers from chronic lung diseases as a consequence of inhaling pesticides and fertilizers for seventy years, who struggle to get the aid they need. Mitchel could have several good years of easy living with the retirement money he had saved, but after the fifth surgery, he was left unable to walk and bankrupt. Now, he has to choose between taking the medication that will let him live to see his grandchildren or paying the electricity bills to run his life-support machinery that keep him alive.

And it's also not a mystery that our nation's spending on foreign conflicts and peacekeeping missions had wiped out any possibility of increasing federal spending on Medicaid and Medicare programs. For instance, did you know that a single tank, used in our military today, costs over two million dollars? Selling one of those alone would practically erase Mitchel's hospital bills. If I am elected to the office of president, I will start a plan that will begin reducing our military surpluses by selling unnecessary machinery and weapons to allied nations. I will also work with those nations in an attempt to reduce the world's dependency on our involvement, thereby decreasing the overall amount of money spent on deploying and supporting troops abroad and allowing more money in our federal budget to spend on Americans in America. I will not, and I repeat, I will not raise taxes, as I believe it is unnecessary. Thank you.

Moderator: I have been informed by... certain members of the organizing committee that I do not have the authority to cancel the rest of the debate and that I must continue. Sure, what the heck, I'll show some professionalism, as much here as the zombie lunatic. There's only time for one more question anyway. You, yeah, you there, go ahead and ask your question so we can get this awful joke over with.

Question: There is a lot of talk these days about "green" companies and a lot of focus, and money, being spent on methods that will help protect the environment. How would you, as a presidential candidate, rate yourself as an environmentalist? Do you think protecting the environment is a major issue in today's politics, and what will you do to improve the condition of our nation's natural resources?

Politician 1: The environment has been a source of major focus for the past several years, especially considering global warming and global climate worries, so yes, I do think the environment is a major issue. However, it would not be a very sound decision, in regard to our economic success, to instigate major or harsh reforms immediately due to the significant cost to our nation's industries, so there will need to be negotiations, compromises, and plans. If I am elected to office, I will begin these negotiations in an effort to create comprehensive measures that will lead to the overall reduction of greenhouse gases and carbon emissions. However, I think it would be ill advised, and even disgraceful to our troops serving for us overseas, to direct too much focus toward issues at home when there are also major issues internationally, issues that affect the safety of our soldiers, their families, and ultimately the entire nation.

Politician 2: Well, in the greater scheme of things, I think foreign conflicts are less important than preparing ourselves and developing or maintaining safe ways of living. I think it's hard to estimate our society's reliance on the environment or how much our natural resources improve our way of life, so in that aspect, it is definitely important that we protect what we have. Personally, I think it's important that we preserve nature as much as we can, that we protect our environment and keep it safe, and I'm not afraid to push Congress to pass more laws to prevent environmental endangerment.

You see, it might be that some day soon zombies will chase us from the cities and areas of dense population, and we will have to live in nature, in unpopulated areas, without technology and without much of our former ways of life. When this day comes, we're going to rely more heavily on nature—the animals it provides, the fruits and vegetables, and the raw materials—so that we can eat, drink, and build fortresses. To do this we'll need wildlife. We're going to need clean water: it won't be purified anymore. And we're going to need trees to build our walls, our fences, our watchtowers. So yes, I think I am very much an environmentalist, and I think it is important that everyone practice living in nature without the support of modern technology, because we will soon be tested on it. As for now, part of improving our nation's security, in plans that resolve to limit human casualties, it will certainly be a major focus to improve and expand state parks for the sake of the overall health of our natural world.

Moderator: Everyone here is sick, part of this sick joke, especially you, Politician 2, you paranoid freak! Worrying about zombies, telling America, on live television, that you're going to prepare for the imminent invasion? You're ridiculous, not to mention out of your mind. There is nothing to fear; there is nothing to prepare for. Really, why am I even bothering, zombies don't exist!

Politician 2: Yet. I beg your pardon, but zombies don't exist yet. Which is why it is so important that we are prepared when they *do* exist, and why we can't let our guard down just because the threat isn't constantly apparent. The terrorists of today didn't target American soil yesterday, but they do now. Cloned corn didn't exist thirty years ago, but I can buy it on the shelf today, at discount prices. The Joker used to be Jack Nicholson, but now he is Heath Ledger, and in ten years could be someone we've never even heard of. The staple and constant in this world is change, for better or worse, and we cannot afford to stand by idly, watching and unprepared, as change envelops us. We cannot afford to constantly be reacting to this change, acting only after the fact. Action needs to take place now so that we anticipate, so that we are ready to fight and not just ready to run, so that we can improve the chances of our survival and that of our children and our children's children. We must act now, before dusk approaches and we are left in the night without light or warmth. To prepare our country is my plan and what I intend to do, because above all, I want to see this nation make it through the night and see the light of dawn unscathed, unharmed, and ready for the future. In closing, let me just say, thank you, viewers and all of us who are here, for sharing this time with me. Bless you and good night.

Moderator: Ah, go fuck yourself!

Chapter 9   The First Forty-eight Hours—a Practical Guide

(Strategized by Geoffrey for your torment)

―

The first forty-eight hours of a zombie invasion. Live or die? It's up to you.

    Hey, Joe (that's you) or Jo (if you're a chick), you are walking around the mall because your eleven-year-old daughter can't have a social life without a minimum of six hours a day at the mall, and the mall has a rule about kids needing their parents after 5:00 PM. You're just walking around, perusing the selections at the various stores that don't really have anything of use to you or anyone else in the world besides eleven-year-old girls. You walk by the bookstore, probably a Barnes & Noble or a Waldenbooks, and see a giant display of *The Ultimate Zombie Hunter's Handbook.* The book looks cool and very informative, and the cardboard cutout of a zombie eating a big-breasted woman's neck meat is very appealing, but you decide you're still in the middle of that unbelievably overdone mystery/suspense novel by Anne Frank. You think you don't really need another book next to the toilet, so you move along.

    Right next to the bookstore, you see a RadioShack with a big wall of display televisions. Luckily, all the TVs are on the same channel, for today's generation, and there is a news story on about people with rabies in your area attacking anyone they come in contact with. The piece was fairly well done by Patricia Morgenstein, your town's hottest star reportress, and you decide it might be worth your time for a watch.

You decide to watch the news ... (*Turn to page 160.*)
You decide not to watch the news and get a salty pretzel instead ... (*Turn to page 161.*)

You decided to watch the news while you're wasting time waiting for your daughter. While the story is interesting, you can't help but notice how Patricia is holding gauze onto her hand where it appears she may have cut herself. Upon completing the story, Patricia signs off to the public, and you sign off to the news channel. People with rabies gets you thinking about zombies again, and it kind of makes you want to go back and buy that book. It wasn't very expensive, and it did look very informative, if not entertaining. It's only five o'clock, so your daughter won't be ready for another three hours, and a new book would help kill the time. But so would a salty pretzel.

You go buy the book ... (*Turn to page 163.*)
You don't buy the book, but you do buy a salty pretzel ... (*Turn to page 161.*)
You didn't buy either the book or the pretzel ... (*Turn to page 158.*)
You buy both the book and the pretzel because, hey, pretzels are good with books ... *(Turn to page 166.)*

Wow, salty pretzels—*argghhhrghhhhrgrghhh.*

As soon as the enigmatic aroma of the almighty salty pretzel hits your nose, you instantly forget if you even watched the news and just need a pretzel. But which one? You could get a jalapeño pretzel, a garlic pretzel, a plain pretzel without salt, a plain pretzel with salt, whole-wheat salty, whole-wheat sesame seeds without salt, low-protein plain, extra salty, butter, a pretzel pig-ina-blanket, or a corn dog. You can get nacho cheese, spicy cheese, sour cream, guacamole, ranch dip, or nothing. Wow, so many choices, so many deliciously awesome choices. What to do?

Get a jalapeño pretzel with any dip ... (*Turn to page 181.*)
Get a garlic pretzel with any dip ... (*Turn to page 175.*)
Get a plain pretzel with any dip ... (*Turn to page 168.*)
Get a plain pretzel without salt with any dip ... (*Turn to page 173.*)
Get a whole-wheat pretzel with any dip ... (*Turn to page 180.*)
Get a whole-wheat pretzel with sesame seeds with any dip ... (*Turn to page 172.*)
Get a low-protein plain pretzel with any dip ... (*Turn to page 162.*)
Get a pretzel pig-ina-blanket with any dip ... *(Turn to page 177.)*
Get a corn dog with any dip ... (*Turn to page 164.*)
Get any pretzel with no dip with it ... (*Go to page 170.*)

Ordering the low-protein pretzel is not just a choice; it's a lifestyle. As you reach up for it, you notice something strange. Your arm just broke. Apparently your low-protein lifestyle has weakened your body so much that you can no longer support your own skin, and a chain reaction takes place. Slowly, painfully, you implode. The guy behind you was going to mug you, but you died. So he mugs you anyway. Luckily, you cannot pose a threat to humanity because even your zombie self will be broken and weak ... just a puddle of rotting flesh in the Dumpster out back.

You are dead. Ouch.

Ah hell, that book does look informative, and you'll never know what kind of effects that genetically enhanced sweet corn people have been eating these days will have. Besides, you have at least three hours to kill, and a new book should help pass the time. You walk into the store and pick up a fresh copy of *The Ultimate Zombie Hunter's Handbook*. You walk over to the clerk so that you can pay for it, and you notice something odd. At first the clerk didn't really seem to notice you, but then the shiny cover of the book flashed in the brilliance of the overhead lighting. It was a moment frozen in time for the two of you, just standing there, breathing and looking confused.

Once the glint from the cover caught the eyes of the clerk, she was instantly hot for you. You could see it and feel it. She wanted you bad. Then the moment was gone, and you had paid and walked out of the store. You felt a little sorry for the clerk. She can't help but be drawn to the animal magnetism that you emit. For a second, you feel her eyes on your back as you walk away, but one quick glance back confirms that she has gone into the back to get something, so it might have been your imagination. Just to check, you go back to see what she was doing ... and then you have intimate relations all over the new stacks of *The Ultimate Zombie Hunter's Handbook*. It was the best experience of your life, or anyone's life on earth, ever. You live to be 104 and have the happiest life ever, on earth, forever.

Not really, but that would be pretty awesome. (*Go to page 165.*)

Corn dogs. Hmm. You could have gotten a pretzel, but you got a fucking corn dog? Remember that commercial for GEICO where the cavemen are talking to a GEICO representative who is apologizing for the slur, "So easy a caveman could do it." You know, the one where one caveman orders the "roast duck with the mango salsa" and the other caveman just stares the representative down as he declares, "I don't have much of an appetite, thank you." That's how I feel right now. A little sick and not hungry at all. But guess who is hungry? The zombies eating your spleen. You really are thick.

You are dead. Worthlessly dead.

Anyone know what dramatic irony is? Well, according to *Britannica Online*, dramatic irony is "a plot device in which the audience's or reader's knowledge of events or individuals surpasses that of the characters." I know that sounds like a lot to swallow at once, but try to focus. You are in a unique situation where you are the character and the reader all bundled into one shining dud of a human being. Well, let's explore how it feels to enjoy all the perks of dramatic irony. You are about to become a zombie. But wait, how is this possible? You are buying the book on surviving zombies, and you couldn't possibly be making a mistake by doing that. Oh, wait, did I forget to mention that you are a freaking moron? For the sake of being awesome, you have to go to page 31 to find out why and how you become a zombie.

Please go to page 189. Don't be a sorry loser.

So you need them both. Good American. Now comes the choice that makes being an American so damn terrible. It makes it worse than being in poor countries without food or clean water. The choice. Those poor kids have no idea how easy they have it. They don't have to decide whether to eat first and then drink clean water, or drink clean water and eat second. They don't have either, so the choice is obvious: do nothing and die. But Americans have it rough. So now, choose you poor little darling. However, just like in the old saying, "To step in front of this train or wait for it to go by," choose wisely, or you may wish you had chosen more wisely.

Buy the book first. (*Go to page 163.*)
Buy the pretzel first. (*Go to page 161.*)

Lol ;-) pwn3d u n00b wh0 41n7 1337.

Now you're a zombie because you can't afford to miss any details in this book. Every single one is required to live. Otherwise you die, since you aren't living due to the missing of said details.

You are dead for missing details. Don't miss details.

Pretty boring choice going with plain, but okay. A guy standing behind you was going to mug you, but of course, you don't know that. When he saw you get the plain pretzel, he felt sorry for your pathetic life and decided to go mug the grandmother at the Maid-Rite earlier. Unfortunately, he knifed her in both kidneys, and she didn't make it. But guess what? You don't care because you have a pretzel, and she was old anyway. All of the sudden, you notice the mad dash toward the televisions at the RadioShack behind you. There is a breaking story on the news about what appears to be corpses roaming the earth, killing everyone that they can get their mitts on. As everyone stands there, at the mercy of the anchorman, a disgustingly obese man, who is too fat to walk anymore and is driving an automated cart instead, has a heart attack, and the cart careens out of control into the crowd. No one survived. Too bad. Just when you were realizing the plain pretzel isn't as good as a garlic or jalapeño pretzel, you no longer crave pretzels. You crave nothing ... zombie!

You are dead, and I am bored of your pretzel.

Well, gosh dern! Put this heavy nonsense with butt wipe 'n' paper in it down and go to the cornfields and get Bubba away from the sheep. You can't read anyway, and nobody around here knows what "reedn" is, so why are you pretending? What you really need to do is go get a shovel and try to go dig some ditches for the government. So you do. And while you are in the trenches of Alabama, you accidentally cut those precious little toes of yours off. God knows you didn't realize they were gone until you fell face-first, on account of not having toes, into your whiskey bottle, knocking the one tooth you had left into the back of your throat and down your esophagus before it lodged itself in your stomach. In a panic from not being able to get your cigarette into that little breathing hole, or your "custom-built cigarette puffmeister," you tragically turn the shovel on yourself. The city almost put one of those little crosses with your name and a wreath of flowers on it, but decided that you died from being an ass, of the dumb variety, and weren't even involved with a vehicle at all, so you didn't really deserve a cross or anything at all. Your mom, however, planted a female ginkgo tree. I find it rather ironic that she planted a tree in your name that drops fruit every year that smells like rancid butter and dog vomit. This is how I imagine a zombie might smell like.

You are dead and smell like Alpo barf. Your mother isn't proud.

Notice something? No matter what type of pretzel you got, no dip = page 170. That's not a good sign. Why isn't it a good sign? Well, because you just got mugged for being a pussy and took a knife to the kidneys. Both of them. Now you just sit in a pool of urine with blood in it and blood with urine in it because both kidneys are done, and you are dying. Good work. Now you're a zombie.

You are dead. Good work.

Deciding to get your daughter and get the hell out of there is a good choice, I think. Her social life is going to take a hit, but you have a feeling that it won't matter in a few days anyway, with the collapse of modern society and all. Luckily for you, it only takes about two hours to find the little brat. Poor little Rosenescra is pretty upset, but you tell her that you'll get her a puppy. That shut her up. You're in a pretty big hurry since you don't feel like becoming a zombie today, or ever, but the little shit won't move her thin little legs. Has she been throwing up again or what? Dammit, she is so slow and keeps getting distracted by the bag of cotton candy that she bought with your money. What are you going to do?

Tell her to put the cotton candy in her backpack. (*Turn to page 174.*)
Tell her to throw that *goddamn fucking bullshit* in the trash. (*Turn to page 179.*)

Wheat pretzels are nice, but add the sesame seeds and you have an attractive treat. A guy standing behind you was going to mug you, but of course, you don't know that. When he saw you get the healthy wheat pretzel, he decided that you might be able to fight him off, even without kidneys. Then he noticed that you had the sesame seeds on it too, adding a little zaniness to the person standing in front of him. He realized, at that point, that he could have just attacked a man with nothing to lose, a man who, no matter what kind of damage sustained, would have killed him in the end with a size 12 boot to the throat, a boot delivered so hard it would have broken his neck and the collar of his shirt.

Being a particularly religious murderous mugger, he decides that God has been testing him, and he has succeeded. He throws his knife down and vows to never steal again. Then he notices the mad dash toward the televisions at the RadioShack behind both of you and heads off that direction to satisfy his murderous curiosity. You unwittingly follow him to see what the fuss is about.

There is a breaking story on the news about what appears to be corpses roaming the earth, killing everyone that they can get their mitts on. As everyone stands there, at the mercy of the anchorman, a disgustingly obese man, who is too fat to walk anymore and is driving an automated cart instead, has a heart attack and the cart careens out of control into the crowd. Luckily, because of your healthy eating habits, you are able to do a backflip out of danger as the cart plows down everyone else in the crowd. None of them survived, but that isn't the worst news you've encountered in the last ten seconds. The anchorman mentioned zombies.

You decide to get your daughter and get home quick. (*Go to page 171.*)
You decide to get an ice cream because zombies aren't real. (*Go to page 178.*)
You gotta get that book. Remember? (*Go to page 163.*)

So plain without any salt, huh? What the *fuck*? So you apparently don't care that a guy is currently knifing you in the kidneys for being a pussy and stealing your watch and probably the earrings you wear in private. Nice choice. Now all you can do is lie in a pool of blood mixed with urine and urine mixed with blood, thinking about how glorious your life could have been if you weren't a wussy. Great work becoming a zombie in record time. I bet a baby in a lion pit would have had a better chance.

You are dead, and your kidneys have been sold on the black market. At a discount.

Rosenescra is not happy because the two of you are on your way home, two hours ahead of schedule. Her life is ruined. And she makes sure that you know all the gruesome details about what you just made happen. So as you two drive down the road, she just keeps on bitching and bitching about how horrible of a father you are and how horrible her life is and how her life is pretty much over. On and on. Just when you think she is done bitching, she draws the air into her lungs with renewed vigor and belts out another epic spasm of bitch. She really is your wife's daughter.

They say that in times of stress, a soldier puts aside all feelings and thoughts and lets the training kick in. Well, this is such a time. Your mind automatically initiates Operation Lungsquall, and your body reacts accordingly. You immediately smack your daughter in the mouth. Not because you beat children, but because sometimes a child needs a little nudge to put her back on the right path in life. She is stunned. Finally, you have time to get what you need to say out. She responds well to the news, that zombies are attacking the world and that life as we know it is about to change, because, after all, she is your daughter. She even mentions that she has been reading *The Ultimate Zombie Hunter's Handbook* at school during her study hall because she had a feeling it might be informative and awesome. You just smile a little. Luckily, the lone tear that escapes your eye is on the left side where she can't see it. You call your wife on the phone and find out that she is already at home. Action has replaced reaction at this point. What comes next?

Go home and get the wife. Get your bags packed with all the supplies you'll need to survive and leave town. (*Go to page 186.*)
Forget home and tell the wife to meet you at her mother's place on Elm Street. (*Go to page 188.*)

Nice choice with the garlic pretzel. A guy standing behind you was going to mug you, but of course, you don't know that. When he saw that you have good taste in pretzels, he decided to go mug the grandmother at the Maid-Rite from earlier. Unfortunately, he knifed her in both kidneys, and she didn't make it. But guess what? You don't care because of the amazingly awesome garlic pretzel that you decided to get. In fact, you are enjoying it so much, you don't even notice the mad dash toward the televisions at the RadioShack behind you. There is a breaking story on the news about what appears to be corpses roaming the earth, killing everyone that they can get their mitts on. As everyone stands there, at the mercy of the anchorman, a disgustingly obese man, who is too fat to walk anymore and is driving an automated cart instead, has a heart attack, and the cart careens out of control toward the crowd. Around the same time, you finish your pretzel and realize what is about to happen behind you. Thinking quick, you hijack the sedan on display in the middle of the aisle and run it straight into the out-of-control motorized obese juggernaut. The car is totaled, the obese man dies, but the crowd survives. But something much worse has come to your attention. The anchorman mentioned zombies.

You decide to get your daughter and get home quick. (*Go to page 171.*)
You decide to get an ice cream because zombies aren't real. (*Go to page 178.*)
You gotta get that book. Remember? (*Go to page 163.*)

You decide to tell the family that you're going to have to sleep off the medication. They agree that they can keep watch on the SUV so that nobody comes close to it without you knowing about it. Trust is one of the most important aspects of a healthy relationship. Too bad it's not about relationships; it's about survival. It's gotta be after midnight by now. Knowing that it's been a long day for everyone and that it is really dark outside, you set your watch and cell phone alarms for four hours. Five is probably what you need, but four will have to do because you can't wait until five or six in the morning to start working. There is a lot of work to do before sunup so that you don't get stranded. And if you do get stranded, hope to God that there aren't more than seven zombies waiting outside. More than seven is just too many.

Since you know this is no time for deep sleep, you sleep in a constant state of readiness. It is kind of like the sleep you get right before you wake up in the morning. Not deep, but ready. And you dream. It was a very strange dream. Some might even say it was peculiar. You dreamed that you were just a figment of the cashier's imagination. You know, the cashier that you blasted for the safety of your wife. Well, you dreamed that he was writing a story, and you were the star. Only problem was, he hadn't written most of the book, mostly just the underlying notes and framework. And when you killed him, you killed yourself. In a way, you dreamed that you had committed suicide when you killed that man. What was that all about?

No alarms. But you're being woken up. Something is happening. Zombies are near. The shotgun is suddenly in your hands. Good. The training is working. But where are the zombies? You look all around the nest, around the SUV, around the surrounding territory. Where are they? Then your wife tells you the problem. They both fell asleep, but the alarms on your phone and watch went off and woke them up. They turned them off before waking you up, assuming that you wanted to get up when the alarms went off. Good. You didn't want zombies to be here yet. This is good. Luckily, the excitement of the zombie scare startled you awake, and you feel energized and alert. You'll need that later.

Go get the SUV situated on page 193.

Getting a pretzel pig-ina-blanket takes balls. I can almost smell the hair on your back; you are so manly. The guy behind you commits suicide for thinking he could mug a man as manly as you are. But you don't care. You expected it because it happens a lot around you for some reason, and you have more important matters. Pretzel pig-ina-blanket. There is a mad rush behind you at the RadioShack, and it pissed you off because of how unmanly it is to rush. You black out. Next thing you know everyone is dead. Not again. Then you hear it. The anchorman said it as if it was nothing.

...

zombie

You decide to get your daughter and get home quick. (*Go to page 171.*)
You decide to get an ice cream because zombies aren't real. (*Go to page 178.*)
You gotta get that book. Remember? (*Go to page 163.*)

Bold choice, sir. But foolish. This isn't any time for ice cream. Zombies are literally all over the damn place. Since you're getting it, you might as well get something good. I suggest vanilla ice cream with hot fudge smothered all over it. Don't get chocolate syrup because it is garbage compared to the glory that is hot fudge. Seriously, don't get chocolate syrup.

Luck is on your side though. Your daughter just happens to walk by as you sit and eat your ice cream, hopefully smothered with hot fudge. You decide to finish the ice cream fast, but not too fast, and grab her quick and get out of the mall. Your immediate game plan is to find your wife and leave town. It's simple and easy. Unfortunately, life is never that easy, so you might have to go back to the drawing board. For now, keep your mind fresh and in the present.

Go to page 171.

So you were the kid in school that cheated off your friends and never read the italics in the main text. Well, those italics were usually full of useful stories that could be enjoyed by all. If you skip the extra stories, you miss out on all kinds of useful information. I know what you are thinking, and no, I'm not a psychic. I just know how stupid people are because only stupid people get to read pages like this. If you had learned anything from the rest of this book that you supposedly read, you would know that cotton candy is the second best thing, behind humans, for a zombie's taste buds. Because you missed this detail, you most certainly missed more details that would ensure your survival. Now, we all know what is going to happen next. Because you're afraid of becoming a zombie, you are going to go back and check out the other option. Go ahead. Turn back.

Turn back to go the other way. (*Go to page 174, chump.*)
Boldly go forward. (*Go to page 167.*)

I suppose I can see the draw of a healthy wheat pretzel. A guy standing behind you was going to mug you, but of course, you don't know that. When he saw you get the healthy pretzel, he decided that you might fight him off, even without kidneys, and went to go mug the grandmother at the Maid-Rite earlier. Unfortunately, he knifed her in both kidneys, and she didn't make it. But guess what? You don't care because of the amazingly healthy pretzel you are now enjoying. All of the sudden, you notice the mad dash toward the televisions at the RadioShack behind you. There is a breaking story on the news about what appears to be corpses roaming the earth, killing everyone that they can get their mitts on. As everyone stands there, at the mercy of the anchorman, a disgustingly obese man, who is too fat to walk anymore and is driving an automated cart instead, has a heart attack, and the cart careens out of control into the crowd. Luckily, because of your healthy eating habits, you are able to do a backflip out of danger as the cart plows down everyone else in the crowd. None of them survived, but that isn't the worst news you've encountered in the last ten seconds. The anchorman mentioned zombies.

You decide to get your daughter and get home quick. (*Go to page 171.*)
You decide to get an ice cream because zombies aren't real. (*Go to page 178.*)
You gotta get that book. Remember? (*Go to page 163.*)

Nice choice with the jalapeño pretzel. A guy standing behind you was going to mug you, but of course, you don't know that. When he saw you get the manly pretzel, he decided to go mug the grandmother from the Maid-Rite earlier. Unfortunately, he knifed her in both kidneys, and she didn't make it. But guess what? You don't care because of the amazingly awesome jalapeño pretzel that you decided to get. In fact, you are enjoying it so much, you don't even notice the mad dash toward the televisions at the RadioShack behind you. There is a breaking story on the news about what appears to be corpses roaming the earth, killing everyone that they can get their mitts on. As everyone stands there, at the mercy of the anchorman, a disgustingly obese man, who is too fat to walk anymore and is driving an automated cart instead, has a heart attack, and the cart careens out of control into the crowd. No one survived. Around the same time, you finish your pretzel and realize the horror behind you. The anchorman mentioned zombies. Oh yeah, and someone spilled unbelievable carnage on the floor.

You decide to get your daughter and get home quick. (*Go to page 171.*)
You decide to get an ice cream because zombies aren't real. (*Go to page 178.*)
You gotta get that book. Remember? (*Go to page 163.*)

Three hours isn't enough, but it'll have to do. You are so worried that three hours isn't going to be enough sleep that you get sloppy. It has to be around midnight, and the zombies have to be growing by the millions. As you lie down, you know that three hours isn't going to take long. You leave the girls to keep watch and tell them to wake you up in three hours. You're going to be tired, but with the help around you, you know that the SUV is going to get situated just fine. The last thing you remember before falling into a deep sleep is resting your head on your shotgun due to the lack of pillows. Pillows are for zombie food.

3:00 AM. Oh shit. You feel terrible still, but it'll have to do. There is a lot to do before the sun comes up to help ensure survival. Survival is what is important, and knowing how is only half the battle. Having the fortitude to do what is needed is important. Having the strength to get it done is important. Having the tools is important. Good thing you have all the above. It's funny though. For 3:00 AM. The sun is pretty high in the sky.

SON-OF-A-BITCH! You startle your wife and daughter awake as you look at your watch. 11:00 AM! How in the hell did this happen? You've lost almost half a day just sleeping. It was foolish of you to not have a backup plan. There is an alarm on your cell phone and an alarm on your watch. Why didn't you set those too, just in case? Both of them had had a long day, just like you. Why didn't you make sure? How could you be so sloppy?

Looking down at the SUV had been your first thought, your worst fear, and the hardest thing for you to do. What if it had been compromised, breached? How would you survive the rest of eternity? One step at a time. Time for a big one. You look down.

Zombies. All over the place. Not hundreds or thousands, but seven. That really is lucky. Seven zombies is the maximum for your contingency plan, in the event that something horrible has happened and you need a way out. But do you have the strength to get it done?

Survival isn't everything. Live the rest of your life with your family. (*Go to page 205.*)

Zombies be damned. It's contingency time! (*Go to page 194.*)

I've got some good news and some bad news. You're still alive, and you have prepared yourself well enough to live for the first couple of days. You have supplies and a place to hide, temporarily. Plus the world is only just beginning to become completely infested with stinking, rotting zombies. That's the good news. The bad news is that you aren't in your bird's nest, adequately named "Raphael Is the Best Ninja Turtle: Alpha Squadron Base A1 Bold and Spicy." You are, in fact, on your way to the Steer Melt to meet your wife. Two main obstacles are going to get into your path to freedom. As a lover of lists, you surely have these conveniently posted to your air bag as a reminder.

List No. 2144233: The Two Things That Might Get Me Killed on My Way to "Raphael Is the Best Ninja Turtle: Alpha Squadron Base A1 Bold and Spicy" with Rosenescra and the Decoy

1. Zombies … lots of zombies. More zombies than I could have anticipated.
2. The Steer Melt. More specifically, the burgers that are so good I would take a knife to the scrotum. Oh damn, those are good burgers. Maybe I should stop writing my thoughts and go get one. Yeah, that's what I'll go ahe—

—

Now, if you carefully look at this list, two things should be obvious. Luckily, a list has been provided on the fly, by yourself, to make note of these things.

List No. 2145694: Things to Notice from List No. 2144233 (The Two Things That Might Get Me Killed on My Way to "Raphael Is the Best Ninja Turtle: Alpha Squadron Base A1 Bold and Spicy" with Rosenescra and the Decoy)

1. Option 1 is unfeasible and will not be a burden. It is impossible to have anticipated less than the possible

amount of zombies. You plan for the worse, more zombies than living creatures on earth. Otherwise, you're dead, and that is not true as this list on the fly proves.

2. Option 2, therefore, is the default worry. Proof of that is also evident from the list itself. You are a self-professed lover of lists, and you couldn't even finish this list due to the thought of the delicious burgers. In the future, we will refer to these ... Oh sweet, sweet burgers. How I need you. How I wish to hold you and kiss you and make tender love to you. No no NOOOO! Get a hold of yourself. The weakness. Yes, that is what they are going to be now. Not delicious, although they really are, but the weakness. What will get you killed. They are dead to you, just like zombies, only delicious.

Now, back to business. How do we get to the Steer Melt, leave without the weakness, and get to "Raphael Is the Best Ninja Turtle: Alpha Squadron Base A1 Bold and Spicy" safely? Well, you can use the main road or a shortcut to get to the Steer Melt. That is the first step. Which one to choose?

Umm, the main road is easy. (*Going to page 187 will do.*)
Shortcuts are fun and quick. Take it. (*Go to page 193, please.*)

You decide that going home, getting the wife, and getting everything you need to survive a zombie invasion is probably the best-effective plan for the moment. You quickly drive home, going about twenty-three miles per hour over the speed limit because you figure that the cops are all dealing with the zombies. After the first ticket and fifteen minutes wasted, you decide that slower turtles win more races than faster rabbits. Why? Because life isn't fair, that's why. So you finally get home, and your wife is bitching at you because your daughter's face is all swollen, and you didn't protect her from the homeless mugger. (You two had a little talk about it beforehand. The wife must never know about Operation Lungsquall.)

After the unnecessary drama, you two work together as a team to get everything that you could possibly need loaded into the car. Then you help your daughter get her things in order so that she can have a little peace of mind. You decide that one last look over the house won't hurt anything, just to make sure that you grabbed everything that you need for the trip. The process is similar to what you would do in a motel room that you are leaving, making sure that everything you brought leaves with you so no one cries later about forgetting their favorite hairbrush. Just then, you notice a quick glint outside your window. You turn on the outside lights and notice something horrible. Your house is completely surrounded by zombies. Just as you notice that the house is completely surrounded, you notice something even more frightening. The house is completely filled with zombies. Just as you notice that the house is completely filled with zombies, you realize something even more terrible. You are a zombie. What the *fuck*?

Pssstt! This is where you go back because you are dead. Go back now. Page 174 if you forgot.

Main roads are quick and safe. Shortcuts are death traps, and only chumps take those. Everyone knows that. Stick to the limited-access highways because it is unlikely for zombies to be there. If they are, just hit them and keep going. Keep a watch on the condition of the engine though. This ain't no SUV, you know. The car only has to last until the Steer Melt, with the weakness, but no longer. It won't be used by you, or anybody, anymore.

About a mile to go before you get to the Steer Melt, and the weakness, you think that something should be done. You cannot be trusted, and the lives of your family, and most importantly your life, are at stake. You quickly pull over and tell your daughter to drive. She is trying to tell you that she is only eleven years old (but she'll be twelve in just 193 days, 17 hours, and 34 minutes) and that she cannot drive. Too bad you were taking a full dose of Nytol, Sominex, melatonin, and Lunesta all mixed in a glass of warm milk. You tell her, "Shut up and drive. It's go time. I'm going to be out in T-minus thirty seconds. Zombies will eat us, Rosenescra! Zombies will EAT USSS!" And you're out.

When you wake up three hours later, you feel so tired and bad that life seems to be without joy. You feel like skin stretched over a rock. And that rock is sitting in an old septic tank from Mississippi. Not good. You knew it was a gamble, but the gamble may have paid off. Taking that much sleep medication was foolish, but the weakness would have ended your life. You know it would have. But where are we?

The journey continues on page 191.

Your wife's mother is dead. She knows this. Elm Street is a fabled street of horrors. Everyone knows this. Naturally, it is all clear and simple. It is a code. It is part of a secret plan that you and your wife have been talking about for a while now, ever since she started reading *The Ultimate Zombie Hunter's Handbook* a week ago. The part about her mother's house is code for "Get the new SUV from the secret garage you built in the back patio under the hot tub. It is already loaded with the main essentials of survival while leaving enough room for three people without blocking any of the prime views of the driver or passenger so that you aren't blind sighted by a zombie flood hiding behind that sleeping bag wrapped around the three-pound chocolate bar."

Elm Street doesn't literally mean "Elm Street." It is an anagram for "Steer Melt," the greatest burger joint on the face of this earth. They only use quality sirloin steaks in their burger meat and the best Swiss cheese in the USA. The burgers are so ridiculously good that I would bring Operation Lungsquall into full force on anyone who dared to oppose me, even my wife. And that could get my balls cut off. Those burgers are so good, I would give up my balls for one. But I digress.

You'll meet her in the parking lot and siphon the gas out of your car because you are leaving it behind. Then you'll all get into the SUV and head for the hills, so to speak. You have a fortress fashioned out of leaves, twigs, random bits of trash, fishing line, and animal hair all mixed with mud. You created this makeshift bird's nest for a few reasons. First off, you only had a week, and a good-sized, adequate fortress would take at least two weeks of prep time and construction. Second, bird's get through all kinds of crazy weather in these things, and for a couple of days, you can weather this storm. It won't do for a long time, but it'll do for the night so that you can get some sleep, off the ground, and come up with a better plan in the morning. If only *The Ultimate Zombie Hunter's Handbook* had come out two weeks ago instead of just one.

Continue surviving on page 183.

Why do you suck? The book has been on presale for over a month, and you could have received your copy in the mail a week ago. You'd already know about the upcoming zombie invasion and taken the appropriate steps. Without the book, you don't stand much of a chance, but it's possible. However, by buying this book, or any other, right now, you throw off the entire time line. There are two ways to meet your end. Both ways lead to the same ending. Let me explain.

Damn that book looks freaking sweet. And informative. So here goes nothing. You're going to buy it. As you pick it up, and the lights above shine off the cover and glint off your eyes, you notice something funny. The cashier looks drunk. You can't see her face because her back is to you, but she keeps standing there, just wobbling back and forth as if she could fall any moment. To give her some time to recover, you browse the selection of all the other bullshit nobody is buying. After a few minutes, you look up and see that your drunken cashier is giving a stranger the hickey of his life. You assume it's a stranger because of his surprised expression. But she is literally going to town on this dude's neck. You look away, partly in disgust, and partly because you are jealous. Off to the magazines. Luckily for you, one of the *Playboy*'s is out of the wrapper, and you peek at it. A lot. You glance back at the cashier, and she is done with everyone else and looks stable, so you decide to get the book and leave.

Now, this is important. Are you getting a pretzel afterward or not? If you already got it or are not getting one, then you are in no hurry and decide to use your cash-back rewards credit card. You have to hand your card to the cashier due to this. At this point, you realize that the cashier is not a cashier at all, but a zombie. You didn't realize this until you noticed her eating your guts though. Funny how that works out when you're not too quick on the uptake.

If you *are* getting a pretzel, you really want that damn pretzel and decide to forgo the cash rewards and use the Visa payWave to purchase the book. This eliminates any contact with the cashier because you slide the bastard over the thing yourself to save time. You didn't even realize she was a zombie. Unfortunately, buying the book takes five extra minutes of time. The pretzel takes only two minutes extra. After a long day of running from zombies and trying to get out of the city, the authorities seal off the city to everything, even rats, which is saying something, just four minutes before you get to safety. Then the zombies eat you. Then you are a zombie. Thank me for saving you the time it would have taken to wind your way through this mess of pages just to find out you were doomed from the start. You're welcome, and I accept your apology for murdering the human race to zombie death by not preordering *The Ultimate Zombie Hunter's Handbook.*

You are dead because you suck at hot hands. And you're lazy.

Well, the wife messed up. After meeting up with her at the Steer Melt, she was driving the family to "Raphael Is the Best Ninja Turtle: Alpha Squadron Base A1 Bold and Spicy" and got lost. Unfortunately, you weren't awake to help her find her way without stopping for directions. So here you are, sitting in a gas station in the middle of nowhere. The odds of a zombie invasion reaching this far so quickly is small, but you don't take chances. It's just not who you are. Knowing that the future may rest in the wombs of the world's women, you cannot give up yours without a fight. You pull the shotgun you keep hidden on your person at all times (you know what I mean) and get out of the SUV. Luckily, the sluggish feeling from the medicine doesn't kick in until you try to move. Instantly, life has been drained of meaning and justice.

KABLAM! You had enough strength to fire the gun. Naturally, your wife and the cashier run outside to see what the commotion is. You notice that he is holding a Tom Clancy novel and a notebook of notes. He doesn't look like a zombie, and she isn't bleeding. Just in time. *KABLAM KABLAM!* The cashier's head exploded like a watermelon three months after harvest. Even if he wasn't a zombie, he would have been. Nobody who has read *The Ultimate Zombie Hunter's Handbook* would ever read another book again. And even if those were notes for plans to survive, it's too late for notes. Take out the enemy now, when they don't expect it. It's a rule I live by. It's a rule they die by. Get the wife and get back in the car. Except that she gets you in the car. Too weak to move.

A few hours go by, and you awaken again. Safe in the SUV with everyone, you recognize the countryside. The cashier knew his stuff. It's a shame that his brain couldn't be put into your wife's body. But the past is gone. Now is the present, and it's time to think of the future. "Raphael Is the Best Ninja Turtle: Alpha Squadron Base A1 Bold and Spicy" is just around the corner. You designed it to withstand the usual weather for this climate at this time of year, and you even made it possible to get the SUV up there too. Good thinking.

The creek that runs next to it is very pretty right now.

Too bad you are too weak to get the SUV job done right now. And your wife and daughter aren't going to be able to get it done either.

The three of you can get into the shelter, and they could make trips to get all the stuff up, but the SUV is essential to the survival of the group. If it is down there, it risks becoming infested with zombies. The drugs should wear off in about five hours, but the zombies could be here by then. It takes about two hours to get the job done, which would leave you three hours of sleep to regain your strength. What are you going to do?

Sleep it off. The girls can keep watch until then. (*Go to page 176.*)
Give it a shot and try to get the SUV situated, three hours from now, with the help of the others. (*Go to page 182.*)

Just like you always say, shortcuts are fun and quick. Let's take the shortcut. You've taken this shortcut on many occasions in an effort to hide from your wife, and you know it well. Just like a soldier, you put your emotions aside, and your training kicks in. You get off the main road and head into a residential neighborhood. It's easy to get through these guys because they don't typically have stoplights to slow you down. You know the speed limit is twenty-five miles per hour, but who cares? The end of the world is here, and tickets won't matter.

One turn leads to another and another. Your speed never slows, and your acceleration holds steady too. In a matter of minutes, you can swear you smell the sweet aroma of blood and grease ... the weakness. As you round the next corner, your mind minutes away at the Steer Melt, a small child runs out from behind a trash can. There was nothing you could do, and you hit him. You hit the brakes and get out of the car quickly to see if he is badly injured. You know that even if he was dead, he couldn't be a zombie already because it takes a little time to do. Mere seconds are not enough time, so it's safe.

You get to the back of the car where you see his body. He is so small, and fragile but he isn't moving. He looks as if he is asleep, but he never is. What you thought was a safe assumption was clouded by the weakness. You let your guard down. You made a mistake. And in this game, mistakes are deadly. Without warning, the ~~child~~ zombie strikes. Without warning, you feel a warm, wet sensation flowing down your chest. In your last few minutes, you wonder what went wrong. The warm, wet sensation acts like a baptism of truth. The child wouldn't be a zombie already if you killed him. But what if he was already dead when you hit him? What if he was already a zombie? Well, your answer came when the lights went out. The last thing you remember is a girl's scream. So close, but so far away.

Shortcuts are death traps. Don't be a chump. Chumps are zombie food. That is an antigoal.

You are dead. Stop doing it wrong.

If this were a movie, it would cut here. Maybe, just maybe, you would get upgraded to montage status so that the slower audience (unfortunately, you probably don't know who you are) would understand what kind of plot advancement is happening now. Here goes nothing ...

Break. Plot advancement commencing. Done.

SUV is situated now. It took almost four hours, but it is ready to go in a constant state of *ride or die*. You've rigged it into the sky so that all you have to do is cut one vine, and a series of sturdy ramps will descend from the heavens to create a master ramp that will allow you to burn rubber out of the trees like a monkey on fire being shot out of a cannon. Anyhow, you've spent nearly four hours on it, and it is getting close to nine in the morning. This is good though. The plans are set for a quick escape, the supplies are safe, and so are the women.

Just before ten, the first of the zombies showed up. At first you thought it might be a squirrel, but it definitely turned out to be a three-hundred-pound zombie wearing a bow tie and a pair of trout trousers. Zombies are strange.

Over the course of another hour, all sorts of zombies start showing up. All in all, you see that there are seven in total. Luckily for you and the girls, an entire army of zombies could show up, and you wouldn't care. The SUV is situated, and it doesn't matter anymore. If you hadn't gotten the SUV taken care of early, it would be a completely different story.

It sure is a beautiful day outside. Good day to be with nature.

And it's a bad day to die. It is also a bad day to be killed by something as unnatural and horrible as a zombie. (*Continue living and run back to page 185.*)

Life isn't fair. Why should death be any different? For some, death comes at an appropriate time for a fairly justified reason. Elderly people live full lives and pass away in their sleep. Lots of people go into the great beyond while doing their favorite activities, such as skydiving, snorkeling, or mountain climbing. A select few get the pleasure, ironically enough, of passing while making love. But others get the shaft, so to speak. Young adults may die in a car accident because of a drunk driver in the other lane. New mothers die giving birth to their children. And some babies die for no reason that medicine can define.

This isn't thinking deeply or being philosophical. This is how life is. And this is how death is. The tragedy of this story is the sacrifice made by a member of your party to ensure the survival of the other two. The reason for this necessary sacrifice is heartbreakingly simple: you fucked up and fell asleep without setting any alarms, and you overslept. All you did was sleep a few measly hours too long.

Your wife was more important to your plan than even she realized. You knew that you didn't have the necessary time to build a good fortress. Because of this, you developed this particular contingency plan. Knowing that your wife can never produce any children, she was the most expendable person in your party, and if humanity is rebuilt because of your actions, she will be honored above all for the sacrifice she made.

You push her out of the tree fort.

As she falls toward the ground, several things happen at once. You grab your daughter, quickly wrap a nearby vine around your left arm, and stow the shotgun for safety. At the same time, you trigger the hidden detonator that will blow up all the barrels of napalm that you have secretly hidden all around you. You tuck your daughter's head down and fall from the nest backward, like a scuba diver off the side of a boat. The backward roll you experience evolves into a downward swing with the vine wrapped around your arm. By the time your wife hits the soft pile of leaves and grass, you and your daughter are across the small creek that flows underneath the nest. It has a quick current and is surprisingly deep for how small it appears. With a sick feeling in your stomach, you remember placing the pile of leaves there in case you would need it, knowing that she would not be worth anything as bait if she died immediately on impact.

Tears blur your vision as your daughter cries out to her mother. You force them back as your wife sacrifices her body, but hopefully not her soul, to your cause and survival. She was a good woman and will be remembered for it.

You are pathetic. (*Continue living, and being pathetic, on page 200.*)

Like most good things in life, your plan is simple and to the point. You are going to wait in your nest for the next day or so, getting some rest while you watch the zombies come, for come they will. You are going to be paying attention to how many and how fast they come as well as how they arrive, in groups or alone. This is going to invaluable information for the survival of the human race in the future.

Thirty hours later.

The zombies have come. There are thousands of them. You aren't particularly sure how they knew you were here, but here they are. They mostly arrived alone, which is good for the survival of the human race. They started as a trickle but began to show up in greater and greater numbers. This is bad for the human race. You've taken notes, created graphs, and doodled plenty. It is time for the next step in survival.

Leaving the nest was always part of the plan, but it is hard to say good-bye to such a vital part of your survival. You pack up all your notes, weapons, and food into the SUV, a Ford Escape, and prepare to leave. Before you can cut that vine, you have to locate something very important to the next thirty minutes of all your lives. The 2007 version of a mix tape, your burned CD with the title "Soundtrack for Kicking Zombie ASS!" written on the top with a Sharpie marker. Ahh yes, next to the shotgun. Good. You whip it out quickly, but not too quickly, and put it into the CD player of your Escape. Now it's time to cut the rope.

Escape (haha!) to page 202.

List No. 2158939: So Long, "Raphael Is the Best Ninja Turtle: Alpha Squadron Base A1 Bold and Spicy"

Body ...   Check
Pulse ...   Check
Wife ...   Check
Daughter ... Check
SUV...   Check

Dead zombies burning in your wake while the rest just saunter off in your general direction without any apparent ambition or emotion.... Priceless

—

... And Check

Everything is going according to plan, but this is where the planning has stopped. You are alive and well and left a pile of rotting zombie corpses in your wake. But what happens now? You have no permanent safety, if such a place exists. What do you do now?

Well, it's been about forty-six hours since the zombie invasion began. You are driving down a lonely road with no other cars in sight. This is not a reassuring sign that the rest of your fellow human beings have faired as well. The longer you drive, the more hopeless it becomes, because nobody else seems to have made it out. You know the zombies didn't get everyone. Others have read this book. Others will have survived because of the planning and the necessary steps that they had to take. You have to find them before it's too late.

True, there is some danger in gathering into large groups of survivors, but it is worth the risk. Human beings are social beings that strive in packs, in numbers. In this way, the zombies will be defeated. Many heads are better than few. Life finds a way.

You pass an abandoned truck on the side of the road. No signs of life anywhere.

Wait! WHAT THE FUCK IS THAT? What is that? Don't you know what that is? Me either ... What is that thing? I've never seen anything like that before, have you? What is that thing? Oh, I know what that is. Yeah. HAHAHA!

WTF? Page 204.

List No. 2158939: So Long, "Raphael Is the Best Ninja Turtle: Alpha Squadron Base A1 Bold and Spicy"

Body ...   Check
Pulse ...   Check
Wife ...   No, but she will be remembered.
Daughter ...   Check
SUV ...   No, I messed it all up.

Dead zombies burning in your wake while the rest just saunter off in your general direction without any apparent ambition or emotion ... Priceless

---

... And Check

Everything hasn't gone according to plan, and you don't have any more plans just yet. You and Rosenescra are alive and well and left a pile of rotting zombie corpses in your wake as well as the life of your courageous wife. But what happens now? You have no permanent safety, if such a place exists. What do you do now? You don't even have a good way to get around the countryside.

Well, it's been about forty-six hours since the zombie invasion began. You are walking down a lonely road with no cars in sight. This is not a reassuring sign that the rest of your fellow human beings have faired as well. The longer you walk, the more hopeless it becomes, because nobody else seems to have made it out. You know the zombies didn't get everyone. Others have read this book. Others will have survived because of the planning and the necessary steps that they had to take. You have to find them before it's too late.

True, there is some danger in gathering into large groups of survivors, but it is worth the risk. Human beings are social beings that strive in packs, in numbers. In this way, the zombies will be defeated. Many heads are better than few. Life finds a way.

After a couple more hours, you feel broken and beaten. Despair has begun to settle on you both, although Rosenescra suffers more. It is at this point that fortune smiles upon you. What you desired to see most has come true. A truck is sitting on the side of the road. If you can get it running by some miracle, you may be able to get yourself and Rosenescra to safety. You try the door. Unlocked. You look for a key. In the ignition. You try the ignition. The truck revs to life. It must have been a hunter's truck. You wonder if the zombies got him or if he is still out there. You cannot afford to wait for him to show up. Your daughter's life is at stake.

On the road again, you finally feel like you two are going to make it. Just an hour later ...

Wait! WHAT THE FUCK IS THAT? What is that? Don't you know what that is? Me either ... What is that thing? I've never seen anything like that before, have you? What is that thing? Oh, I know what that is. Yeah. HAHAHA!

WTF? Page 204.

Why the Escape? It has a manlier name, but it also has less power than the Hummer. Its shocks aren't as good either, or are they?

Well, think about this. What would you rather be doing? Would you rather be driving Miss Daisy to the grocery store for her morning coffee and gossip while listening to John Denver and Patsy Cline on the AM radio while you wonder if you are going to have the beef brisket or the pork pot roast for dinner tonight? And what are Ralph and Loren doing tonight anyway? Don't they have to get their tax information for the last four years together because of that audit? I tell you what: the government is out of control these days, just like the weather and gas prices. The whole world has just gotten itself into a big damn hurry, and nobody spends time thinking these days. Maybe I will have the pot roast. That sounds good. Yeah. The pot roast.

Or would you rather be kicking some serious zombie ass, smoking a fat Cuban cigar while listening to skull-crushing hits like "Welcome to the Jungle" by Guns N' Roses, "e" by Queen, and "Rock You Like a Hurricane" by Scorpion? Seriously, these songs make you want to power morph into a *chupacabra* and suck the blood out of all the goats in a five-mile radius while your wife is cooking leg o' lamb corn dogs in the fat fryer at home. You can't listen to a dynamite soundtrack like this while cruising smoothly through a forest of zombies. You gotta feel the bump and the grind and the crunch of every zombie skull that you smash with the grill of your SUV. Wasn't it you who decided on the slogan "Their grill into our grill ... I want to feel that." This is the very reason you got the Escape in the first place. Bose would make you feel like a pleasant ride out to the country club for a round of golf and a gin and tonic. Springs make you feel like you are maiming, crushing, smashing, and killing any and every zombie that crosses your way while shooting Fighting Cock Whiskey and eating tacos. Hell, it was half the reason you waited for thousands to show up in the first place.

And crush some zombies you do. There is a bloody smear across the countryside visible from space because of you. For the first time in your life, you can be proud of something. Can you imagine what kind of song Björk would write that was inspired for what you did?

Crash, smash, clang, slurp,
crunch, gurgle, wheeze, burp.
There is so much music in the world,
Even when zombies try to eat me, girl.

Well, maybe her song would sound a little different, but who cares? You're still alive, and you're kicking zombie ass. You get to share this beautiful moment with your wife and daughter. Feel good about life for now.

Continue to page 199.

What appeared to be a Porta-Potty in the middle of the woods turned out to be a secret entrance to a secret military base in a secret part of the state. It wasn't marked on any of the maps you studied, which is why you hadn't planned to just go there when the zombie invasion began, and that's when you begin to realize that the government almost ruined your chances of survival. You begin to realize that if the government had prepared, taken precautions, publicized the safe houses of America, the last great vestiges of our great nation, all this madness, and horror could have been averted. And who is there to blame but yourself for not casting your vote to the man with the contingency plan. But at least you found a safe house, despite their best attempts. I would say that it is pretty lucky that you happened to come across this thing out in the middle of nowhere.

But how did you recognize it as a secret entrance? Well, the first clue was the fact that it was out in the middle of the woods. The whole place is a toilet if you need it to be, so why put a Porta-Potty out here? At first you thought it was just some dumb politician wanting to feel important and wasting your tax dollars, a thought that instantly made you shake your fist at the Porta-Potty in vain. But then something happened that you didn't expect.

Unexpected diarrhea. Yep, it happens to the best of us, at the worst of times. Because of the diarrhea, you were thinking it was lucky that you found a Porta-Potty out in the middle of nowhere (hey, even a Porta-Potty can be better than a pinecone and a thornbush), not knowing how lucky you actually were. After what seemed like two hours, you were finished stuffing your intestines back inside yourself when you realized something very peculiar about this particular Porta-Potty. The toilet had a flusher.

Why would a flusher be on a Porta-Potty? They don't have a tank. They don't really have any water to speak of. There is no plumbing. Yet here it is, a flusher. You flushed.

The back of the Porta-Potty opened up like a doorway, unmasking the hidden world behind that was filled with men, weapons, tanks, and food. There were refugees here, from the cities, and soldiers training for battle. Apparently if you had traveled any farther along the road, you would have crashed into the impossibly lifelike wall around this facility that was painted to blend in with the surrounding forest. Camo. God bless it. After a few minutes, you have explained the situation to the people that guard the entrance, and you are allowed to bring your family and belongings inside the facility. It is here that you will begin the rest of eternity. Good luck, Joe.

You have survived ... for now.

Despite your best efforts, you made a mistake that will cost lives. It could be just one now, or it could be the lives of many. Even after anticipating for mistakes and coming up with a contingency plan for them, you don't know if it was really worth it. Life is to be treasured, but at what price will you pay to keep it? The price was high in this case. So very high …

Nobody likes to make decisions that are tough. Life-or-death decisions are sometimes the toughest anyone can make. Choosing life is almost always the preferred option, but sometimes death can be a better substitute. If the quality of life following this particular point in time would be worse off to unbearable degrees, then life may not be the best choice. You've already decided what is to be done.

The contingency plan involved betraying your wife and running while you still could. But you can't do it. Life without her wouldn't be any different than life as a zombie. You would be devoid of the one thing that keeps us human: emotion. No more laughter, no more happiness. Survival is important, but maybe it isn't the most important thing in the world.

You explain the situation to your wife and daughter. You explain to them that you made a mistake and that it might be the end of their future in this world. You are prepared to take their lives so that they will be spared the undead existence of a zombie. Zombies are unnatural and tortured. They accept the gravity of the situation and the enormity of the decisions that you have made. They appreciate the sacrifice that you are making on their behalf and the gift that you are giving them. If the time comes, you will send them into the afterlife, not to hunger or to become zombies.

But suicide is not your cup of tea. You know what zombies are good for. Nothing but for an ass whooping. Even with just seven, your chances of survival are slim. Now that you have spent the last hour talking, the number has multiplied by four. Your gun only has four shots in it, and the ammunition was lost or forgotten in the SUV. Four shells. One for the women. You trigger the hidden detonator that blows up all the hidden barrels of napalm in the area. Three for the zombies.

As you leap over the edge of the nest, a smile carves the hate onto your face. Maybe today is a good day to die.

The end. You get points for being valiant. Points that mean so little.

You are dead, but at least you went out in a blaze of glory.

Chapter 10 Applying Knowledge to Tactical Situations

Ladies and Gentlemen, Please
(As imagined by Matthew)

Scenario

At some point during the past week or month or who knows how long, you blacked out. You've just come to and find yourself sitting in the midst of a large group of people, watching some great debacle of color in what looks to be a huge dimly lit tent. You realize from the clowns and the trapeze ninjas that you're at a circus, and no one else has a splitting headache but you. That's when you see the zombie wobble in through the front tent flaps and take the neck out of a guy. You reach for your shotgun but find only a hunting knife. What do you do?

What You Should Do

In order to respond to this scenario, you'll have to understand a little about the mob mentality. When people catch on to the gory zombie glee going on near the entrance, they're going to go bat-shit nuts and run for Jesus. Everyone will panic and do as quickly what they can to move toward what they perceive to be an escape. Problem is, some people are clumsy and fall, some people are ruthless and throw elbows, and everyone generally moves at a different pace. The result? Chaos, confusion, and a hot sweaty traffic jam: a man buffet, ripe for the infectious blood vomit.

In the jumble of limbs, the zombie will have plenty of time to take a nibble here and there, until the zombiism is spreading as fast as fire in a furniture store. You don't want to be caught down in that crap because you hate people rubbing their sweat all over you, and your knife won't protect you from a thousand zombies already rubbing you the wrong way. That's why you're going to be smart and avoid the mob.

Instead of running down the stands to join the death sentence below, move upward, toward the top. There will be very few people at the top, so you won't be bothered by strangers you may or may not hate. Also, the zombie will be distracted by the mass of people, and even when zombies start to head your way, they will probably be even slower to advance due to their general inability to scale a set of stairs. Even better, you'll have a bird's-eye view to watch the madness or otherwise check its progress.

That just leaves you with the escape part. Well, it's a good thing you brought your knife, because if you hadn't noticed, your cage is nothing more than some heavy-duty fabric. Since you're at the top of the stands, you should be at the wall of the tent, so use the knife to slash your own exit. Now, you'll probably be at least forty feet up in the air, so don't haul ass skydiving because you'll never walk away clean. Instead, check the ground for zombies, climb out of the tent, and use the knife to slow your descent as you slide your way down to the ground.

What I Would Do

Since I'm always watching for zombies, blacked out or not, I spotted the zombie before it even knew what a second chin tasted like. The quick observation buys me precious time. Before anyone else would even have a chance to recover from the shock of a man bleeding out, I would have vaulted over the heads of a hundred men down to the main attraction. Every circus has a clown and a cannon, so I'd use both in a maneuver I like to call "keeping the bull off the cowboy." Shooting the confused and abused clown out of the cannon and into the zombies would keep the macabre at the entrance and slow their advance for only the cost of a creepy vintage funny man.

With the zombies busy feasting on number three, I would duck and roll over to the lion tamer and cut his Achilles' heel so I could steal his whip. The lions, as their kind has been known to do, would grow wild at the scent of blood and devour the weakest, then naturally fall in behind their new ringleader. With whip in hand, I would approach the three zombies, whipping them from twenty feet like the real Indiana Jones from when his movies were good. First, I would take out their eyes. *Whip! Whip!* Then I would knock out their teeth. *Whip! Crack!*

After rendering the zombies helpless, I would likely be attacked by circus folk seeking revenge for the loss of their old whip master. This would, of course, be a minor annoyance, as I would unleash my ferocious man-eaters on them. The carnies' thirst for vengeance would only whet the appetite of my four-legged bodyguards, so some innocent bystanders might also be consumed, as could be expected. Free from distractions of my own, I would continue whipping at the blind, toothless undead until I had backed them into the elephants' cage and locked the door. Then I would continue whipping the zombies through the bars of the cage while the fire-breather set 'em alight, just to build up a thirst for the heavy drinking in which I would be about to partake.

—

Lemon Drops in the Afternoon Sun
(As dreamed of by Geoffrey)

Scenario

You're a ridiculously old person, and you have bad credit. AHHHH! But seriously, AHHHHHHH! Anywho, you're out trying to find a new refrigerator. Apparently, trying to keep forty-two gallons of prune juice cold in the dead heat of August was too much for your previous effort, so you need something with a little beef to it. You open up the largest fridge you find. As a sales pitch, the staff kept an entire zombie frozen solid in the freezer portion of the fridge. Unfortunately, you're old, and the zombie thawed out before you could decide what to do (and move to do it).

What You Should Do

AHHHHHH, old people! As an elderly American, you must get away quickly. If anyone in the near area has an IZRM, you will fall in the reaction. Unfortunately, that old football injury is acting up, and quick movements are all but impossible. You'll need to get on a Segway and get on one quick. While scooting away in style, blow your zombie whistle (if you don't have one, get one).

Zombie whistles were created by aliens as a weapon to quickly combat zombiism. The whistle causes a zombie to remain immobile while the tune plays. The aliens first gave them to Jesus and Moses, two Mexican brothers completely unrelated to anything religious. The two brothers were deeply religious and believed that the whistles were given to them by God. Because of the confusion, God got angry at them for worshipping a false god and forced them to eat each other. They each started at the other's foot and continued eating until they both disappeared, and that is how the Chihuahua was created. Some believe that the whistles were redistributed throughout the family, but you might find them on eBay.

If you wreck your Segway before an observant zombie killer can dispatch the abomination, I hope a washing machine falls on you, and you die.

What I Would Do

I wouldn't be old, for starters. That aside, I would definitely use a little technique I like to call "lemon drops in the afternoon sun." To successfully pull this off, you need a healthy supply of marbles, boiling water, salt, a stockpot, rope, and a screen. Luckily, I keep all these things on me at all times, which is ideal.

To start, I have to put the boiling water and the salt in the stockpot. This allows the water to become super heated without spilling everywhere. Take the screen and wrap it around the marbles and tie the rope to the end. Drop the sack in the water. Watch for splashing because it can sting. Once the screen begins to glow red, it's time.

Since I am faster than an old person, the zombie is still partially frozen by the time the marbles are ready. I have to pull the sack out and begin spinning it above my head, as if I were a cowboy with a lasso. After reaching a top speed of 1,200 revolutions per minute, catapult the sack toward the zombie. Just as the rope is running out of length, pull it back with the force of 1,200 mules (see the symmetry here?). This will force the hot marbles through the red-hot screen, creating a million tiny red-hot zombie-killing bullets. The mixture of cold zombie and hot swarm of marble shards creates a phenomenon known as pink mist. It is rare, but beautiful. If the sun catches the pink mist at twelve noon, it creates a leprechaun with 1,200 pieces of gold in his pot o' gold. Nobody ever expects that.

—

I Drive a Dodge Stratus
(As prophesied by Geoffrey)

Scenario

Holy shit! You stole a car and are driving so fucking fast your teeth are digging into the headrest. Not only that, but it's raining, and the tires of the car are bald. Plus the floorboards have holes in them, and so do your shoes, making your toes wet. Why did you steal that crappy car in the first place? Suddenly, right in the middle of a two-tire turn, you hear a ripping sound in the backseat. Lucky for you, it's just a zombie tearing its way toward you from the trunk. Also, something smells like gasoline. What do you do?

What You Should Do

Never, and I mean never, steal a car with a zombie in the trunk. You can get yourself into a predicament such as this. What could be worse than the deadly combination of a zombie, gasoline, and a stolen car that sucks? A zombie with time-traveling abilities, but that is for another time. In this moment, nothing is worse.

First of all, get all four tires on the ground. Stabilizing the car is the only thing that will get you out of this mess alive. There should be no attempt to kill the zombie at this point in time, only escape. The best defense is a great offense, but only when the board is stacked for you, not against. So I repeat, get the tires on the ground.

Second (of all?), tuck and roll, baby. No, I know you're all hot and bothered over Chinese food right now, but this ain't no spring roll, honey. You need to literally jettison your body out of that car and into (traffic?) safety.

Finally, stop some cars that are passing by. Chances are at least one of them will have a gun that you can blow the zombie's brains out with. If you don't find one quickly, get out from the Dodge. I know it doesn't sound responsible, but you're obviously not equipped (mentally) to handle a zombie in the open.

What I Would Do

Well, I wouldn't steal a car because I am not a moron. I'd steal a tank because I know it'll be secure. But let's say that I got high on propane and Tylenol, and I stole a car, and the car happened to have a zombie in it. While I'm turning the corner, I'd pull my trusty shotgun out of nature's pocket and blast the damn thing back into the trunk. Now, assuming you've never seen *Mythbusters*, the zombie would probably catch on fire at this point, setting the entire trunk ablaze. Pull the e-brake. Get out of the car. Take a bus home. Done.

—

The Office
(As masterminded by Matthew)

Scenario

You work at the office, watching over the little people as they do your bidding. You have the power to make things happen, and you make things happen. They call you the manager, but you shorten it to the man. You don't worry about the coming zombie invasion, you anticipate it, and that means preparation. Unfortunately, you have four hundred employees and a big building with lots of windows. What do you do?

What You Should Do

Launch a campaign of preparation like a modern general against primitive bush people. Fast, intelligent, multipronged, and bloody. In order to whip your crew of wheezing lax-ass moneybags into shape before the future comes, you're going to have to use every skill you've amassed during your several years viciously clawing your way to the top.

Consider what's more devastating, a fire that burns down the building or the failure to contain a zombie infestation? Make the right choice and replace those fire extinguishers with handfuls of automatic shotguns. Keep the antizombie sticks behind highly shatter-prone glass so that when your employees punch through with shards embedded in their knuckles, they are reminded of what it means to be a man. Randomly hide extra boxes of shotgun shells in desk drawers, vases, bigger boxes, or out in the open for the occasional future freedom fighter to find.

Replace the glass on the lower levels (at least) with bulletproof glass. Also, add extra security to every entrance so that when the zombie alarm is pulled, the doors seal shut and can only be opened from the inside by a warm hand. Add an armored company bus to the secret underground parking garage you'll need to build, or just make it a secret bunker with plenty of supplies for your employees to hold out for three months or more.

Start Zombie Emergency Response Team (ZERT) training classes. Here, teach members how to manage the panic of their peers, how to kill walking croaks, how to "cure" those who've been bitten, how to bake a cake, how to organize, fight, survive, and purge the zombie disease from the planet. Teach employees how to tap into their dormant IZRM and use it to their advantage. Have plans, backup plans, subbackup plans, and drills testing combinations of plans. Dress hobos up as zombies and trip the alarm. We're talking timing here, speed, efficiency. We're talking survival here, and anything less is just fucking bullshit.

What I Would Do

No one has ever said I'm not a team player, but I don't need everyone. Sure, manpower makes the world turn round, but on my team, manpower takes on a whole new meaning, and if you're not on my team, you're nothing better than a shield or a target. As a manager, it's my job to make sure my employees are the best, most ruthless trained paperwork assassins in the industry; it's the only way to get ahead in this cut-throat world we live in. If those same employees can't carry their skills forward into a world dominated by death, then they're as worthless as pennies to Bill Gates.

Obviously this means that part of my interview process would include a "zombie mojo" test, a test of their ability to fight the good fight. Those who rank high would be able to survive if thrown into a pit of zombies with nothing but a chicken leg, and that clearly means they can outperform in any random middle-management situation. As an extension of this test, before I give anyone a job, they have to pass the In Case of Zombie entrance exam. In this, I show up at the person's house around one in the morning, convince the hobo-zombies that the prospective employee has swallowed some quarters, and then let them loose. Can I hire you if you have hobo hands in your stomach? Only if you ate 'em.

ZERT wouldn't be just a mandatory class for every employee; it would be a way of life. During my drills, shotguns would be dismantled and their parts spread throughout the building. That doesn't make it easier to fight zombies, but in the real world, it's not very often one will just find a whole shotgun lying around. Also, my office would have a "zombie imminent" alarm, and it would be going off the entire time.

Some Last Words Before You Start Rereading

Whether you know it or not, your life has just been changed forever. Not only can you tell your family and friends that you've practically finished a book, a great book, perhaps the first great book you've ever read in your entire life, but you've also just had your mind blown again and again like a recycled shell casing. On the cusp of victory and worldwide domination, you can look back behind you, back down the hill of your upward struggle, and say that here is where it all began. At the end. Of this book.

And why? Why should you be more awesome than other people who haven't read this book? Because you have the knowledge necessary to make the world a better place, right after it becomes a worse place? Because you know about zombies, their threat and that very real danger? Because you know about identifying them with what you might recall was a litmus test, or how to become a better person that can detect zombies always forever sleeplessly? Because you're constantly vigilant, like a McDonald's drive-through? Because, right now, you're oiling the shotgun you bought as soon as you finished the first chapter?

You're goddamn right.

If you don't have a diary, go get a diary, then open it up to the first empty page, and take note of this occasion. Say something like, "Dear Diary, today I have become a man, and I don't need you anymore." Then set the diary on fire and throw it at your neighbor's house. Don't worry about damages; if something happens, it only means they aren't as prepared as you are now, and it doesn't matter anyway because I'm assuming you've already packed the car to move into the country.

You know what to do, you know what to buy, you know how to plan. You know what lists to make and how to get your drink on. There's nothing left now but to go out, out into the world, and decide for yourself how to make it the best place for you to survive. Our only advice is that you tell those you think might be worth saving, tell them about the zombie apocalypse and about this book, share with them the light that might guide them to a brighter future while everyone else stumbles around in the dark.

Find your own place to survive, and once you've done that, turn to the first page and read this book as if it were your first time. Don't worry, you can thank us for it later, after those no-good fucking zombies are blown to bloody hell.

Appendix A

List No. 63701: Geoffrey's Dream Fighting Team, v. 6912.1

1. MacGyver
2. Dr. Quinn, Medicine Woman
3. the Terminator
4. Private Vasquez
5. John Rambo

MacGyver. He has to be on the list. Not only does he have to be on the list, but he also has to be on *your* list. Not only does he have to be on *your* list, but he also has to be the *first one* on your list. If he isn't on your list, then you should stop reading this book and eat it instead. The whole thing. And wash it down with a nice glass of cool, thick white Elmer's Glue. Why? Because you are going to die, so you might as well end your pathetic life, get it over with, and not be a zombie that I will be forced to enjoy obliterating.

MacGyver is the cream of the crop when it comes to quick thinking and blind luck. Seriously, go back and watch the show. He is one lucky son-of-a-bitch. Honestly, who else could take a rubber band, paper clip, and a stick of chewing gum (to be as cliché as possible) and create a parachute that could safely land a Boeing 747-100, with a takeoff weight of 735,000 pounds, while simultaneously disarming the hijackers and throwing all the guns out the window (even the one in the cockpit, since he hates guns) without disrupting the cabin pressure? Nobody. That's why I have wet dreams about having his baby. He is *so* dreamy.

PS: If you had him on the list at place 2–5, just pinch yourself on the arm, right above the elbow, really hard, for being a twit.

Dr. Quinn, Medicine Woman. Oh, baby. Not only can she go into nature and find medicine and use that shit to fix people up, but she is hot. We know she is fertile. How else could she have twins? Honestly, though, who could you imagine that would be better suited for on-the-go survival medicine than a woman who lived in the nineteenth century? No one. She knew all the tricks to keep fevers down, prevent infection, and stop the spread of smallpox in Indian villages. And she is hot. Not just a little, I mean smokin' hot. Plus if I ever get bitten, she can cut my arm off just like that. She is already used to finding sharp rocks and hacking body parts off for survival, and somehow, that makes her even hotter. Way better than any modern-day doctor can do. Especially Doogie. What a turd.

The Terminator. I know what some of you are thinking. You're about to go cry to your mommy because you think I am breaking the rules, because the Terminator doesn't exist. Well, for your information, you are an idiot. There have been great leaps in robotics recently, and some scientists think that we can even have sexual relations with them soon. Now, imagine a few hundred years of this kind of progress, and the terminator is not a far cry from reality. He doesn't have superpowers; he is a fucking machine! If you are having problems with this, go back up to the Elmer's Glue thing and take some advice from me.

But why him? Easy question to answer, friend. He is a badass and almost impossible to kill. I have a penis paired with a ball sack filled with manliness that can satisfy multiple women, so his unreproductive nature is neglected here. Also, he is a robot with living flesh over his metal frame. We can use him for what he was built for: a spy. How nobody else thought of this is beyond me, but it could just save the species. He can get bitten and let his skin turn into zombie flesh and walk around for a while incognito and then kill the hell out of them. Oh lord, I have a chubby just thinking about how glorious that would be.

Private Vasquez. Who? Oh yeah, that butch chick from *Aliens* that isn't Ripley. Why not Ripley? Well, that's another easy question to answer, you ass. If you don't start impressing me, I might have to glue your mouth shut, if you know what I mean. Ripley is a pussy. If you go to the movie where she is a badass, she is a clone with alien DNA mixed in. If anything screams, "Start of a zombie invasion!" it would be clones, clones with alien DNA infested throughout. Fuck that mess. And if you go to the part where she isn't an alien, she risks her life and the lives of everyone with her to save the life of a little kid, and that's not badass. That's Elmer's. Just get Vasquez. She is a tough broad who doesn't back down in the face of danger and the completely unexpected. Ripley almost had a nervous breakdown. Vasquez went in charging. The only reason she died was because she had bigger balls than most men today. And a grenade exploded in her fucking hands. On top of that, she is a woman. Women are important to survival because they can make babies. This is almost like having a man who can make babies in the team. What could be better for the end of the world?

Finally, John Rambo. He is a badass who is almost as resourceful as MacGyver, except not at escaping death, in creating it. Yep, he can hide out in the woods for weeks without any weapons or supplies and take down an entire police force. He has also been known to ignore pain to do what has to be done to survive. He is pretty much the ultimate survival warrior. I'm pretty sure he is immune to cold, heat, thirst, hunger, disease, bullets, bombs, women, and a whole mess of other stuff. The funny thing is, he still likes all that shit and a bag of Charlie's hair.

With these five people on my side, I can pretty much handle anything that zombies can dish out. Even if it is cold, cooked spinach mixed with unheated spam and Elmer's glue. Ew.

Appendix B

List No 112358: List of Lists

I. List No. 112359: Things That Even I Wouldn't Punch in the Face

1. A baby with Down's syndrome
2. Chuck Norris
3. A zombie bear
4. A meat loaf sandwich

II. List No. 112360: When I Discover the Neighbor's Daughter Is a Zombie

1. List of five ways to kill her immediately
2. List of places to sweep for zombie threats
3. List of six snacks to celebrate killing her (Because she was a bitch, and nobody tells my daughter she smells.)
4. List of twenty-one orders to shout at family
5. List of items to load into the car
6. List of things not to order at Taco Bell (optional)
7. List of people to remember to leave the house with
8. List of 1,315 ways to destroy the house after evacuation
9. List of places to go in order of likelihood of survival

III. List No. 112362: List of Baby Animals We Would Be Sad to See Become Zombies

1. Ducklings
2. Mice (pinkies)
3. Kangaroo (joeys)
4. Piglet
5. Kitten
6. Harp seal (pups)
7. ManBearPiglet

IV. List No. 112363: What Not to Do When Making a Zombie Movie

1. Include zombies that think or talk.
2. Forget it's a movie about zombies.
3. Leave out random nudity.
4. Do not cast John Leguizamo.
5. Make zombies walk underwater.
6. Have zombie fish.
7. Devise a cure and act like it's real.
8. Make nonthreatening zombies.

V. List No. 112364: Top Ways to Become a Zombie

1. Choose not to read this book.
2. Get all sexy before anyone knows your name.
3. Go back … for any reason.
4. Hold on to the sweet childhood dreams of your sodomized past.
5. Ignore the very real threat of a zombie invasion.

VI. List No. 112365: List of Things to Load into Your Car

1. Twenty boxes of ammunition for the 9-mm Glock in your holster.
2. Remote detonator for the bomb strapped to your gas tank.
3. Verify bomb is prepped on gas tank.
4. Remote for the remote detonator attached to key chain.
5. Board with a nail in it (ammoless weapon) (For those with extra trunk space: bigger board with bigger nail in it.)
6. Fifteen cans of baked beans and can opener.
7. One gallon of water.
8. Ten gallons of extra gas and siphon.
9. Bag of boiled-down black coffee to be inserted "up tha butt."
10. Sunglasses.

VII. List No. 112371: Top 6 *Imaginary* Weapons to Fight Zombies

1. Holy hand grenade
2. *Predator*'s shoulder-mounted energy cannon
3. Spiky turtle shell from *Mario Kart 64*

4. Moonraker
5. Lightsaber
6. A cure

VIII. List No. 112373: List of Thoughts When the Doorbell Rings

1. The doorbell rang! Holy crap!
2. Zombies!
3. Grab the gun!
4. Don't open the door until I've swept the lawn!
5. Stop opening the door!
6. Provide cover fire!
7. Holy crap! Zombies!
8. False alarm, whew!
9. Make plans to rediscuss proper door-opening procedures with family!

IX. List No. 112374: Top 6 Favorite Beans

1. Black beans
2. Kidney beans
3. Pinto beans
4. Mexican jumping beans
5. Magic beans
6. Frank 'n' beans

X. List No. 112375: Must-See Zombie Flicks

1. *Night of the Living Dead* (Watch it till it turns you on.)
2. *Undead*
3. *Dawn of the Dead* (both of them)
4. *Shaun of the Dead*
5. *28 Days Later* (Alternate title: *Running-Spitters and Bandits, Oh My!*)
6. *The Serpent and the Rainbow*
7. *The Ultimate Zombie Hunter's Handbook: The Movie*